Praise for Jay ~~~~~~~~

Perfect Victim

"Eerie and mindbendingly imaginative, *Perfect Victim* plumbs the depths of evil—and the result is a chilling ride with scares all the way."
— **Tess Gerritsen,** *New York Times* bestselling author of *The Keepsake*

"Jay Bonansinga's latest novel to feature Ulysses Grove, *Perfect Victim*, is a nail-biting cycle into terror and madness. Cross Patricia Cornwell with Stephen King and you'll get some idea of what's in store for you. Here's a book that's not for the faint of heart, but for everyone who enjoys a staccato-paced thrill ride into the heart of darkness. It'll leave you gasping for breath up to the very last page."
— **James Rollins,** *New York Times* bestselling author of *The Last Oracle*

"I loved the book! In *Perfect Victim* Bonansinga's prowess as a storyteller reaches a new level. This stunning thriller, which includes a light dusting of the paranormal and a touch of history, is unputdownable. Bonansinga's prose is addictive, the plot roils with suspense and action, and his FBI profiler protagonist, Ulysses Grove, grows more appealing with each novel. Well done!"
— **Libby Hellman,** Edgar-nominated editor/author of *Easy Innocence*

Shattered

"M. Night Shyamalan, meet Harlan Coben. *Shattered* seamlessly blends the frightening metamorphosis of a serial killer with a race-against-the-clock chase. Who is more haunted, the serial killer or the FBI profiler chasing him? The head-spinning plot turns and fascinating characters put *Shattered* at the top of any reading list. This novel will stay with you long after you finish it."

—**David Ellis,** Edgar Award–winning author of *Eye of the Beholder*

"A great hero, a truly sinister villain, and a riveting game of cat and mouse between them—*Shattered* is a gripping, compulsively readable thriller."

—**Joseph Finder,** *New York Times* bestselling author of *Power Play* and *Killer Instinct*

"A first-rate suspense thriller, as compelling as it is frightening. . . . Bonansinga never lets the intensity flag while balancing believable characters, forensic science, hard-nosed detective work, and paranormal flourishes. Grove proves to be one of the most genuine, flesh-and-blood suspense-thriller protagonists out there, and the foe Bonansinga pits against him is truly chilling."

—*Publishers Weekly*

Twisted

"Scarily real and really scary . . . everything a great thriller should be—and more."
> —**Lee Child,** *New York Times* bestselling author of *Nothing to Lose*

"Suspense, thrills, action—*Twisted* has a pulse-thumping pace all the way. Highly recommended!"
> —**Raymond Benson,** author of *A Hard Day's Death* and several James Bond novels

"The chills don't stop . . . Bonansinga has a talent for painting suspenseful scenes in vivid colors, put to especially good use in the final showdown."
> —*Publishers Weekly*

Frozen

"A relentless chiller that leaves you guessing and gasping again and again."
> —**David Morrell,** *New York Times* bestselling author of *Scavenger*

"A captivating novel of cold and meticulous suspense, Bonansinga's *Frozen* rings a bell that defines eternal evil in all its manifestations, in fact spanning six thousand years of the entity we call evil. This thriller is like no other serial killer novel. It has everything—a unique setting, a compelling lead character, a new twist on forensics, and the latent evil of mankind."
> —**Robert W. Walker,** author of *Absolute Instinct* and *Final Edge*

PERFECT VICTIM

JAY BONANSINGA

PINNACLE BOOKS
Kensington Publishing Corp.
www.kensingtonbooks.com

PINNACLE BOOKS are published by

Kensington Publishing Corp.
850 Third Avenue
New York, NY 10022

All Kensington titles, imprints, and distributed lines are available at special quantity discounts for bulk purchases for sales promotions, premiums, fund-raising, educational, or institutional use. Special book excerpts or customized printings can also be created to fit specific needs. For details, write or phone the office of the Kensington special sales manager: Kensington Publishing Corp., 850 Third Avenue, New York, NY 10022, attn: Special Sales Department; phone 1-800-221-2647.

PINNACLE BOOKS and the Pinnacle logo are Reg. U.S. Pat. & TM Off.

ISBN-13: 978-0-7860-1878-9
ISBN-10: 0-7860-1878-X

First printing: December 2008

10 9 8 7 6 5 4 3 2 1

Printed in the United States of America

This one is dedicated to Mikey Stein
and the Bad Boys.

ACKNOWLEDGMENTS

Major thanks to Michaela Hamilton, Peter Miller, Adrienne Rosato, Keith Scherer, Tina Jens, The International Thriller Writers, Lee Child, Harlan Ellison, The Landlocked Film Festival, Terrence Rogers, David Cushing, Richard Walter, Bruce Ingram, Anastasia Royal, and especially my family—Bratch, Joey, and Bill—for giving me the ultimate gift.

PROLOGUE
Raw Material

Woe to you, O earth and sea, for the devil
has come down to you in great wrath.

—REVELATION 12:12

Barbara Lynn Allison noticed things. Little things. Seemingly trivial things. It was partly her nature, and partly the curse of twenty-first-century motherhood. Before giving her children packaged cookies, for example, she would notice in the small print below the Nutrition Facts legend whether the product contained trace elements of peanuts. Last year, when she and her husband, David, upgraded to the split-level in Eden Prairie, she noticed all the sharp corners in the kitchen, the questionable second-floor banister, and the lack of a sturdy fence around the pool. "Kid Hazard Radar" is how her pal and fellow mah-jongg player Cyndee Kaiser characterized the talent. More than likely it was this preternatural mommy-vision that caused Barbie Allison to first notice the gray panel van that afternoon, parked way off in the corner of the mall parking lot.

As she pulled her Dodge Caravan into the south lot of the Mall of America, temple of consumerism and eighth wonder of the retail world, she never really got a good look at the van—or at the dark figure huddled behind its steering wheel—as the vehicle was nearly a football field away, sitting out there all alone. Plus Barbie was too busy scanning the jammed parking lanes near the entrance. She needed to find a spot close to the doors so that she wouldn't have to lug her sample case full of cosmetics farther than necessary. Distracted, craning her neck to see an opening, she only caught a fleeting glimpse of the van out of the corner of her eye before losing it in sunspots flaring off the high-gloss hoods of parked cars.

Somewhere in the back of her mind, she made a mental note. It was probably nothing. Lots of vans park in the far reaches of parking lots. Still . . . just for an instant, something about it strummed a nerve.

Shrugging it off, Barbie parked her minivan, killed the engine, and gathered her things. She had a full itinerary of sales calls ahead of her—her cruelty-free cosmetics, developed as an independent project during her days at the University of Minnesota, had been catching fire as of late—and she wanted to take advantage of this rare eight-hour workday afforded her by the playdates she had arranged for Carrie and Casey that afternoon.

She got out, her keyless alarm chirping as she thumbed the control and started across the traffic lane, her glamorous yet sensible wares in tow. The sun was high and wan in the pale spring sky that day, the air redolent with the scents of Cinnabon and coffee wafting out of the massive brick façade of Macy's. The endless ant farm of glass boutiques rose up before Barbie like a Mayan rampart, four levels high, housing hundreds of upscale stores, creating an audible thrum—the whirring of a great particle accelerator bubbling with voices, fountains, and perfumed air.

The sound of commerce.

Barbie paused near the entrance, digging her PDA out of her purse to double-check her first appointment. An elfin woman with a spray of freckles across the bridge of her nose, she looked a decade younger than her thirty-three years. Rigorous postpartum jogging and Pilates had staved off the requisite midriff bulge, and a burgeoning small business had done similar wonders for her self-image. Now, clad in her smart, formfitting, navy DKNY dress, she put her iPhone away and strode through the mall entrance with the high-chinned confidence of a color guard leading a victorious regiment. She was ready to rock.

Thoughts of errant vans parked in unlikely places had already faded from her radar screen.

She got a lot done that day.

After Macy's she bopped over to Bath and Body Works, then on to Perfumania, then Sephora, then Nail Trix. All told, Barbie took eleven orders. The gal at Nail Trix bought an entire carton of organic yucca moisturizer and Teddy Furniere at Regis Salon ordered the entire line of avocado body lotion.

It was a good day, and by the time Barbie, her sample case empty, made her way down to the food court, exhausted and famished, it was nearly five o'clock. Mrs. Kamin would be dropping off Casey and Carrie soon. Dinner would have to be made, homework supervised. There was just enough time to fill out the sales log and have a quick frozen yogurt, and then back home for mommy-work.

But first things first. Barbie's bladder was screaming. That venti mocha that she had snuck between Bare Escentuals and Your Body Repair Shop was threatening to pop.

She made her way down a side corridor toward the restrooms. The mall had cleared significantly since her arrival that morning, and now the narrow corridor leading to the ladies' john was deserted. Barbie reached the last door on the right and stopped.

The CLOSED FOR REPAIRS sign taped over the knob sent of zing of frustration down her spine.

She turned and trundled back out into the main corridor, found the directory kiosk, and saw that the next-nearest public restroom was at the other end of the east corridor, next door to the Sheraton Hotel, between Martini Cove and the Wine Shack. Barbie had no choice. In rush-hour traffic she would be wetting her pants, so she marched eastward, toward the darker, muskier, smokier regions of the mall.

The ladies' room was inside a tile-brick alcove tagged with the international symbol: stick-figure-woman in skirt. Barbie slipped into the silent fluorescent chamber, immediately flinching at the peppery stench of ammonia and human spoor. The restroom was deserted. The muffled drone of a nearby jukebox thrummed behind the walls, the bass lines of some garish hip-hop tune vibrating the tiles. Barbie hurried into the last stall, latching the door behind her. She set her empty case on the floor, then got her dress hiked up in seconds flat.

She was tinkling when she heard someone else enter the ladies' room.

All at once her urine stream halted.

Her heart started racing, a current of amorphous alarm flowing through her brain. The hair on her arms bristled. All because of what she saw underneath the gap at the bottom of that stall, crossing the tiled floor of the restroom: the pointy-toed black shoes of a man.

"Excuse me," she blurted, her voice cracking with tension.

She could hear a thick, deep breathing out there as those onyx wingtips paused and pivoted toward the stall. Barbie held her breath, her heart thumping in her ears. She could barely muster another word, her saliva all dried up. "You're in a ladies' room, sir."

No answer.

"Sir?"

Nothing.

"Sir!"

Cold panic sluiced down Barbie's backbone. Her joints felt stiff and cold all of a sudden, her mind swimming with contrary undercurrents. Were these the shoes of a harmless, scatterbrained janitor? Maybe. But *wingtips?* Didn't janitors wear work boots? Perhaps it was a security guard. But why wasn't he responding? Was this a stylish, oblivious, *hearing-impaired* janitor?

"There is someone in here!" she barked at the pointy shoes, taking a different tack. Perhaps if she got angry he would leave. "Hello? Sir?"

Then she heard something coming from the man with the black shoes that chilled her to the bone.

A low, breathy *shushing* noise.

Barbie instinctively rose off the toilet seat, yanking her panties up over her privates with a dry wheezy sound. The back of her dress accidentally slipped into the toilet water. She gasped, whirling around, pulling the expensive silk-rayon blend out of the muck. Her hands trembled as she wrung the fabric dry.

She glanced back at the floor under the stall door.

The shoes were gone.

Barbie took a couple of girding breaths. She told herself to calm down, take it easy, it was probably just a maintenance man who didn't understand English. She smoothed down her dress. Another deep breath and she opened the stall door.

The ladies' room was empty.

Inadvertently leaving her sample case in the stall, Barbie went over to the sink and ran water over her shaking hands. This was so silly. What was wrong with her? She let out a pained sigh as she dispensed a dollop of cleansing foam on her hands. She washed and shook her head and let out another sigh, glancing absently up at her reflection in the mirror.

The man behind her smiled.

"OH!"

Barbie hardly had a chance to turn around before the man lunged at her, grabbing her from behind, pressing a big rancid-smelling hand over her mouth.

So many impressions flooded Barbie's brain and body at that moment that she could only writhe in the man's iron grip as he tugged her toward the southeast corner of the bathroom. She could smell smoke on him, not just cigarette smoke but brimstone and wood smoke, like the smell of burned buildings.

White-hot terror knifed through Barbie's midsection as she dug her heels into the floor and bucked wildly in his arms. *She would not be raped.* That notion crackled through her brain with the cold abruptness of a lightning bolt. *She would rather die than be raped.* If she had to perish at the hands of this freak she would go down fighting. And that's when she thought of something she had learned in a self-defense class she had taken with Cyndee Kaiser many years ago.

She lifted her right foot suddenly and slammed her stiletto heel down as hard as she could on the man's instep.

It was as though a switch had been thrown, the man yelping suddenly like a stuck pig, his arms instantly loosening, his body seizing up. Barbie slipped out of his grasp, lumbering toward the door but stumbling over her own feet. Those four-inch heels proved to be a blessing *and* a curse. She tripped and landed on her face.

Out of the corner of her eye, in the row of mirrors, she glimpsed the reflection of her assailant. He was doubled over now, ass against the back wall, cringing with pain. Face obscured by shadow, he wore an anachronistic old stovepipe hat—a midnight-black topper, as Barbie's grandfather might have called it once upon a time—along with the black suit of a mortician. In fact, even amid her debilitating terror, Barbie Allison latched onto an odd stray thought: *He looks like a mad chimney sweep.*

He was also digging something out of his pocket. A gun? A knife? Barbie crawled toward the door in a panic.

She never made it.

A viselike grip closed around her ankles, and she screamed then, a primal cry for help, a last-ditch shriek for deliverance that bounced off the tile walls and reverberated out into the corridors, reaching countless ears. *"Help! Somebody help!"*

The man in black calmly and relentlessly dragged her back into the shadows, a slipstream of charred BO trailing after him, Barbie kicking and clawing at the floor. She would not give up. She would not give this monster the opportunity to rape her. She would chew his testicles off before she would allow him to rape her.

The odor of menthol filled Barbie's nostrils as a cloth was pressed down over her mouth. Outside the bathroom door, frantic footsteps were approaching. The jangle of keys. The sound of the locked door rattling.

The light was fading, Barbie's flesh cold and tingling, her mouth so cottony now she could hardly open it. She felt herself sliding back along the tiles, and it felt as though she were slipping into a warm bath of darkness. There was a second door in the ladies' room, a service door in the corner, and Barbie saw it through the gauze of her dwindling vision. The man in black was prying it open in slow, blurry motion—a time traveler from some Dickensian nightmare.

Barbie was dragged into darkness, her last conscious thought a prayer to some vague supreme being that she wouldn't be raped.

She needn't have worried.

The man in the hat had something completely different in mind for her.

PART I
The Archetype

What we seek, we shall find.

—EMERSON

The true motive behind most multiple
murders is a hall of mirrors—an insatiable
beast feeding only on itself.

—ULYSSES GROVE, *The Psychopathological
Archetype: Toward a Statistical Model*

ONE

"This morning we're going to build the perfect serial killer."

The man at the front of the room made his pronouncement in a measured voice, unaware of the tremendous portents in his words. He was a trim, light-skinned African American in a smartly tailored houndstooth sport coat, black V-neck, and jeans. His deep-set eyes and sculpted features revealed very little, and about the only thing that differentiated him from a stylish hip-hop A&R man was the laminated FBI faculty ID clipped to his outer pocket.

He turned and scratched a phrase in large letters across the blackboard—

THE ARCHETYPE

—as the hushed, scuttling sound of note-taking filled the oblong classroom.

"Webster's defines *archetype* as the model or the original version of something." He clapped chalk dust from his hands, raising tiny puffs of yellow smoke as he casually surveyed the room. "That's not exactly what I'm talking about here. And I'm definitely not talking about some B-movie version of the serial murderer. You can forget all that bogus mythology. What I'm talking about here is the mathematical average. The standard. The *monolithic* murderer."

Fourteen eager recruits sat in orderly rows before Ulysses Grove, twelve men and two women, bathed in stark fluorescent light. Each bore the telltale formality of the junior field agent on the come, from the Brooks Brothers jackets draped neatly over chair backs down to the meticulously buffed Florsheims. They all listened intently to the dapper instructor's words—all of them, that is, except one.

Edith Drinkwater sat next to the windows, near the reeking coffee service, chewing her pencil eraser. She was a short, stout, copper-skinned Haitian girl in an ill-fitting black dress, with tight cornrows of inky black braids curving down the back of her skull like ribs of armor. She had the plush curves of her mother—the matronly hips and bosom—which for years had been concealed behind the starched breastplates of boardroom dress codes. But when your cleavage starts a few centimeters south of your chin, there's not much you can do in the way of disguise.

The youngest field agent in the room, Drinkwater had difficulty focusing on the dapper instructor at the blackboard due to an undercurrent of emotions ebbing and flowing through her. She felt a vague distrust for the mostly male faculty here at the Academy—the old patriarchy was alive and well at Quantico—and yet at the same time she wanted so badly to rise through its ranks, to get to the *good part*—the actual casework.

Back in the mid-nineties, fresh out of junior college with a BS in Law Enforcement, Drinkwater got a job as a radio dispatcher for the Cicero, Illinois PD's Violent Crimes Division, a position for which she was woefully overqualified. After burning out on the edgy ennui of the gig, she spent a few years in the private sector—first as an investigator for American Family Insurance, and later as a skip tracer for Maksym Bail Bonds in West Chicago. All of it conspired to make Drinkwater want more. She was too smart, too tough, and too talented to be the token black in an understaffed suburban bond shop.

"Okay, let's start building the killer," Agent Grove was saying, pacing across the front of the room with his own bad self all decked out in Armani denim.

Drinkwater noticed Grove's mismatched eyes from the back of the room—one eye, the left, looked droopy, unfocused, and dead—and she wondered about the visual acuity in that left eye. Would they let *her* in the Academy with an eye like that? She knew all about the incident that had nearly blinded Grove two years ago. In fact, she knew more about Ulysses Grove, the only African American man ever to reach the status of senior consulting profiler in Bureau history, than most field agents who had spent months on cases with him. She made it her business to know such things.

"First question," Grove said, looking around the class. "Man or woman? Quick. Anybody."

Drinkwater heard somebody murmur, "Man . . . what else?"

Grove was nodding. "That's right, men are dogs,

and they also thrill-kill about eighty-nine percent more than women. What about age, race, religion?"

A portly black man with thick glasses in the third row raised his hand. "Middle-aged, white, Christian, red state Republican probably."

Scattered laughter. Grove acknowledged the joke with a terse nod. "Very good. The archetype is forty-two, to be exact. He's married and has a family. Usually in some middle-management job. Very few serial killers are drifters, as the movies would have you believe. On the other hand very few are geniuses. On the surface, the archetype is a bland, ordinary, run-of-the-mill person with no outward eccentricities. That's too easy, though. Let's go back to the perp's childhood and the old chestnut, the homicidal trinity. The early childhood attributes of tomorrow's serial killer are . . . what? Anybody. Give me the three traits of the junior sociopath."

Around the room scattered arms levitated. Edith Drinkwater put her hand up.

Grove gave her a nod. "The nice lady in black over here."

"Bed-wetting, fire starting, and animal torture." Drinkwater uttered the words with the plainspoken confidence of a country lawyer resting her case, as Grove proffered a pleasant smile in response.

"Excellent, thank you." He turned and wrote the three traits on the board, the sound of his chalk rasping and squeaking.

BED WETTER
FIRE STARTER
ANIMAL TORTURER

"This formula is overused," Grove went on. He turned and scanned the room as he spewed his rapid-fire lesson. "It's probably a little misleading, maybe even a little apocryphal, but it's still to this day a good starting point. Sixty-two percent of all children between the ages of six and ten wet the bed on a regular basis, and they're not gonna kill anybody. But when you add a fascination with fire you reduce the percentage to eleven percent."

Throughout the classroom pens madly skritched and scrawled the numbers.

"You know where I'm going with this." Grove paused for dramatic effect. "If our little problem child also has a propensity to pull the wings off of flies, he's part of a much narrower band of the population. We're talking about maybe point-zero-five percent that will pee the bed, play with matches, *and* kick the dog. Why is this percentage important? Anybody? What's the big deal with point-zero-five percent?"

Fewer hands shot up. A couple in the back. And, of course, Drinkwater.

Grove grinned at Drinkwater. "You're on a roll, go ahead."

"It's basically the same percentage of the human race that will murder somebody."

"Very good. Now let's push it further. Let's say a huge percentage of that point-zero-five percent will kill out of passion or opportunity. Cuckolded husbands, drive-by initiates, robberies gone bad. That's not our boy."

Grove paused again. He played his gaze across the room, and for a brief instant Drinkwater thought he was going to say, "Boo!" Ulysses Grove had that effect on people. Something behind his dark, almond-shaped eyes hinted at volatile chemicals being mixed.

Not surprisingly, many of the students had entire MySpace pages devoted to speculations about Special Agent Grove's mysterious personal history. He had been instrumental in more infamous homicide closures than any other single employee of the Bureau, including Melvin Purvis and J. Edgar Hoover combined, and yet he seemed like a major flake. One rumormonger swore up and down that Grove was the reincarnated spirit of some African witch doctor. Most believed there was something mystical about the man's intuition, but Edith had a feeling the only mystical thing about Ulysses Grove was his ability to manipulate the media, play politics at the Bureau, and maybe even use people to get ahead, to close cases, to build his legend.

Right now, in fact, the legend was turning with a dramatic flourish and pulling down a small projection screen on which a gun-range silhouette was pasted. "Our boy fits into a much smaller shard of that murderous pie chart," Grove said, jerking a thumb at the silhouette, then shooting a sidelong glance at the class.

Drinkwater stared at the paper effigy. She had seen similar silhouettes many times. The black, featureless cutout was rendered with the simplicity of an international symbol for PERSON. Depicted from the waist up, overlaid against an intricate crosshair bull's-eye, it looked like an inverted cast-iron skillet.

"We're talking about one hundredth of one percent of that point-zero-five percent." Grove indicated the black oval head and rounded rectangle shoulders.

Drinkwater knew target silhouettes well. She had happily riddled many of them with .44 caliber holes over the years. At the Cicero police academy she had won a trophy in the quick-draw contest, managing to get her Colt Desert Eagle out of her shoulder holster in 1.5 seconds, then squeezing off eight rounds over the course of another 4.2 seconds, five of them head shots. But today, for some reason, the target looked strange to Drinkwater.

At the front of the room Grove posed another question: "What we're talking about here is a person who will kill out of . . . what?"

Only Drinkwater's hand went up.

Grove gave her a nod. "Go for it."

"They'll kill out of need."

"Define need," Grove said.

She looked at the target silhouette, that big bulbous black head like a dead lightbulb. "Need . . . in terms of . . . like addiction."

Grove nodded. "That's not bad. But it's more than a controlled substance to feed an addiction, it's fuel for the fantasy. The killing is actually secondary. What do I mean by that?"

Drinkwater didn't exactly get what he meant by that.

Neither did anybody else.

"The murder serves a purpose not unlike pornography," Grove explained. "This guy—our mathematical average, our *every-killer* if you want to call him that—he kills to feed that furnace."

Pens scribbled notes across the room. But Drinkwater could not tear her gaze from that silhouette. Something about it was profoundly bothersome.

"What is this furnace anyway?" Grove scanned

the room, looking for a participant other than Drinkwater. "Anybody, what is it?"

"Sadism?"

Grove nodded at the Pakistani gentleman in the second row, the one with the bow tie and eager-beaver expression. "Interesting but not exactly correct, not for our archetype. Somebody else take a crack."

"Cruelty," another voice suggested.

Grove shook his head. "Actually, cruelty is more of a baroque, external modifier. When I say furnace I'm talking about something fundamental, the source of the fantasy—the *source*—somebody else?

Nobody said anything.

Drinkwater stared at that black bulbous outline, that perfectly generic figure. "Ego."

"Excuse me?" Grove glanced at Drinkwater with a half smile. "Say again?"

"Ego."

"Give the lady a gold star, that's exactly right. Hubris, ego. It's that Nietzschean superhero comic book in his head." Grove walked over to the target. He reached up and ran the tip of his index finger around the contours of the silhouette. "When you strip away the fantasy, our typical killer here murders out of the need to dominate. To be superior. That's where the torture component comes in."

More scribbling.

Grove cocked his head at the silhouette. "Yes, ladies and gentlemen, our boy's a torturer. Most are. Even physical positioning echoes the ego. Somebody tell me what I mean by that. The physical positioning echoing the ego component."

Drinkwater looked up, didn't even raise her hand. "You're talking about the missionary position."

Uneasy laughter.

Grove stopped smiling. "Go on."

"Man on top," Drinkwater said.

"That's right . . . and what else?"

Drinkwater looked at the silhouette. "He needs to do it to them slowly."

"Good, what else."

"He needs to have eye contact."

The class got quiet then. Grove nodded. He started down the row toward Drinkwater's chair in the back. "Interesting. *Why*, though? Why eye contact?"

Drinkwater took a deep breath. At the age of eleven she had been raped by her stepfather. It happened late one night in a tractor shed out behind the Robert Chambers housing project.

After a long pause she said, "Because he needs to see the desolation in your eyes."

Now the class was stone silent. Some of them stared at the floor. Most realized Drinkwater had said "*your*" instead of "*their*" as Grove approached her desk. He gave her an encouraging smile. "Ms. Drinkwater, you go to the head of the class."

"He needs to see it," she reiterated softly with a level, unblinking gaze.

Drinkwater was raped during a lightning storm, in the midst of a blackout. For most of her life, right up until the year she went through some heavy therapy, she only remembered the flicker of cold, icy light on her stepfather's grizzled face while he thrust himself into her.

"Let's go ahead and take a break," Grove suggested, his overly cheerful voice finally breaking the spell. "We'll pick it up after lunch."

Chairs squeaked. Voices murmured with relief. Drinkwater let out a sigh and gathered her things, feeling Grove's silent benevolent presence beside her like a phantom.

Even as she made her way out of the room she felt him watching her.

TWO

That evening, just after sunset, an inexplicably large cloud of gypsy moths formed around the giant sodium lights that blazed down on the Dixie Boy truck stop out on Highway 264 east of Greenville, North Carolina. Of the genus Lymantria, the gypsy moth is the color of toasted almonds, and features delicate, papery wings the consistency of snakeskin. Close up, a single moth is quite lovely, but when coalesced into a massive swarm they can take down a two-hundred-year-old oak or rival a biological attack of noxious gas.

In the thirty-one-year history of that dilapidated roadside complex, nobody had ever seen such a thing. And these people were not unaccustomed to bug infestations; every summer, Greenville becomes the mosquito capital of the Old South—"skeeter season," the old-timers call June down here—but *this*? This was something else altogether.

By 7 P.M., the density and volume of insects churning around those oblong overhead vapor lights reached the level of desert sirocco. From a distance, it looked as though the air was billowing with thick brown smoke. The moth cloud sparkled and undulated with its wheezing, dry-husk roar of feathery wings ticking and pinging against the glowing chevrons. Third-shift mechanics came out of their grease pits to watch. Busboys and fry cooks emerged from the main building and stood in awe, wiping their hands in towels, eyes gaping.

One person who was present that night thought of Revelations.

She watched the moth storm from inside the two open rear doors of her Kenworth eighteen-wheeler, fingering the tiny gold-plated crucifix around her sinewy neck. Karen Wanda Finnerty had just finished unloading a pallet full of raw coffee beans for the Dixie Boy grill, and now was fixing to get back on the road. A rawboned woman with a platinum blond dye job and forearms strong enough to crack walnuts, Karen had been a gypsy trucker for most of her adult life. Not only did the freedom of the open road appeal to her, but the lifestyle seemed a healthy way to rebel against her strict Pentecostal childhood. She was fully assimilated now, but those old Bible stories died hard, as did the marks left by the lashes of her father's belt.

Then from the smoke came locusts on the earth and they were given power like the power of scorpions, she thought as she watched the pulsating thunderhead of bugs swarming around the lights.

A noise from somewhere nearby splintered her attention, and she glanced over her shoulder. The asphalt stretched behind her, deserted, bathed in shadow. Along the periphery slept rows of idling semis. Most of the drivers were inside now, filling their bellies, getting jacked up on either French roast or little white pills.

Karen turned back to her work, securing the empty pallet with nylon shipping straps. All at once she heard the odd noise again: the scuff of a shoe on cinders. Very close. She looked down at the pavement at her feet and thought she saw the flicker of a shadow moving behind one of the truck's open rear doors.

She got very still, then carefully dipped her hand into her jeans pocket, where she kept a small folding stiletto knife. Then she grasped the edge of the door, took a deep breath, and suddenly yanked it shut.

There was nobody there.

Karen Finnerty let out a sigh of relief. She released the knife. Something was giving her the willies tonight and she had no idea what it was or why it was working on her. Maybe she needed a vacation. She turned back to her work and finished securing the straps, then shut the other door.

The tall man standing there suddenly lunged at her with something white in his hand.

Karen had no time to fight back, no time to react, no time to even scream—and she could have put up a fairly decent fight, given half a chance—because the big dark assailant immediately pressed a narcotic-soaked cloth over her face, then held it there with the pressure of an iron vise.

Karen Wanda Finerty sank to her knees, then sank through the pavement into a black void.

She regained consciousness only twice that night, the first time a brief instant of gasping for air as though she were underwater, blinking fitfully, desperately trying to focus on something. She had no concept of how long she had been out, but she sensed immediately, in some deeply buried compartment of her brain, that she had been moved indoors.

Head lolling to one side, she registered a sensation of cold—a metallic smoothness—beneath her; yellow light gleamed off steel devices hanging from a low ceiling. Eyes adjusting to her dim surroundings, she saw glimpses of gauges, dials, instruments. And then the realization—maybe *revelation* was a better word—pierced her consciousness with the icy abruptness of a nail from a nail gun hitting her between the eyes. She realized in that one groggy glance, right before blacking out again, just exactly where she was: *lying on a giant scale.*

She was being weighed and measured like a slab of meat.

Or more appropriately, as she would soon learn, like a sacrificial lamb.

THREE

After dinner that night, Ulysses Grove enjoyed another lively performance—rendered in the mixed media of peas and mashed potatoes—by his precocious three-year-old son, Aaron. "Big gween lady bugz all fly away Daddeee!" the little tyke enthused, pushing his plump little finger through the uneaten food on his plastic plate, his terrycloth bib a Jackson Pollock of gravy. "Big gween ladybugz all fly awaaaaaaaay! Look, Daddeee, look, look, look, *look*!"

Grove grinned over the top of his newspaper. Shirt sleeves rolled up, collar unbuttoned, he still had the stink of the academy on him, the chalk and coffee smells in the pores of his light bronze skin. "Wow, that's a lot of green ladybugs."

"All fly awaaaaay!" The boy furiously agitated his peas. A cherubic tyke, Aaron Grove had the pale eyes of his mother and the caramel complexion and tight frizzy curls of his father. He was already exhibiting a bubbly little personality, which he probably got from his mother, as well as a volatile temper. But there was something else about the child that worried Grove. The older the boy got, the more he seemed to hook into his father's moods, the angst and the obsessive brooding.

A voice came from across the kitchen. "All of which begs the question: who's on dishwashing duty tonight?"

Maura Grove was fiddling with the coffeemaker across the room, dressed in her floppy 49ers football jersey and Capri pants. A pale, whippet-thin woman with pewter blond hair, high cheekbones, and smart, hard eyes, she had an air of self-possession about her, the sanguine calm of a soldier who had served her tour and now had settled into the graceful banalities of homemaking.

"I believe I had that job *last* night," Grove replied with a gentle, needling smirk, gazing at the mess on the table.

"Fly awaaaaaay!"

Maura came over with a cup of decaf and set it in front of her husband. "Man sounds pretty sure of himself, Aaron. What do you think?"

"Fly-fly-*flieeeeeee*—!"

Grove winked at his wife "I recall a particularly nasty crust of macaroni and cheese I had to deal with."

Maura gave him a rueful smile, hands on her hips. "Fair enough. You can take bath time tonight." Her grin widened. "Since you're so handy with the macaroni and cheese."

"Touché." Grove put his paper down, pushed himself away from the table, and scooped his son out of his high chair. Aaron squealed as Grove bounced the sticky toddler in his arms. "C'mon, slick, let's go get you cleaned up."

Grove carried the boy out of the kitchen and across the spacious living room toward the stairs.

The house was a quaint, two-story Cape Cod overlooking a rugged stretch of mid-Atlantic coastline just south of Pelican Bay, Virginia. This upscale bedroom community was home to all manner of government types, from well-heeled policy wonks to senior intelligence analysts. The place was a little rich for Grove's blood, but the Bureau had helped him relocate here last year after his Alexandria home burned to the ground in a terrible, inexplicable fire. It was, in a way, another in a long line of compromises he had been making lately.

The truth was, the teaching gig had been a compromise as well, a mutual decision made last year between Grove and his benefactor, confidant, and section chief, Tom Geisel, in the aftermath of a profiling assignment gone bad. On that job, the predator Grove had been obsessively hunting had somehow learned the location of the Grove family safe house in rural Indiana. Fortunately, in the eleventh hour, Grove had managed to save his wife and his baby son. But the incident had taken its toll. For months afterward the memories had wormed their way into Grove's dreams. It wasn't the first bout of post-traumatic stress that he had ever experienced, but it was turning out to be his first full-blown identity crisis. He didn't know who he was anymore, and he was increasingly defensive about his new job, especially when VIPs visited, especially since he was supposed to be this big rock star at the Bureau. So what was he doing slumming down at the Academy?

"Make you a deal, slick," he murmured into the boy's ear as he carried him up the stairs. "You take your bath like a good boy, and I'll tell you another exciting tale of romance and adventure."

The boy had no idea what romance and adventure were, but from the sound of his squeals, it was clear that he thought a story was a good idea.

A few hundred miles to the south, on a leprous outcropping of mid-Atlantic coastline known as Emerald Isle, a battered, rust-pocked panel van pulled into the vapor-lit darkness of a deserted public parking lot. The lot was adjacent to a public pier known as Bogue Inlet. The van parked near a column of weather-beaten steps.

Nobody saw the dark presence emerge from that vehicle like a moving shadow.

Presence, because the individual with the odd headwear seemed to absorb light like a black hole. Face shaded by his shopworn top hat, broad shoulders draped in a black oiler, hands gloved in black rubber, the figure might as well have been invisible—despite the strange headgear and imposing height.

The stranger went around behind the van, opened the double doors, and pulled out a large canvas duffel bag that seemed to be loaded with cinder blocks from the way the big man hefted the strap over his shoulder.

He went over to the stairs and descended with an almost robotic stoicism, the hat tilted forward just enough for the brim to shade most of his face, which looked from a distance as though it were covered in soot. The hat itself—which had begun to show its age (a little shiny at the edges, the felt tattered and pilled along the top)—had an elaborate history.

Stolen from the British Museum in the late 1980s, it had floated around on the black market for decades, traded and relished by collectors of the outré, before coming into the possession of this tall, mute man in black. The hat was originally found at a murder scene in Whitechapel, London, in the year 1888. It was believed to have once belonged to Jack the Ripper.

Now the tall man was crossing the deserted beach, the sea wind buffeting his coat, flapping his hood, and threatening to toss his hat off, yet he remained oblivious to the elements. The inky black waves, shimmering with moonlight out beyond the sandbar, were merely vectors and angles of light to this unseen presence. Nature mattered only as a grid across which a higher purpose played itself out. It was nearly 9:43 P.M. It was almost time.

Ulysses Grove was leaning over the upstairs bathtub, reciting to his boy with great melodrama. His voice echoed off the bathroom tile as he traced the washrag around the tiny convolutions of the child's ear. " 'The brave knight heard a voice then. He looked around the dark and saw no one present other than the tall dark trees.' "

"Looks like talking tweez!" Aaron exclaimed, pointing a chubby little finger at the illustrations of the Golden Classic book his daddy was holding over the bathwater.

"That's right," Grove said with a nod. "It's the tree that's talking to him."

The boy was on a roll. "Like in *The Wizard of Oz*."

"Exactly . . . the ones that threw their apples at Dorothy."

Aaron looked at his dad excitedly. "Do these tweez throw apples?"

Grove shrugged. "Wouldn't surprise me."

The boy looked back at the book.

"Keep weading, Daddy, keep weading," he insisted.

Grove grinned. " 'Beware,' said the great old oak. 'Beware the troll that lives under the bridge!' "

The little boy's eyes widened with awe.

The dark man paused, the tide licking across the deserted beach brushing the edge of his black wingtips. His face cloaked in shadows, his muscles flexing under the coat, he felt something moving inside his giant duffel bag. He tightened his grip on the strap, then started toward the pilings.

A woman's leg burst suddenly through the end of the duffel bag.

The tall man dropped his human cargo in the sand. In the moonlight, the leg appeared sunburned, peeling here and there. On closer inspection, the wounds revealed themselves as horrible bloody divots, still oozing.

The stranger stood over the wiggling mass and watched with a blank, poker-faced stare. The bag teetered in the sand, once, twice—accompanied by a strangled cry—and then began to roll. It rolled over and over again, toward the water.

The figure watched impassively. It was nearly time. The duffel bag landed in the water just as the flailing woman inside it tore through the broken seam.

"HHHEEEHHHHHHH—HHHHEEEHH-HHP—!!"

Karen Finnerty—voice strained to the breaking point—attempted the word *help* but was impeded by a birth defect or injury of the soft palate. Somehow she had gotten her bloody hands free and had torn the duct tape from her mouth, and now she crawled madly out of the bag, trailing the canvas behind her like a giant slimy pupae in the dark breakers foaming across the beach.

The truck driver's garbled shrieks were drowned by the crash of waves against the breakwater. Her bottle-blond hair sticking to her horrified face, her sinewy muscles defaced by all the superficial wounds across her sacrum, she kept crawling and crawling, and she got nowhere.

The shadowy figure behind her watched with the implacable calm of a nineteenth-century gentleman judging a croquet match. He looked at the moon, then glanced across at the cones of vapor light shining down on the parking lot.

A nearby rust-pocked sign demarcated the distance to the next town on the island, which the figure had calibrated carefully.

It was 9:48. The peroxide-blonde woman had two minutes to live.

" 'You must answer a simple question in order to pass over the bridge,' said the Troll."

In the bright, gleaming, soapy atmosphere of the bathroom, Ulysses Grove lowered his voice to nearly a whisper. The boy sat upright in the tepid water, rapt, his little mouth slack, his eyes huge.

Grove continued reading: "The Brave Knight nodded and said, " 'Very well. I am ready.' " And that's when the troll smiled a crooked smile and said, 'The question that I'm about to ask is the only question that matters. The only question there is.' "

Aaron gawked. Grove paused for dramatic effect, as he always did at this juncture in the story, then read the kicker at the end.

" 'The question is *"Why?"* ' "

"PLLLLLLEEEEEEEEEEEEATH!!" In the salt-cured moonlight, Karen Finnerty rose up on wobbling legs and started hobbling through the sodden sand toward the higher road, unaware of the presence closing in behind her.

A second later he pounced.

His hat never left his head.

It felt to Karen like a hornet had stung her between the shoulder blades, except for the fact that the initial sting erupted into a maelstrom of cold fire spreading down her spine. Her legs buckled.

She stumbled to the ground, eating a mouthful of sand, legs already going numb. She tried to crawl through the darkness, but the paralysis was setting in from the eight inches of tempered steel sunk into her back. She gasped for breath—the knife had, unbeknownst to her, punctured a lung—as she managed to traverse a few more inches before giving out, the cold shade of unconsciousness drawing down over her.

The last thing she saw was a tiny hermit crab crawling through the moonlight toward her, its beady little eyes fixing on her, seeing her but not seeing her.

The woman expired in a swirling black corona of blood and salt water.

The figure loomed over her. The luminous sweep-second hand on his watch had reached twelve. The minute hand pointed to the fifty-seventh minute past nine. He knelt down and rooted the blade out of the victim's spine. It came free with a satisfying, wet, smooching noise.

Perfect.

The second blow came down exactly six inches to the left of the initial wound. This time the body lay as still as a stone, as blood bubbled around the blade's hilt. The woman's vitals had shut down at 9:57:21 P.M., Eastern Standard Time.

Perfect.

The third blow landed precisely four inches below the original killing blow. The lifeless woman absorbed the impact like a pincushion, as blood bubbled and flowed in rivulets off the corpse and down into the black tide pool created by her own body.

Perfect.

Again the knife came down, piercing warm flesh, baptizing the sacred sand in sacrificial blood, marking the scene for posterity. Again and again and again and again and again and again and again.

Eleven times.

The perfect average.

As written in the Prophecy.

FOUR

Later that night, at a few minutes after 11 o'clock, the Groves' phone rang. It was an odd time for a call, even for the telemarketers, who had been plaguing the Grove household for months.

Ulysses was in Aaron's room, watching his child sleep, lost in his thoughts. Maura was still in the kitchen, dealing with the disaster otherwise known as the dinner dishes. Throughout all the scrubbing and rinsing, she had been idly thinking about all the things she wanted to do to the new house, vacations she wanted to plan, romantic getaways she wanted to enjoy with her husband. She loved—in fact, she *cherished*—having him home now, safely ensconced as a teacher, out of the danger zone of fieldwork. Maura had vigorously encouraged this conversion from soldier to sage, even urging him at one point to publish his class notes as a book. The more successes he had behind his proverbial desk, the more normal his family life would become.

And Maura adored being normal.

To say that she had gotten her fill of high-level criminology over the last few years was an understatement. Never mind that she had gotten mixed up one too many times in the macabre minutiae of her husband's work. Never mind that her own life—not to mention the life of her child—had been endangered on more than one occasion. The worst part was trying to believe the promises Ulysses kept making to her: he was done, he was getting out of it, for good, period, end of story.

Now she went over to the cordless on the wall and looked at the caller ID display as the phone rang a second time.

A current of nervous tension trickled coldly down her solar plexus as she recognized the area code; 703 usually meant Bureau business, and Bureau business usually meant a restless husband. It was not unlike a liquor store calling a recovering drunk just to tell him about the latest bargain prices on grain alcohol. Bureau people often called Ulysses for a quote for some profile, or even a few hours of consultation. "It's just a little light reading," he would assure Maura, "just a glorified book report." But Maura knew the truth: every time the FBI called with some new abomination of nature, some new monster on the loose, Ulysses got restless, like a bloodhound getting the scent.

The phone rang a third time, and Maura finally snatched the cordless off its cradle and answered.

"Hello," she croaked in an anxious voice, hoarse with nervous tension.

The voice on the other end of the line was not the voice she had expected.

A thick roux of fog had rolled in over Emerald Isle beach, and now the air stewed with a gray

briny mist pushing down from Kitty Hawk. Somewhere out in the black opaque distance, a lighthouse bell sent a melancholy clang echoing over
the breakers. The only other sound was the shrill
babble of an old lobsterman who stood between
two policemen on the beach, gazing down at the
human wreckage on the sand, the ragged form
barely visible in the magnesium-silver beams of
their flashlights.

"I tell ya, it's the drugs, it's the crystal meth and
the bathtub speed and them college kids comin'
down here from Duke every Easter. Just last year
we had some drug addict commit suicide off that
same dad-blamed dock right up—"

"Sir, please," one of the cops broke in, raising a
beefy hand in an attempt to stem the flow of babble. The older of the two patrolmen, Officer Ted
Stenowski had been on the Outer Banks beat for
most of his twenty-seven years with the force, but
he had never seen anything on the beach quite
like *this*. "I'm going to need you to hold that
thought and be quiet for a second."

The old salty dog stuck out his lower lip and
gave the cop an indignant grunt.

Stenowski went over to Karen Finnerty's remains, his Wellington boots sinking down to the
ankles in the muck. High tide had come in only
minutes ago, and now the waves licked at the
woman's corpse, gently nudging it sideways with
every sudsy ripple. Stenowski shone his flashlight
down at the victim. Darkening blood swirled on
the seafoam like threads of raspberry syrup.

"This is no suicide," Stenowski muttered, somewhat rhetorically, more to himself than anyone
else. He shone the light off to the left of the

corpse, then off to the right. Then he took a second look at everything. He saw the remnants of something scratched into the sand vanishing on the waves.

They looked like letters.

"Johnny, get on the blower to Raleigh, get Dave Van Teigham and the whole CSI bunch down here."

Behind Stenowski, the younger cop frowned. "You want the Bureau in on this thing?"

Stenowski didn't answer—he had too many things running through his mind at that moment as he stared down at the meticulously mutilated victim.

The door to little Aaron's room clicked open softly, and Maura peered into the darkness.

Ulysses Grove sat in a bentwood rocker next to his child's crib, rocking and thinking. Only the faint yellow glow of a night-light and a pale strip of moonlight coming through the blinds illuminated Grove's chiseled features. One of Aaron's coloring books sat on his lap.

For the last hour he had been absently doodling in the margins of the book with a black crayon, drawing the same symbol over and over—the bulbous gun-target silhouette from his class. *The faceless effigy of the every-killer.* It was a symbol that had been haunting the periphery of his dreams and visions for nearly a year, ever since he had turned his elaborate 125-page class syllabus into a forensic textbook ponderously titled *The Psychopathological Archetype: Toward a Statistical Model.* Somehow, in his fervid imagination, Grove had anthropomor-

phized that human target silhouette into a mon-
strous *individual*, an individual *he* had birthed into
the world.

He closed the coloring book and looked up at
his wife like a man stirring from a dream. "What's
wrong?"

"Lois Geisel just called," Maura whispered as
she approached her husband. She was holding
herself as though she were cold.

Grove reflexively looked at his watch. Lois
Geisel rarely deigned to make personal calls, especially not at this late hour. She was a very private,
very introverted, very patrician woman who had
served her husband well over the years as the un-
official "first lady" of the Behavioral Science Unit.
She was a party-giver and a function organizer, but
never a kibitzer. Grove got along well with her, and
had nothing but respect for any woman with the
good taste to stay married to Tom Geisel. The
aging patriarch of the BSU was Grove's mentor, his
best friend, his moral compass. Without Tom
Geisel running interference for him over the
years, Grove would have been chewed up by the
Byzantine politics of the Bureau long ago.

"Uly . . ." Maura stopped, something terrible
glittering in her wet eyes.

"What is it?"

She swallowed. "Tom Geisel's had a stroke."

By 3 A.M. the soupy air over Emerald Isle beach
flickered with the silver strobes of forensic cameras.
The field office in Raleigh had dispatched two ad-
ditional special agents to accompany the senior investigator, David Van Teigham, to the scene, and

now the sand—most of it staked off with yellow tape and patchworked with plastic drip cloths—bustled with crime scene technicians.

"What I'm trying to figure out here is why the first on the scene shoots an immediate call to us," Van Teigham was saying, standing off in the darkness by a weathered piling, his thick head of chestnut hair tossing in the sea breeze. He was young for a senior investigator, with a stylish look about him apparent even in the wee-hour dark. He had surgical gloves on his hands, and a laminate ID card dangled across his Bill Blass tie, twisting and flapping in the wind. "In other words, what gave you the idea this was anything more than, you know, a one-shot deal?"

Officer Stenowski stood next to the agent, his burly arms crossed defensively against his chest. "Honest truth? I really had no idea."

Van Teigham gazed at the scene, the blatant array of footprints, the darker patches of sand, the black arterial stains fanning out from Karen Finnerty toward the sea grass to the north. "That makes two of us."

The cop licked his lips thoughtfully. "You mind if I ask you something?"

"Shoot."

"Does it look like a series?"

Van Teigham looked at the cop. "You didn't really answer my original question."

Stenowski looked at the victim, then shrugged. "The thing is, I read a lot."

Van Teigham cocked his head. "Reading is good. What do they say—reading is fundamental?"

"I know it sounds corny."

"Not at all. We're all friends here." The agent

gave the cop a smile that faded almost immediately. "You got a theory about this situation?"

"Theory? No. Well . . . I wouldn't exactly call it a theory." Silver strobes flashed in the fog like heat lightning. Stenowski looked at the agent. "Am I crazy or does it all look familiar?"

"All what?"

"Everything, every little thing." Stenowski gestured at the victim, the scene. "The body, the pose, the evidence. I don't know. Everything."

The agent ran fingers through his thick, sandy hair. "You're thinking we got a copycat on our hands?"

Stenowski shook his head. "No . . . not exactly. It's just . . . *familiar.*"

The agent thought about it for a second, then said, "Lemme ask you something, Stenowski. When you say you read a lot, you're talking about, what? Sherlock Holmes? Forensic stuff? Mickey Spillane? What?"

Stenowski shrugged. "Textbooks, mostly. Forensic science, criminology, behavioral profiling, stuff like that."

The agent glanced at the evidence flags, the blood-mottled sand, the huge black oval under Karen Finnerty's torso. "That's very interesting."

Stenowski looked at the younger man. "Why's that?"

Van Teigham pondered the victim's pale, mildewed corpse, and the fact that it perfectly matched another random, motiveless killing in Minneapolis just a few weeks ago. "Because I was thinking the same goddamn thing—how familiar it looks."

FIVE

Grove was dozing fitfully in a cheap armchair in the corner of Tom Geisel's hospital room when his cell phone began trilling incessantly in his pocket.

Grove had been maintaining his lonely bedside vigil since 4 A.M. Not long ago he had told Lois to go get something to eat, and the subsequent silence had made Grove drowsy. He needed to rest his eyes. For hours he had been doing nothing but staring at his comatose boss, praying that the man would come back to the land of the living. Now the chirping cell phone seemed an affront to the older man's dignity. "Should've turned this piece of shit off," Grove grumbled under his breath as he rooted the cell phone out of his pocket.

Across the room, a cold, gunmetal dawn rose behind the Venetian blinds, bathing the gurney bed in cameos of pale light. The section chief, nestled in his white linen sarcophagus, did not stir, did not move. Eyes closed, his strong, cleft chin shadowed with whiskers, Tom Geisel looked almost serene. Regal, even. Lois must have combed his hair, because it still had his trademark ruler-straight part, the iron-gray wings sweeping back over his large ears. His enormous, gnarled, liver-spotted hands lay in repose at his side. The soft beeping noises of the vital monitors drowned his shallow breathing.

The section chief's prognosis, according to the young, sober-faced resident who had been periodically charging in and out of the room, was still inconclusive. They were still studying MRIs, still analyzing CT scans. They suspected either a massive stroke or an aneurysm of some sort, but they were not ruling anything out, especially in light of the man's symptoms. According to Lois, her husband had been dozing in front of the TV last night when he suddenly awakened from a terrible nightmare with blurred vision and chest pains. He had stumbled into the bathroom, and minutes later Lois found him on the floor, mumbling, disoriented, a part of his face slack and twitching.

Grove looked at the caller ID display on his buzzing cell phone and saw it was a Bureau field office calling.

An unexpected twinge of dread stabbed Grove in the chest: *Bureau field offices never called him directly unless there was a time crunch on something.* Was this the other shoe dropping? Was this the *second* act of this inexorable little tragedy he had stumbled into? *Bad news comes in threes,* his mother used to say. But right now, one was enough for Grove. At the moment, in fact, he wasn't even sure he could handle a new case. Not with his lifeline—his anchor, his voice of reason—fading away in front of him.

Tom Geisel had been Grove's benevolent ring

man from the very beginning: recruiting Grove
fresh out of the military, and always present in
Grove's corner; carefully selecting Grove's assign-
ments, protecting the wonder boy. Grove and Geisel
had caught dozens of elusive criminals together, and
had also gotten to know each other on that bone-
deep level shared by fellow trench warriors. They
had attended weddings and funerals together, had
burned CDs of old jazz tunes for each other, and
on alternating mornings had even brought each
other lox and bagels. Without even being aware of
it they had become like brothers. And now Grove's
only brother in the world was dying, and it made
Grove's guts twist with anguish, and it made him
curse this goddamned cell phone for squeaking
and vibrating in his hand like a viper.

"This is Grove," he snapped into the cell.

An unfamiliar voice said, "Agent Grove, this is
Dave Van Teigham, special agent out of Raleigh-
Durham. Sorry to bother you so early in the morn-
ing, sir."

Grove frowned. He didn't know anybody out of
Raleigh-Durham. The voice on the other end had
a youthful quality to it, and a calibrated drawl that
suggested New South, maybe a college degree
from someplace like Duke or Tulane. "Listen, uh,
Agent, uh—"

"Van Teigham."

"Right, um . . . look. I'm a little tied up this
morning. Can you leave a message at Quantico?"

There was a tense beat of silence, then the voice
said, "The thing of it is, I would normally go
through channels, but this thing is . . ."

Grove waited. "I'm listening."

"Okay. In a nutshell. We got reason to believe we got a series going now—and it's a little unique."

"Go on."

The voice took a deep breath. "We just taped off a scene outside a little resort town in North Carolina, along the Outer Banks, called Emerald Isle—female, white, early forties, name of Karen Finnerty, apparent cause of death sharp trauma. Signature matches up with an unsolved killing in Minneapolis two weeks ago."

"You mean the MO?"

"Actually there's a real signature here, looks like a ritual type deal."

Grove let out a pained sigh. He felt slightly guilty talking about this stuff in front of his unconscious boss. He turned away, toward the wall, as though this conversation might actually infect Geisel with its tainted backwash. "Look. Van Tiegham . . . I'm going to have to get back to you—"

"If you just give me a chance to—"

"I'm sorry." Grove rubbed his eyes. "I'm going to have to pick this up next week—"

"It's just like your book."

Grove frowned. "I'm sorry?"

"I said it's just like your book."

Grove stood up, turned toward the wall, his voice suddenly low and urgent. "What the hell are you talking about?"

On the other end of the line, Van Teigham's voice dropped an octave. "I didn't want to just drop this in your lap like this."

"What do you mean, just like my book?"

"I think we got a situation here—I don't think

copycat is the right word for it: the evidence is staged *exactly* the same way it appears in your book."

The door to Geisel's room whooshed open, and Grove lurched into the corridor, his sweaty grip tight on the cell phone, the back of his neck tingling with nervous tension. "I'm not following what you're telling me here," he said under his breath, oblivious to the nurses brushing past him, the orderlies pushing carts down the hallway.

"Let me repeat what I'm saying," the voice in his ear said. "The evidence—both in Minneapolis and North Carolina—it matches down to the last fiber the model in your book—what did you call it? The archetype?"

"How did you even—?"

"I caught your lecture at the annual AFP meeting last March, met you afterward at the banquet, got a copy of your book. I probably wouldn't have connected anything up if I hadn't seen that illustration."

"What illustration is that?" Grove stared at the scuffed tile floor, chewing the inside of his cheek. He did not notice the frail, gray-haired woman approaching from the bank of elevators fifty feet away. Dressed in jeans and a fleece vest, her eyes raw from crying, Lois Geisel carried a large purse, a brown paper bag, and a newspaper under one arm. She walked with the somnambulant, zombie gate of the traumatized.

Van Teigham's voice kept crackling in Grove's ear: "It was in the chapter on spatter patterns, bloodstain pathology—the artist rendering—I checked it again this morning—compared it to the CSI shots from the Finnerty scene. Pretty damn uncanny. Same exact pattern in the smudge marks across the sand, same exact volume. In the alley in Minnesota, too. Same story—"

Lois Geisel walked up to Grove and put a cold, slender hand on his arm.

Grove patted her shoulder, and made a "gimme one second" gesture, as Van Teigham's drawl continued sizzling in his ear.

"—which got me to thinking, what about the other averages from your study? You can look at the two scenes yourself. They're identical, they perfectly match the averages in your study. The MO, the body dump, the print dispersions, victimology, the whole shot. The archetypal killer. And I'm thinking, is this even possible? I'm wondering is this even within the realm of—"

"Okay, Van Teigham, I get it." Grove chewed on his lip, thinking. "Where are you right now?"

"I'm at the Raleigh-Durham field office."

"Okay, look, I'll call you back. Stay put. I'll call you back in fifteen."

"I'll be here."

Grove thumbed his cell off and folded it shut, then put an arm around Lois Geisel's thin body.

She gazed up at him through strands of gray hair. Her eyes, spiderwebbed with wrinkles and running mascara, looked parboiled. She managed a halfhearted smile. "Always working, you boys."

"Sorry about that."

"I forgot to tell you." She dug in her purse for something. "He wrote you a note."

"Excuse me?"

"It's here somewhere. He was lucid in the ambulance for a while. Managed to scribble something before he . . . lost consciousness."

Grove looked at her. "Tom wrote me a note?"

"Here it is." She pulled out a folded piece of ruled paper. "He said something about getting this to you as soon as possible."

Grove took the note.

Lois shrugged. "I didn't even read it. I'm not even sure it's legible. By that point, he was"—she swallowed the end of the sentence, her eyes welling up—"he was—"

"He's gonna be okay, Lois." Grove gave her a hug, the note crumpling in his fist. "Just a bump in the road—he's gonna pull through."

From the look on her face it was clear she didn't believe a word of what Grove what saying.

For that matter, neither did he.

By two o'clock that afternoon, Grove was on a commuter flight to Raleigh-Durham.

Before embarking, he called Maura from the airport, assuring her that Tom was stable and that there was nothing to worry about—something had come up that necessitated a quick trip down to North Carolina. Just for the day, no big deal. He'd be home by suppertime. From the resignation in Maura's voice, Grove could tell that she was suspicious, worried, even a little aggrieved. But Grove would have to deal with that later.

Now, seated in the rear of the small Jetstream

aircraft, coursing high above the steel-gray coastal plains of the Chesapeake—one of only three passengers in the narrow cabin of twenty-nine seats—Grove was on his own dime. He hadn't taken the time to notify Operations of this unexpected consultation. He hadn't bothered telling anybody at the Academy; luckily he had no classes. But the truth was, he wasn't even sure he was authorized to go on such a trip.

None of these factors, however, currently occupied his thoughts. None of these considerations even entered his mind as the plane pitched and bumped over angry turbulence. He was too busy staring at the damp, wrinkled note spread out on the tray table in front of him.

Grove had read and reread Tom Geisel's hurriedly scrawled message, at least a half a dozen times now, and it still remained as cryptic and foreboding as the first time—especially the last few lines, when the spidery handwriting disintegrated into illegible gibberish, probably due to the onslaught of convulsions.

Ulysses—
Minds a little scrambled now, bear with me. Full disclosure time. Been having nightmares last few years. Thought it was stress. Now, I think has something to do with this thing inside the perps that you're in the habit of mentioning. This entity you speak of. Let me start over. Having trouble organizing my thoughts. Tonight had the worst dream ever, a dark figure, like a shadow. No face, just an outline just not feeling too good about not tellin

yo s'thing they tol me bac then
tht thee ws an o her b y a
b d one who_ yo have to UI h
ss yr tn

And that's how the note—and ultimately Tom Geisel's time on earth—ignominiously came to an end.

SIX

"It's just up ahead, near the end of the causeway, another mile or so," Van Teigham was saying, pointing a manicured finger at the distant overcast horizon visible through the windshield. They were driving to the north end of the island, a scabrous stretch of marshland and trailer homes rusted out by the salt winds and Carolina sun.

"Where is the scene exactly?" Grove wanted to know as they thumped over traffic-control bumps. The fishy smell of the low country filtered through the window vent. It was nearly four o'clock, and the daylight was already starting to soften. The sky had a cellophane texture to it. Distant streaks of faint lightning veined the horizon-like tinsel.

"What do you mean? The street address?" The young field agent in his stylish haircut and Ralph Lauren suit made Grove nervous. There was an edge to the man that Grove couldn't quite put his finger on.

"No, I mean in relation to the rest of the community. Is it in a gentrified area? Upscale resort area? Industrial pier—what?"

Van Teighman shot him a glance from behind the wheel. "My guess is you already know."

"You folks use the zone system down here?"

"Yep, just like the big guys up north."

"My guess is Zone II."

Van Teigham gave him a nod. "You got it."

The zone is a method of defining populated areas in terms of criminal activity. Zone I is usually a central business district. Zone II is a transitional area of warehouses, alleys, and mixed-use buildings sandwiched between a populated area and an unpopulated area. Nearly 80 percent of all violent crimes occur in Zone II. The average body dump also happens there.

"Lucky guess," Grove muttered under his breath as he stared out the window. "I assume you got all the ME photos of the vic ready to go?"

"Absolutely, got the whole series on a light table back at the office."

"How about evidence logs?"

"Yep, and we got the autopsy report an hour ago."

"Pathology report?"

Van Teigham gave a nod as he made a sharp left turn, then headed down a sandy access road bordered by palmettos swaying in sea winds. "Got the lab stuff in my briefcase."

"And?"

Van Teigham didn't say anything for an excruciatingly long moment.

Then the young field agent finally looked over at Grove, and replied in such a somber tone it sounded as though he didn't believe it himself. "It's like when you wrote that book . . . you were *thinking* of this guy."

* * *

The actual murder scene—at least the taped-off portion of the beach—was barely a hundred square feet, now crisscrossed in late-afternoon shadows from the adjacent pier. For nearly fifteen minutes, Grove silently circled this patch of coarse, weedy sand without saying a word, his eyes watering from the sting of ocean wind. Every few moments, one of his designer loafers would sink into the mire, and he would pull it free with a *smucking* noise. He wore surgical gloves and he carried a notepad, but he made very few notes. All he could do was marvel at the mathematical precision of the scene.

The murder had occurred fourteen to sixteen hours earlier near one of the massive salt-eaten pilings of the ramshackle Bogue Inlet pier. The positioning of the body, which had been carted away by the medical examiner earlier that afternoon, was marked by an outline of waterproof tape. The tide had sucked away half the bloodstains, leaving a sluggish leech trail of pink foam in its wake.

In his book Grove had discussed the average blood-spillage during the typical stranger-murder. Metrically speaking it was precisely 1.2 liters, and at the end of the chapter on patterns and signatures he included an illustration based on a computer model. Right now Grove was staring at a life-size, three-dimensional version of that illustration—especially the fan-shaped stain soaking the sand above the place at which Karen Wanda Finnerty's head had come to rest.

Other aspects of the scene were stunningly faithful to the book. The perpetrator's footprints—size eleven and a half E, according to Van Tiegham, the perfect average—tracked around the periphery.

Tiny evidence flags marked each one, each position identical to the computer models of the book. Even the victimology—female, white, independent, age 42—matched the study down to the exact age.

Traces of buprenorphine, a form of methadone, were found in the bloodstreams of both women, as well as sodium thiopental, which Van Teigham attributed to the killer's MO of sedation and control—yet another trait of the Archetype. A perfect rendering down to the chemical ratios.

"What's that?" Grove pointed at a lone evidence flag jutting out of the sand a couple of yards to the left of the body-outline. He could only see a tangle of seaweed near the flag.

"I'm told there was writing," Van Teigham replied from behind Grove. The young agent was watching Grove stalk the scene with a mixture of fascination and envy. The winds shook his pants as he shot a thumb at the ocean. "Tide got the better of it unfortunately."

Grove blinked. "A note from the perp?"

"That's right. Beat cop that was first on the scene saw it washing away in the tide."

Grove glanced back at the lone evidence flag. A cold feather of dread ran down the back of his neck. He could feel the light darkening around him like a fist. In the back of his mind he saw that black, featureless target-silhouette of the every-killer. He closed his eyes and remembered the splintery handwriting of Tom Geisel, scrawled in the throes of a stroke: *a dark figure, like a shadow . . . no face, just an outline.* Grove shook off the errant thoughts, then pointed off to his right, indicating the four-foot square blanket of canvas that had been duct-taped up over one of the pilings. "What about that?"

"Oh yeah, forgot about that," Van Teigham replied. "They put that up before the media showed up this morning, didn't want to freak out the rubberneckers."

The young agent trudged over to the piling, ripped off the canvas, and dropped it to the sand.

Grove gaped.

He heard faint voices whispering in his head, speaking foreign tongues, sounding like a million match tips striking all at once. A vague panic seized his chest as he stared at the bloodstain defacing the salt-silvered wood like a Rorschach of black ink in the dying light.

Van Teigham kept on chattering. "What I'm thinking here is, we start selecting anybody with the right background who has actually *seen* your book. I'm already running down Internet orders at the publisher. I'm sure you've got some ideas of your own?"

Grove could not form a reply.

The piling was the problem. Two distinct smudge patterns blossomed up from the point where the worm-eaten wood met the sand—less than five feet from the final position of the victim—like bloody leaves shooting up the stem of a flower. Grove gaped at these smudges with the awe of a Paleozoic ape staring at fire.

"Agent Grove?"

Grove could not make his mouth work, despite the fact that alarms were going off in his brain. The marks on the piling swam in his vision.

"Agent Grove? You all right?"

For reasons that were lost to him now, Grove had pulled three diagrams from his book prior to publication. One was a computer model of the most favored angle of entry found in the majority of wounds. Another was an artist's conception of the most popular weapon used in the average motiveless murder—a twelve-inch Bowie-style hunting knife. And the third illustration—based on a computer-assisted rendering—was the median smudge pattern found at the average serial murder scene.

The winglike floret of smudges had been created on his own computer, and currently existed only in digital form on his hard drive at home.

Ulysses Grove was the only human being on earth who had ever seen that pattern.

The same pattern now adorned a rotten wood piling near a chalk outline on a deserted North Carolina beach.

On the trip back to Raleigh-Durham, Grove didn't say much. Van Teigham did the driving, and did most of the talking. He wanted to get headquarters involved and maybe get more personnel working the case, and perhaps even form a task force with Burt Milliken and the folks up at the Minneapolis field office. He also wanted to know if Grove could dedicate himself to the case 24-7. Grove was noncommittal, stoic, lost in his own thoughts. He did not mention the inexplicable bloodstains on the piling.

By the time they rolled into Raleigh-Durham International Airport, it was after dark and Van Teigham had taken the hint. "You sure there's nothing wrong?" he asked as Grove climbed out of the car with this briefcase.

"I'll be in touch, thanks," Grove muttered without even shaking the guy's hand.

Grove entered the terminal and went directly to the bank of pay phones. His cell reception was atrocious down here in the wide-open spaces, and he needed to check in with Maura before he did anything else. He needed time to think. Time to figure out what was happening.

She answered on the third ring. "Uly?"

"Hey, kiddo."

A beat of silence. "Oh God, Uly."

"What's the matter?"

"I tried to call you."

"Maura, what's—?"

"Honey, Tom Geisel passed away at four-thirty this afternoon."

SEVEN

Thomas Edward Geisel
1941–2008

PIONEERING CRIMINOLOGIST
SHAPED STUDY OF
SERIAL KILLERS

WASHINGTON, D.C. – One of the most important figures in the world of crime scene investigations has died at the age of 67. "He was a force of nature in the field of behavioral science," said longtime colleague and protégé, Ulysses Grove. "He virtually invented protocols that are still used today by investigative units and detective squads around the world."

Mr. Geisel died on Saturday, at Cedars-Sinai Medical Center in Washington, from complications resulting from a brain hemorrhage. He is survived by his wife, Lois Renata Geisel (née Moorland); his four children, Joseph (Brittany) of Pittsburgh, PA; Nathan (Karen) of Grand Rapids, MI, Cynthia Standiger (Jerome) of Sarasota, FL; and Peter (Mae) of New York, NY; and nine grandchildren. "He was a very special man," his daughter, Cynthia, said from her home in Florida. "The children just adored him."

Born in Ossining, New York, Mr. Geisel was educated at the prestigious Henniman School for Boys, and later at Harvard, where he received his doctorate in psychology. A stint at Bellvue Hospital's violence ward in New York City led Mr. Geisel to a career in criminology, first with the NYPD, and later, in the 1960s, with the FBI.

During his long and notable career at the Bureau, Mr. Geisel took part in the apprehension and study of such infamous murderers as John Wayne Gacy, Jeffrey Dahmer, Richard Ackerman, Michael Doerr, and Henry David Splet.

Services will be held on Monday, June 12th, at 10:00 A.M., at the Shalom Funeral Home, 2000 N. Marsh Road, Richmond, VA. Interment to follow. In lieu of flowers, memorials in Mr. Geisel's name may be made to the Temple Emanuel or the Jewish Children's Bureau, 1278 S. Highland, Alexandria, VA.

For more information, contact the Shalom Funeral Home at (917) 765-4435.

The next day, Grove left the obituary as his home computer's wallpaper throughout the afternoon for reasons that he would be hard-pressed to explain. It was his modest little shrine, a reminder of his loss imprinted in pixels of light, a temporary kaddish for the section chief. Grove remembered a Judaic blessing spoken at a crime scene once. *Baruch dayan emet*: Blessed is the one true judge.

"Get you anything?"

Maura's voice startled Grove, who was standing at the window, gazing out at the darkening sky above the bay. He whirled. "What?"

She came over and put a hand on his shoulder. "Can I get you anything?"

"No. I mean . . . no, thanks. Where's Aaron?"

"He's down for a nap."

"Good."

"You okay?"

"No."

She stroked the edge of his jaw. Her hand was cold. "I know. You might want to take something."

He looked at her. "What do you mean? A sleeping pill?"

"It might be a good idea if you slept a little before the funeral."

He turned and looked out at the dwindling daylight. "I'll be fine."

He hadn't slept for thirty-six hours, and he was starting to see bright white spots on the edge of his vision and feel dizzy with fatigue. He had no appetite, and had no energy to open the e-mails piling up on his work account, most of them from David Van Teigham. He knew he had to face the Archetype Case—which was how he was coming to think of the strange murders ripped from the pages of his book—and he knew he had to face the possibility that the killings were connected in some bizarre way with Tom Geisel's death.

But right now all he could see in his mind was a crack in the universe.

"I got Martha Washington to babysit tomorrow during the service." Maura's voice sounded odd, brittle, humorless, as she stared at the back of his head.

"Very funny," Grove muttered, not taking his gaze off the ashy dark clouds over the Atlantic. "I don't get it."

"What."

"The joke."

Maura kept looking at the back of his head. "What joke?"

Grove turned and looked at her. "Martha Washington?"

"That's her name, Uly. The lady from the day-care center. Big heavyset gal?"

Grove remembered now. "Oh right, right." He turned back to the window. "I'm sure she'd make a fine first lady, too."

"You bet your ass she would."

Tears gathered in Grove's eyes. He felt something break inside his chest. "You realize I never even knew my dad."

Maura didn't say anything, just put her hand on Grove's shoulder and kept it there.

"I never even met the man." Tears clouded Grove's vision.

"Uly—"

"This is my fault." His voice began to crack. "This happened because of me."

"Uly, shut up now—"

"This all happened because of me." He turned and put his arms around her and pressed his face into her neck. This horrible notion had been swimming around, sharklike, beneath the surface of his thoughts all day: that he was somehow responsible for his friend's death in the wake of that hideous black silhouette of the every-killer.

"Hush now, Uly, hush," she whispered and held him.

Grove let his tears come then, until he couldn't see or hear or feel anymore.

EIGHT

The funeral came and went the next day in a solemn, melancholy blur. By mid-afternoon, trapped at the Geisel shiva, alone among a house full of grim-faced strangers, Maura Grove realized something was wrong. She realized this even before she saw her husband having an intense, clandestine conversation with the FBI director across the dining room of the crowded farmhouse.

The stately old home, which belonged to Lois Geisel's brother, famed D.C. divorce attorney Danny Patton, had been seething all day with quiet undercurrents of nervous tension, most of which seemed to be radiating from Ulysses. He kept pulling various Bureau staffers into quiet alcoves to have hushed, tense conversations about some pressing matter that had nothing to do with mourning Tom Geisel. After four glasses of tepid chardonnay, Maura became convinced that her husband was being drawn into another dark labyrinth. She had seen it too many times—the mood swings, the cryptic dissembling.

Now, standing alone in the Patton kitchen, staring out the window blinds at the overcast after-noon, Maura could see her husband strolling the far reaches of the backyard with one of his stu-dents, both their faces looking dour and grave as they talked.

Maura felt a pang of jealousy, standing there with her glass of room-temperature wine, watching her husband confer with a voluptuous black girl named Drinkwater. Maura knew how much the students idolized Grove. Still, it was a ridiculous notion that Grove would have an affair with one of his pupils. It stemmed from Maura's own projec-tions, her own insecurity about the current state of her marriage, and her uncertain future.

Standing there, nervously sipping her sour char-donnay, her thoughts drifted back to that bizarre moment last year when she herself had been the object of a young person's desire.

The key incident—Maura had come to think of it this way, an *incident*, like a fender bender or a sprained ankle—had unraveled in such an innocu-ous series of events, it hardly seemed worth remem-bering. Ulysses had been out of town, consulting on a kidnapping in Indiana, when an unexpected vis-itor appeared on their doorstep. A young Bureau trainee named Benjamin Bard had come over os-tensibly to hand-deliver, as was Bureau policy, a hard drive loaded with case files for upcoming ex-pert-witness testimony. The kid had a lanky, rangy swimmer's physique and a long blond ponytail, and when Maura offered him a cup of coffee, he smiled and pulled a joint from his pocket.

"You realize you're married to a freaking leg-end?" he had asked her at one point, sitting at the kitchen table across from her, puffing his blunt, tossing his long blond straggles out of his face.

Then came the touch.

It wasn't much as physical flirtations go, just a light squeeze of Maura's bare forearm, which was resting on the table. But the young man's hand had lingered just a millisecond longer than the duration of a friendly pat. "Must get lonely around here, though, with the maestro gone all the time," the kid had murmured then, just in case Maura had missed all the blatant signals.

"Yeah, um. . . ." She had immediately pulled away. Then she went over to the sink to regain her composure. She busied herself with the dishes, grasping for something to say, searching for just the right combination of rakish indifference, wry humor, and tart wisdom. But the perfect response remained out of reach, just beyond the limits of her improvisational skills. And she was just coming to this conclusion when she felt a presence skulk up behind her.

"Don't fight it, just let it happen," a voice purred into her nape. Maura felt arms slinking around her midriff. Her heart raced.

She squirmed out of his grasp. "Um . . . you know . . . I'm thinking that maybe it's just about time you finished up that little marijuana cigarette and hit the road."

"I just thought we—"

"Yeah, I'm sure you had all kinds of thoughts bouncing around that noggin of yours, but right now I'm thinking it would be best if you got the hell out of here."

The surfer dude finally gave up and made his exit in a flurry of muttered profanities.

Afterward, Maura had felt so flustered and alone that she drank an entire bottle of pinot noir that she was saving for Ulysses' birthday. Part of it was outrage at the gall of this kid, this snot-nosed slacker who'd had the nerve to hit on the wife of a principal player in the FBI hierarchy. But part of it was the guilty excitement, the cheap thrill of it all. What was wrong with her?

The strangest part, though, was what had happened a month or so later. Around the dinner table one night, Grove had idly mentioned that the Bureau was having staff problems. "One kid in IT just up and left," he marveled, morosely picking at his tabouli salad. "Big gangly surf-punk kid, name of Bard, Ben Bard, decides to just not show up for work anymore. Wrote an e-mail to his supervisor telling him to eat shit."

After a long moment, staring at her food, Maura said, "Punk is right."

"Pardon?" Grove looked at her.

"He hit on me, Uly."

"Bard?"

She nodded. "Right here, in this very kitchen, he comes over one night—you were away—he comes over to drop off a file and he comes on to me."

Grove waited. "And?"

She shrugged. "That's it. I kicked him out. End of story."

After a moment's thought, Grove wondered aloud, somewhat rhetorically, like a professor posing a Socratic question, but with an edge to his voice: "Why would you not tell me about this?"

She didn't have an answer. She couldn't explain it to *herself.* How was she going to explain it to her husband? All the mixed emotions—the shame, the morbid curiosity, the guilty thoughts—had kept her awake at nights and made her wonder if she needed more therapy.

Now, alone at the Geisel shiva, woozy from too much wine and worry, these thoughts swirled through Maura's mind as she watched her husband through the window, out there in the overcast afternoon, talking about something very upsetting with one of his students.

NINE

"I understand you were a PI in another life." Grove was leading Drinkwater down a flagstone path along the edge of the Pattons' expansive lawn. The backyard was deserted. Off to the east, a child's swing set, long abandoned, lay in cobwebs. Along the western edge of the lawn, chicken coops bordered a split-rail fence. Nothing stirred, no sound came from within the barns or from the densely wooded Virginia farmland in the far distance.

"Yessir, I was." Drinkwater seemed jumpy, apprehensive, maybe even a little defensive, as she strode along in her good heels and dark dress.

"Tracked down bond jumpers?"

"Yessir."

"Accident scenes?"

"Yep."

"Affidavits?"

"You bet."

"Missing persons, I'm assuming?"

"Yessir, um—"

"Why don't you call me Ulysses? You still have your license?"

Now the woman looked at him. "Last time I checked. Got my passport, too."

Grove sighed. "Look, I don't mean to give you the third degree. I need to talk to you about something, and I want to make sure I'm not wasting time for either of us."

They walked in silence for another moment. Grove took in a deep breath of musky country air, and tried to clear his mind. Drinkwater was his star pupil, but also an outsider. He needed to handle this situation delicately, but he was too distracted by the loss of his best friend and the improbable connection between the Archetype killer and the strange death note that ushered in the section chief's last moments on earth:

A dark figure, like a shadow. No face, just an outline.

Grove could not get those disturbing phrases and fragments out of his mind. They festered and fomented there like tangled cancerous threads:

Not tellin yo

Grove wondered if Geisel's reference to "not telling you" concerned something that Geisel had not told him about a case, maybe a recent one, maybe a cold one; perhaps that was what Geisel felt bad about, which led to the most disturbing part of the note, and the reason Grove was dragging Drinkwater into this right now:

j'thing they tol me bac then

Grove let out another sigh and tried to clear his mind. He looked at Drinkwater. "Bob Wexler over at Justice says you're a regular bloodhound."

"Deputy Wexler said that?"

"Yes ma'am, he did." Grove gazed out at the distant hills. "Says you could find the needle in the proverbial haystack."

"I don't know about needles." Edith Drinkwater had a defensive sort of tang in her voice. "But you got an individual wants to hide out, they're a little shy, I can usually dig 'em up."

"Good, I'm glad to hear that. Because I need your help on a case."

Drinkwater cocked her head ever so slightly at him then, and the way she did it—that trademark sister-girl double take—sent a faint jolt of recognition through Grove. Drinkwater still had some of the playground in her, some of the street. Grove admired that more than anything else about her.

Right now she was giving him an incredulous look. "An *active* case?"

He looked at her. "That's right. On the down low, if possible."

"Pardon?"

"Think of it as independent study."

She gave him a look. "I'm getting a grade on this?"

"As a matter of fact, you're getting something better than a grade."

"Which is?"

"The chance to save somebody's life."

After a moment she asked, "What am I going to be doing exactly?"

Grove gritted his teeth, thinking of that next female, white, forty-two-year-old victim—an unlucky winner—he would find mutilated and left for the maggots. Pain throbbed in his jaw, a sensation not unlike biting down too hard on an ice cube. It was a symptom of his compulsive teeth-grinding. He saw a dentist about it once, who had prescribed a rubber bite-plate to avoid tooth wear, but the mouthpiece did little to alleviate the pain. Later, a doctor told him he also had early signs of TMJ—or temporomandibular joint syndrome due to a subtly misaligned jaw—which made the grinding all the more excruciating. But Grove had very little control over it. "You cannot tell your closest family member about what I am about to tell you," he said finally.

"Okay, sure."

Grove took a girding breath. "There is a serial murderer at large who may or may not have some connection to me, to my history at the Bureau, and maybe even to my relationship with Tom Geisel."

Drinkwater took this in, kept walking, didn't say a word, just nodded.

Grove went on: "The clock is running. I do not have time to pursue the two parallel tracks of this investigation. I need you to dig into something that happened to me."

Now Drinkwater looked more intrigued than nervous. She waited for him to continue.

"When I was a kid, way back in the Stone Age, I have reason to believe some people were following me." Grove paused and measured his words. "To this day nobody knows for sure *why* they were following me. Or who they were, or just why the hell they picked me to follow."

Drinkwater nodded and asked how he knew all this.

"Tom Geisel told me."

A beat of silence. Drinkwater cocked her head again. "Mind if I ask how old you were when you were allegedly being followed?"

"I was ten, eleven . . . something like that. Geisel was a middle manager at the Bureau in those days, moving up the ranks. One day, these people came to him out of the clear blue. Six old men. Told him to keep an eye on me, told him someday I'd make a pretty good FBI agent."

Drinkwater was frowning. "He didn't find out who these guys were?"

Grove rubbed his eyes. The grief and shock had dragged down his normally handsome, sculpted-bronze features, making his dark eyes darker. "He got their names, addresses. Not much else. He thought they were a bunch of senile old coots. Didn't worry about them that much. They all checked out fine, too—no jackets, no records whatsoever. I guess Tom eventually looked me up out of curiosity."

A long pause, Drinkwater absorbing all this. "When did you find out about this?"

"Last year."

"Does anybody else at the Bureau know about it?"

Grove told her no, nobody other than Geisel.

After another pause Drinkwater asked, "Why do you think he told you about this just recently?"

Grove had expected this question, and had been torn about how much he should tell her. Over the last few years, working some of the strangest investigations in law enforcement history, Grove had stumbled upon a bizarre phenomenon running like an undertow through his work. It involved a vague, undefined personality buried in the fractured psyches of those he hunted—an alter ego—which Grove had come to think of as Factor X.

Factor X seemed to have an agenda *beneath* all the killings—an agenda that had something to do with *Grove*—and this revelation had poisoned the profiler's dreams. It tainted his private ruminations, and it appeared in symbolic form in visions, hallucinations, portents. It also reverberated back through the years to his early childhood in Kenya, resonating in ways he would be unable to fully explain. Tom Geisel was the only other human being on earth privy to all this.

Now, in his deathbed note, the section chief may have provided a linkage to this dynamic—maybe even to the Archetype itself—through his odd reference to the six old men. Near the end of the note, Geisel had cobbled together phrases such as "something they told me back then." Was he referring to the six old men? Something they told him back then? And what was Grove to make of the gibberish at the end of the note:

thee ns an o her b y a b d   one who_   yo
have to Ul h ss yr tn

And now, today, flashing back to these fragmented words, Grove finally looked at Drinkwater and broke the spell of silence. "I'm sure you've heard rumors. About my methods, my background. You can't work here without hearing all sorts of crap—how I manage such a high closure rate on a lot of these serial cases, how I got some kind of African mojo working all the time."

She had a strange look on her face now. "Well?"

"Well what?"

"Is it true?"

Grove gave her a nervous grin. "Oh absolutely, I'm a regular bogeyman."

"And now you want me to find out who these guys were, the ones came to Geisel . . . where they came from?"

Grove nodded, said nothing.

"Why me?"

"Because you're an outsider. You're a skip tracer. Woman like yourself, all those tricks up your sleeve. What do you think?"

The young lady stared at Grove. She seemed to be sizing him up, which, in all honesty, made Grove more than a tad uncomfortable.

For a long moment Drinkwater considered her response carefully. She wondered if she had perhaps stumbled into a pivotal moment here—a crossroads, a once-in-a-lifetime opportunity. Maybe this was the back door to success she had been seeking. Maybe, just maybe, Drinkwater could manipulate the master manipulator.

The biggest irony here was that Grove had no idea how diligently Drinkwater had investigated *him* before coming to the Bureau, how she had spent the months leading up to her arrival at Quantico digging up details on his life. She had used FBI websites, city directories, academic records, and military archives to build his biography. She had also used the Freedom of Information Act to get transcripts of public hearings, cold case files, and declassified memoranda among investigators.

On the surface, of course, Grove's background, albeit very cosmopolitan, didn't give Drinkwater much to go on. Born forty-one years ago in the small Kenyan town of Kinyasha to an African mother and a Jamaican father who vanished shortly after Grove's birth, young Grove had emigrated at the age of two with his mom to the United States. Raised on the mean streets of Chicago, the boy kept to himself, got good grades, and stayed out of trouble. Undergraduate studies in criminology at the University of Michigan were followed by basic training, followed by three years as a noncommissioned officer in the Army—first as an MP and then as an investigator in the military's CID unit.

But none of that interested Drinkwater as much as the stuff that was *missing*.

Nobody knew how Grove did his "thing" at the Bureau, how he tracked these monsters down. Notwithstanding all that hooey about his spooky African juju, or his eerie connection to the perps, Drinkwater was starting to wonder if she had been wrong about his insincerity. During his lectures, something had sunk a hook into her. She had been dreaming about that shooting range silhouette from his Archetype talks—and some of these dreams had been nightmares. During the daytime, every now and then, she would close her eyes and see that disgusting, coal-black, featureless outline of a head.

"Before I agree to do this, I'd like to ask you something," she said at last, pursing her lips thoughtfully. "If you don't mind."

Grove looked at her with an inscrutable expression now. "Go ahead."

"There's only a half dozen field agent spots waiting for us this spring."

"That's true."

"What I'm saying is, let's say I do this thing. Will I get one of those spots?"

Grove kept looking at her with that unreadable expression. Then he smiled. "Seems fair."

"And if there's any legal question, you're gonna have to take the heat."

"I understand."

Drinkwater took a deep breath. "I'm gonna need access to Geisel's files."

Grove nodded. "Got them all on hard disk. I'll have them delivered to your hotel. I'll pull his personal journals, too, if that'll help."

Drinkwater chewed the inside of her cheek, and then stopped walking. "Okay." She gave him a hard, determined look. "Fine. I'll do it."

"Good, good." Grove shook her hand. "Go home. Get some sleep. You can start tomorrow. I'll square your absence with the dean."

"There's one more thing."

Grove told her he was listening.

She looked at him. "What if I find out something—something about *you*—something you don't really *want* found out?"

Grove stared at her for a long time.

He didn't have an answer for that one.

PART II
Cold Metal Misery Machine

The future overcomes the past by
swallowing it.

—José Ortega y Gasset

Once upon a time the psychopath wore the
skin of legends—folktales, witches,
werewolves. It was the only way we could
comprehend an evil so perverse it defied the
physical laws of the universe, an evil we take
for granted today.

—Ulysses Grove, *The Psychopathological
Archetype: Toward a Statistical Model*

TEN

The following Tuesday evening, exactly a thousand miles west of Quantico, just outside of Galveston, Texas, around 7:35 P.M. Central Standard Time, a forty-one-year-old junior college student named Madeline Gilchrist, unaware she was about to become the third sacrificial lamb, heard a noise in the darkness behind her.

She kept walking.

That's what Grandma Rose always told her to do if she found herself in a pickle such as this. *Just keep on truckin', Maddy.* Clad in a halter top and shopworn jeans plastered with patches and embroidered messages like IMPEACH SHRUB and GO GREEN, she was carrying an empty plastic gas tank, heading along the gravel shoulder of the weed-whiskered Intracoastal Highway. About a quarter of a mile back, her VW bug had mysteriously run out of gas. This made no sense. She had topped the tank off last night. Now everything felt wrong. The back of her neck crawled with heat chills.

Footsteps—furtive, quick, powerful—circled

around the Joshua trees and the scrub brush to her right, then abruptly halted.

"Hello? Anybody there?"

No answer.

Madeline picked up her pace. Off to her left the roar of the Gulf waves hitting the breakwater called out in the distance like a giant invisible lung. The footsteps loomed somewhere ahead of her now. *Ahead of her?* Madeline faltered, slowing down, dizziness washing over her. Was there more than one figure out there in the darkness? The drone of crickets and frogs suddenly ceased.

In the silence Madeline stumbled to a sudden stop, paralyzed with panic, dropping the plastic container. She stared into the darkness ahead of her.

A lone figure had stepped into her path about twenty yards away.

Madeline could not believe what she was seeing. Garbed all in black, a big chimney hat shrouding his face in shadow, the figure stood very still, facing her in a column of flickering light from a faulty streetlamp. Moths swarmed above him. He dripped with menace, and every fiber of Madeline's being told her to turn tail and run like bejesus, but for one horrible instant she was transfixed.

It wasn't the great big knife in the man's hand, dully gleaming in the streetlight, that held Madeline rapt for that single moment. Nor was it the air of weird, unearthly calm about the figure, standing there in the middle of the road with the cruel indifference of a wax figure in a museum.

On the contrary, it was a subtle little detail of behavior exhibited by this strange figure that positively hypnotized the girl.

It was the fact that the man was holding a pocket

watch in his other hand, consulting it like a train engineer diligently keeping a schedule.

Ulysses Grove stood alone in the far reaches of the Beth E'met Cemetery. Situated in the high woods along the Mason Neck nature preserve, about twenty miles south of Alexandria, the cemetery was now deserted, bathed in the shadows of tall white pines. The waning light of dusk had already closed in like a predator.

Grove turned up his collar against the chill and gazed down at the recently dug and manicured grave. Yellow light spilling from a nearby lamppost shone off the headstone. "I know what you're thinking," Grove murmured, addressing the departed mentor. "I should be home with Maura and the baby."

The headstone said nothing. No ghostly reply, no Dickensian whisper from the ether.

"I need you on this one, Boss." Grove stared at the waist-high block of clean, white granite. The epitaph etched into the stone—*Geisel, Thomas Edward, 1941–2008, Father Husband Friend*—called out to him. Twisted in his guts. Made his eyes sting in the cold breeze. "This one's different."

Only the rustling leaves answered.

Grove wiped his moist eyes. "I gotta shut this one down, Boss."

Silence.

"Wish I knew what you were saying at the end of that goddamn note."

Leaves skittering.

"I want this one bad. I cannot wrap my head around this guy."

No reply.

"What were you thinking, leaving me on this one?" Grove wiped his nose on his sleeve. "I'm being selfish now, okay, so sue me."

Then, almost on instinct, Grove looked over his shoulder, as though somebody might be eavesdropping. He turned back to the headstone. "Never should have published that goddamn book . . . never should have done it . . . this one's my fault . . . this one I created somehow. I . . . I don't know how yet."

The gravestone said nothing. A couple dozen smooth little stones—tributes from the previous week's mourners—still lined its top edge.

Grove closed his eyes. "He's out there, Boss. Right now. Hard at work. Because of me."

Madeline Gilchrist regained consciousness that night in fits and starts, writhing out of her drugged slumber like a diver struggling to the surface of a dark ocean, sensing a presence hovering nearby before actually seeing him. She could not move her head or breathe through her mouth due to the duct tape across her lips. She was barely able to see through her watery, mucousy eyes.

She peered to her left, registering the blurry patterns hanging from the ceiling, crisscrossing the air, slashing through the middle distance all around her. At length she began to understand at least the gravity of her situation if not the purpose of all the diagonal lines in her field of vision. Strapped to a workbench in a windowless chamber (which would turn out to be the back of a panel truck), she was clad only in her underwear and wet with perspiration, urine, and oily grime. She felt prickly sensations all over her body, like mosquito bites.

Eyes focusing gradually, irises adjusting to the dim light, she sensed—mostly in her peripheral vision—a tall dark man moving beside her. She looked up. He stood in front of her now. His back was turned to her. He wore some kind of tall hat, and maybe a black raincoat or an old overcoat— her eyesight was so bleary it was hard to tell. Hovering there, glimpsed in her watery vision, he looked like a big, shapeless, *silhouette* of a man: an empty-souled, generic, international symbol for STRANGER.

He seemed to be hyperventilating, flexing his broad shoulders.

He slipped off his oiler.

He was nude.

Maddy Gilchrist started screaming.

Grove had one of the worst nightmares of his life at precisely the same moment that Madeline Gilchrist was living one out within the corrugated metal walls of that windowless panel van. The two events—separated by nearly a thousand miles— were connected in ways that Grove would not decipher for many, many hours.

But right now, in the moist, clammy folds of his sweat-soaked sheets, only centimeters away from his slumbering wife, Grove dreamed he was moving down a narrow, dark passageway toward the third murder scene.

Somehow, in his dream logic, he knew this was

the third and final scene, and when he reached the squalid alcove of crumbling brick at the end of the passageway, he saw the victim supine in a pool of dried black blood. He opened his mouth to say something, but he couldn't make any sound come out of his lungs, because he was staring at his mother. Vida Mae Grove, her slender brown legs protruding from her torn sarong, her proud face stippled with blood, looked up at her son and uttered two words in a dissonant, sibilant stage whisper that pierced Grove's soul like a clap of thunder and violently woke him up: "*It's you!*"

Maddy Gilchrist ran out of breath just as her captor began to turn around to face her.

Her muffled scream dying in her throat, she strained and strained against the leather straps holding her to the workbench, the airless cargo hold of the van closing in on her. The terror swirled up through her brain stem like a squall until she ran out of both air and sanity.

The captor—a muscular simulacrum of a man— had tattoos over 90 percent of his body, his back virtually covered with them. At first Maddy thought they were serpents and vines and barbed wire, and all manner of billowing ribbony designs, but soon she realized in her hysteria that all the tattoos were of the same category: *measuring devices*. Long, flowing tape measures tattooed around massive, rippling triceps . . . rulers running down a sweat-glistening spine . . . delicate calligraphy spaced evenly along prominent ribs . . . fractions and hash marks and scientific calibrations along every bulging muscle and sinewy.

The killer turned, and Maddy got her first and only glimpse of his face.

White-hot terror choked the breath out of her. In any other context, this guy might be passed off as a run-of-the-mill street person, with the slack, empty gaze of ordinary madness dragging down his features; but here in this horrible, stifling truck, in the flickering light of a faulty dome lamp, with his profusely tattooed body—*Jesus Christ, even his penis is hatched with tiny numbered measuring lines!*—he appeared omnipotent, godlike.

Maddy couldn't breathe anymore, mostly because she finally realized, over the space of a single terrible instant, right before the torture began, what all the diagonal wires and cables and ropes crisscrossing the cargo hold had in store for her. *Oh Jesus sweet Jesus no I don't even want to know this anymore I don't please please—*

The tattooed man was holding, in each hand, a tiny wooden cross, each device connected like the controls of a puppeteer to the cables fanning around the workbench. And rigged at the far end of each cable—each and every one—was a sharp instrument, such as a hunting knife, a scalpel, a needle, each pointing at Maddy, each carefully cocked on tiny loops and ready to slide home.

The cables were attached to Maddy.

Oh my God, that's what the prickly sensations had been—the mosquito bites: the ends of those hideous cables stuck to me with some kind of adhesive, all over me, ohmygod, the ends of the cables marking me like I'm a voodoo doll or, or, or, or a specimen or God GOD GOD!!

A dark shade came down across Maddy's vision then as the silent tattooed man consulted the clock on the wall: It was almost time.

Maddy passed out.

Three minutes and thirteen seconds later, she was wrenched back to consciousness as the knives slid down their guylines with a chorus of zinging noises.

ELEVEN

The next morning Edith Drinkwater lit out on her below-the-radar branch of the investigation. With a little help from New York City directories and phone book archives, she had discovered, much to her amazement, that one of the old men who had visited the section chief all those years ago was still alive in an extended care center outside Newark, New Jersey. This old coot, as Drinkwater was about to discover, would turn out to be a connection between Grove and the Archetype.

Drabbed down in her gray sweatsuit and sneakers, her hair pulled back in braids, Drinkwater spent most of the flight time out to Newark studying Geisel's journal.

She had made Xeroxes of key pages, then bound them into her other notes on the Grove job—bios from the Internet, Mapquest directions, names and addresses of key people in Grove's life—and today she read and reread key entries written in the section chief's neat, tightly coiled hand:

17 July 1978
Strange day. Just when I'm feeling halfway confident
about managing new department (HQ thinking of
calling it Psychological Research and Metrics) I get this
strange call from lobby receptionist. "Group of gentle-
men here to see you." What? No record of any meet-
ings, nobody on the fourth floor knows a thing.

Curiosity got the better of me I guess.

Met with these six old men in first floor conference room.
Claimed they were part of a community religious council.
Multidenominational antiviolence group, something like
that. But that's not the weird part. Weird part is why
they came. Said they read about me. How I'm a natural
leader, a mentor. I remember that word for some reason.
Mentor. They went on and on, how I'm going to change
the world by studying evil and quelling violence. They
gave me tips on who I should watch out for, people I should
pay attention to, blah blah bah.

End of day, asked Briskin to run checks on all the old
codgers. Strictly routine. Don't expect to find anything.

Geisel never saw any of the old men ever again.
The Bureau ran all the standard and customary
background checks on the six geezers ("The Order
of the Owls," as Geisel had come to know them), and
the results turned up a week later in Geisel's diary:

24 July 1978
Not much to report today. Got rundowns on six old
owls. Nothing much there. No jackets on any of them.
Legitimate church group, DC address. Only thing out
of the ordinary is variety of origin-countries. Names go
in VICAP just in case anything crops up:

Goodis, Arthur S. (US)
Schoenbu, Bernard J. (Israel)
Okuba, Baruk (Sudan)
Pelsoci, Gerald H. (Czechoslovakia)
Norgaru, Ten-Sin (Nepal)
Achmadra, Mohammad (Morocco)

Drinkwater ran her own checks, and found no immediate family members and all but one of the owls deceased. The second name, Bernard Schoenburg (or baum, as the original pen had smudged at that point), was listed as terminal at St. John the Baptist, age ninety-eight. Drinkwater immediately headed north to Newark to check it out.

The hope was not only to find out why the old men had gone to the trouble of telling Geisel about this alleged wonder kid in Chicago, but just exactly how the old men had latched on to young Ulysses Grove in the first place. As did Tom Geisel those many years ago:

9 September 1978
Clipped more news items from Chicago. Following the whiz kid becoming a hobby of mine. He won a chess championship in August, got bumped into a gifted program this fall. Starting to feel a little weird about watching from a distance. Not sure about ethics. Old men knew what they were talking about though. This kid is one-of-a-kind. More than a prodigy. Something profound here. Something deeper going on behind this kids eyes. . . .

This brief entry, as far as Drinkwater could tell from surviving documents, was the last time Tom Geisel would mention the mysterious old men—or the prodigious young whiz kid whom they brought to his attention.

While Edith Drinkwater's plane was descending into Newark airspace, the whiz kid from Geisel's journal—all grown up now and bearing the invisible scars of his dark fate—was nervously pacing the outer waiting room of FBI Director Louis Corboy's office in D.C., waiting for the old man to get off the phone. Clad in his best sartorial armor—Armani suit, crisp rep tie, and spit-shined Italian shoes—Grove was dressed for psychological battle, ready to negotiate the bureaucratic shark tank.

He had spent the bulk of that morning marshaling resources, making sure the full range of CSI materials from Minneapolis and North Carolina were delivered via secure e-mail to Ben Sehgal, his trusted analyst in the Behavioral Science Unit, for a second opinion. Shoe-print impressions, blood samples, hair and fibers, tire prints, wound angle data, pathology reports—all of it arrived on Sehgal's computer before 9:00 A.M. Eastern Standard Time.

Sehgal—a transplanted New Yorker assigned to Moses DeLourde's Violent Crime Analysis Center at Tulane—finally got back to Grove on his cell phone around lunchtime. "If you'll pardon my impertinence, this has gotta be a joke," Sehgal said in his rapid-fire Noo-Yawk accent. "Any chance one of your students could be pulling a very psychotic prank?" Grove told him it was no joke, and yes, they should indeed be looking at Academy students, as well as anybody else familiar with the Archetype, including fellow agents and investigators.

And they would have to do it in a timely fashion because all the hard evidence had a shelf life.

Both Grove and Sehgal knew this all too well. They'd learned it in the Academy: *the Natural Law of Exchange.* All living organisms exchange matter with their environment. A perpetrator not only leaves a part of himself at a scene, but the victim leaves a part of herself on the perpetrator. And today, with the advent of genetic analysis and nanotechnology, the minutest trace of a fiber or tissue cell—down to the atom—can provide the crucial link between murderer and murder scene. This theory even extends to psychological issues, behavioral aberrations. Killers often trade raw experience with their victims, quid pro quo, trauma for trauma. But secretions can evaporate. Cells degrade. Even psychological extrapolations fade in importance. A scene must be consumed within its freshness date.

But what Grove didn't share with Ben Sehgal that day was the *impossibility* of any suspect knowing about the unpublished computer models on Grove's hard drive. Sehgal did confirm the fact that the MO and signature at both scenes—Minneapolis and Emerald Isle—precisely matched just about every *other* average in Grove's book-length study. The only part that Sehgal did *not* confirm was the exact reproduction of that leaf-shaped blood pattern on the salt-rusted piling near the Emerald Isle body dump: the pattern known only to Grove.

Had the unpublished illustrations—those thorny, delicate computer-generated bloodstains that resembled the stems of a deadly rose—somehow leaked into the digital universe? Had Grove inadvertently cast them adrift in the data stream by clicking the wrong link or pressing the wrong key? Or had they been *extracted* by more metaphysical means?

On that chaotic Wednesday afternoon, Grove had no idea how close he was to learning the answer.

"Here we are," the birdlike nursing home manager murmured over her shoulder as she paused outside a blemished oak door that was slightly ajar. The odor of urine hung faintly in the stale air, which made Drinkwater shudder slightly as she hovered behind the scrawny staffer.

The manager was a dour, officious little woman named Jayne Symons; she seemed slightly put off by this intrusion into her daily routine as she knocked lightly on the ancient doorjamb. "Mr. Schoenbaum? Are you decent?"

From within the room came an odd sighing noise like steam escaping a radiator.

Jane Symons shot a glance at Drinkwater. "We're catching him at nap time. Which is most of time, I'm afraid."

"Should we come back later?"

The woman waved a dismissive hand. "He'll be fine, a visitor'll probably do him good."

She pushed the door open, and Drinkwater followed her inside the dim chamber.

"Afternoon, Mr. Schoenbaum." Symons spoke as one might to a slow child, with exaggerated enunciation and volume, as she roused the grizzled old man curled up in a fetal position in a tangled knot of yellowed sheets on a rusty hospital bed. Sunlight seeped around the edges of a faded, stained window shade above him, giving him and the rest of the cluttered room a sickly, yellow cast. The air was choked with dust. A large, aluminum Star of David hung on the wall over a bookshelf brimming with old newspapers and ancient oil-spotted grocery sacks. "Look what I brought you— a visitor!"

"Macaroni and cheese again?" The bullfrog voice belched out of the old man as he struggled to sit up against the wall. He looked to be about a hundred and fifty years old, although the nursing home records, contrary to public documents, had him at ninety-nine. His sunken chest was barely covered by a damp, sleeveless T-shirt, the gray hairs poking out the top like corn silk. His bony arms and legs looked as delicate as balsa wood, and from the jaundice of his loose flesh and the red-rimmed edges of his eyes, it was clear he was close to the end.

"A visitor, Bernie, you have a visitor."

Drinkwater stepped forward. "Sir, hello. How you doing tonight?"

"I can't shit."

A quick glance between the two women. Drinkwater smiled at the man. "I know how that goes."

A chirping sound rang out suddenly; Symons reached for the beeper attached to her belt. "Unfortunately I'm going to have to cut this short," she said, staring at the beeper. "I assume we've established the man exists."

Drinkwater looked at her. "Ma'am, would you have any objection if I stuck around for just a few minutes? I can show myself out."

The bird-faced lady puckered her lips skeptically, then shrugged. "Mr. Schoenbaum agitates easily, so if you could make it quick I would appreciate it."

Drinkwater assured the woman she would do just that. After a reluctant pause, the supervisor shrugged again and whisked out the door with her clipboard in tow. Drinkwater took a deep breath and glanced around the room. She didn't have much time, and wasn't exactly sure what she was looking for. She turned back to the old man and spoke softly and quickly, yet loud enough to penetrate aged ears. "Sir, do you remember visiting a man at the FBI in the late seventies by the name of Geisel? Thomas Geisel?"

The old man chewed the inside of his sunken cheek. "I've got some pain in my testicle area, I don't mind telling you."

"How about the name Ulysses Grove? Ring any bells?"

Something sparked behind the old man's eyes, just for a moment, then vanished. His toothless mouth worked but made no sound.

"He would have been a child when you knew him or knew about him, maybe twelve years old? Again, the name is Ulysses Grove."

Drinkwater studied the wizened, shriveled face, the blood-rimmed eyes. Was there a faint glimmer of fear in those milky gray pupils? Reaching into her purse, Drinkwater pulled the binder out, then paged through the Xeroxes until she came to the names of the rest of those old men in the Order of the Owls. She asked Schoenbaum if he remembered any of his old colleagues, slowly reading off each name.

His back pressed against the wall, his gnarled

hands shaking in his lap, the old man mouthed something, a faint whistle of a sound coming from deep within his throat. It sounded like a word.

"What was that, sir?" Drinkwater leaned down close so she could hear.

"Long way . . ."

"What's that, Mr. Schoenbaum? Did you say 'long way'? What's a long way?"

Barely a whisper: "Long way to fall."

Drinkwater looked at the wrinkled visage of the old man, his wormy lips moving impotently, moist with spittle. "I'm sorry, I didn't quite get that. Long way to what?"

No answer.

"Sir?"

Nothing.

Glancing at her watch, Drinkwater wondered how long she could safely linger in the room with the old man. She thought about making some notes. *Long way to fall? Is that what he said?*

She turned and went over to the bookshelf. A quick glance inside the stuffed grocery sacks revealed yellowed back issues of the *Jerusalem Post* and the *Forward*. She glanced down the spines of old dog-eared texts stacked between the bags: books on Kabbalah, Jewish mysticism, and the occult. Drinkwater dug in her purse for her cell phone and took a few still frames of the literature.

For what it was worth.

Drinkwater was about to give up and say goodbye to Bernard Schoenbaum when a trio of framed pictures in the opposite corner of the room caught her eye.

She went over to the wall and took a closer look: a framed photograph of a sixtyish woman with thick glasses—presumably the late Mrs. Schoen-baum—and a group photo of six middle-aged men lined up outside an ivy-covered building on some unnamed college campus. Some of the men were dark-skinned. Middle Eastern, perhaps. Drinkwa-ter felt a tingle in her spine. Was she looking at the group of six who had visited Geisel? Maybe, maybe not.

Between the two photographs hung a faded, rainbow-colored eight-by-ten-inch broadside—the kind that adorned bulletin boards at taverns and nightclubs, or perhaps might be found taped to telephone poles or the sides of buildings to adver-tise forthcoming musical acts.

The performer on the lobby card was a young black man with a steel-plated guitar, looking world-weary and brooding with his boot propped up on a garbage can, a classic blues pose that brought to mind Robert Johnson or Howlin' Wolf. The venue advertised was the Cherry Pit in Charleston, South Carolina, August 27th through September 3rd, in some unnamed year. But it was the name at the top of the placard that mesmerized Drinkwater.

David "Chainsaw" Okuba.

How many Okubas could there be in an old Jew-ish intellectual's circle of friends? Her heart quick-ened as she remembered the name in Geisel's diary, listed among the six old men—*Baruk Okuba (Sudan).*

Leaning down close enough to fog the glass with her breath, Drinkwater saw a messy inscrip-tion scrawled across the bottom of the picture, a blue ballpoint pen long faded to gray chicken-scratch. The best she could tell, it said, "For Uncle Baruk, the last true African American."

Glancing over her shoulder to make sure the old man was still gazing off into oblivion, she quickly snatched the framed poster off the wall and stashed it in her purse. She did this all in one fluid movement, then turned to face Bernie Schoenbaum as if nothing had happened.

"You take care of yourself now," she said with enough volume to register out in the hallway. "I'm gonna be on my way."

Then she turned and marched out the door, her heavy purse banging her in the ribs.

If she hurried she still might be able to catch a commuter flight to Charleston that evening.

TWELVE

"Earth to Agent Grove . . ."

The voice shook Grove out of his troubled ruminations.

He had been pacing a rut into the floor of Corboy's outer office, his adrenaline spiking for what seemed like hours but was probably more like fifteen minutes. His work at the Academy was a million light-years away now, as though it were from another life. He kept thinking of the inevitable third murder; how he burned to prevent it, to catch this beast before it fed off another innocent. But like a shortwave radio crackling with interference, Grove's thoughts kept returning to that nightmare about his mother. She was the source of all things inexplicable for Grove—his heritage, his bloodline, his inchoate connection to the metaphysical. So was this why she had made such a surreal entrance into his consciousness? For years now, Vida had lived in her son's memory as a series of sensory impressions: the musky smell of curry in an iron pot; the itchy sandpaper texture of her dresses; the mismatched irises of her huge, sad eyes, one gray, one brown, always seeing beyond the rational. Over the years she had given her son talismans, charms, magic trinkets, all manner of paraphernalia to ward off evil. Grove wondered if he needed those things now more than ever.

He blinked away the daydream as he looked up across the reception area at the deputy assistant to the director.

A meticulously groomed thirtysomething dressed in a sharp linen jacket, Jake Bloom peered out from behind the door to Corboy's inner office. "You can come on in now, Ulysses," he announced with a smile on his face.

In the macho gun culture of the Federal Bureau of Investigation, few employees felt comfortable exhibiting alternative sexuality. Not Jake Bloom. As one of the only staffers who was proudly out, he had always harbored a schoolboy crush on the dapper Grove, and Grove had always found it amusing, if not flattering. Today, however, Grove was too preoccupied to notice any subtle flirtation as he crossed the outer office, buttoning his coat with one hand, carrying his attaché with the other.

"Very sorry about Tom," Bloom said as Grove passed. "I know you two were very tight."

"Thanks, Jake."

"Word to the wise." Bloom lowered his voice as Grove stepped up to the doorway of Corboy's command center. "The big guy's in a mood today, so step lightly."

"Thanks."

Grove went in and found Corboy talking on a headset behind his massive teak desk on the far side of the room.

"They got a time of death yet? Who's the primary down there?" The Director was pacing across a shuttered window with his jacket off and his shirtsleeves rolled up, his belly straining the buttons of his shirt.

Louis Corboy had a jock-gone-to-seed look about him, as well as the flat pallor of a born bureaucrat. Whenever Grove was around, the man seemed to radiate contempt. In his early years at the FBI, Grove had pegged Corboy as a racist, but now the hostility seemed more specific. Louis Corboy didn't like things he couldn't understand—things he didn't *get*—and Grove was at the top of that list.

The big man motioned for Grove to wait a second. "Spell that, would ya?" Corboy wrote a name on a pad. "Okay, let's teleconference the scene when you're ready. You can work it out with Bloom. Okay . . . thanks."

He thumbed a switch on his earpiece and turned to Grove. "What is it with you and these redline cases?"

"Funny you should mention that." Grove let out a nervous sigh. At the Geisel shiva, he had confided the broad strokes of the Archetype killings to the Director. Now Grove needed more time and money and personnel for the case—things with which Corboy hated to part. "I just talked to Ben Sehgal about the—"

"I know all about it."

Grove looked at Corboy. "Pardon?"

"Walk with me, Ulysses." Corboy scooped his suit coat off a chair back, and came around the side of his desk. "The shit is hitting the fan, and I for one don't want to get it all over me. C'mon."

The portly director lumbered out of his office,

taking big robust strides, like an angry parent leading a recalcitrant child. Grove followed, a little
dazed, a little nonplussed. Crossing the vestibule
office, Grove heard Jake Bloom jabbering on his
own headset, talking with somebody about patch-
ing through forensics from a hot crime scene somewhere.

"Got a new scene I want you to explain to me,"
Corboy was saying as he led Grove through the outer
door and down the corridor.

"What do you mean, '*explain*'? What new scene?
You're talking about Emerald Isle?"

"Galveston, Texas."

"Texas?" Grove felt a faint vibration in the base
of his neck.

"Got it fresh this time," the Director went on.
"Same-day service. Gonna telecon it on the big
screen in the conference room." He turned a cor-
ner and nearly ran over a secretary. "Sorry, Carol.
Excuse us. Grove . . . don't get me started on North
Carolina. You definitely have a talent for trouble."

"What do you mean?"

"Some cop down there, Stenowski I think his
name is, he got a burr up his ass about this field
agent—Van Teigham. This nosy uniform proceeds
to call the Mid-Atlantic section chief and chew his
ear off. Gets the whole goddamn region bent outta
shape over this copycat thing."

"What exactly did Dave Van Teigham do?"

Corboy turned another corner and led Grove
down a narrow carpeted hallway lined with red
warning lights. Windowless steel doors stood entry
to audio labs, latent print rooms, and fiber analysis
suites. "They're waiting for us," Corboy said, motioning toward the last door on the right.

"Boss, what did Van Teigham do?"

Corboy paused outside the teleconference room. "Stenowski was first on the scene, claims he saw the connection first, the similarities to your book. Now he claims Van Teigham is stealing his thunder."

"Who cares?"

Corboy gave him a hard look. "*I* care. That's who. Understand something, Grove. I spend fifty percent of my time dealing with congressional oversight committees—time better spent running the circus. Now somebody leaked this latest freak show to the media, probably this Stenowski character, and I gotta go into PR mode again. Which means I need this thing closed down. Now. Which means I need you to pay attention."

Grove met the man's angry glare. "You have my undivided attention."

Corboy shoved the door open, and the two men entered the noisy teleconference room.

THIRTEEN

Three young middle-management types with laminate badges and sport coats bustled around the oblong teleconference room, which was lined with acoustic tile and blazing with fluorescent light. A large plasma screen hung on the far wall, flickering with an image of color bars. A shrill tone rang out from speakers embedded in the ceiling, and the air smelled of burnt coffee.

Corboy took a seat at the head of the conference table, motioning for Grove to sit across from him.

Grove did so, opening his briefcase, pulling out his notebook. "What are we looking at here?" he wanted to know.

The Director gave a terse nod to one of the underlings, and the sport coat fiddled with a keyboard. The screen flickered with shaky handheld video footage of a deserted beach—presumably Galveston Island—framed in a window on one side of the screen, an unidentified talking head on the other.

Corboy spoke up: "Are we on yet? Agent Phipps? Can you hear us?"

The talking head, a square-jawed man with a buzz cut and cheap sport coat, was wrestling an earpiece into his ear. "Keith Phipps here, Houston field office." The man's southwestern drawl crackled out of the speakers, slightly out of sync with his mouth. "Who am I speaking with?"

"You've got Louis Corboy here, along with Ulysses Grove, Quantico."

"Fellas, I gotta be honest with y'all . . . I'm not sure what we got here."

"Go ahead and run it down for us."

Onscreen the man read off a small spiral-bound notebook in his hands: "We got a white, female victim, looks like multiple stab wounds. Latent has nothing. Looks like smooth gloves." He looked up into the camera. "Y'all gettin' this?"

Grove watched the shaky footage on the opposite side of the screen. The camera panned to the left, then tilted down, revealing drag marks in the sand, a dark smudge—most likely blood—and footprints. Like a Xerox copy of North Carolina. The camera panned to the right and a dark bundle came into view. The camera moved in closer, finally revealing the pale, sodden remains of Madeline Gilchrist.

"We're seeing it," Corboy commented flatly. "This footage was taken this morning?"

"No, actually, it was early this afternoon, at low tide," Phipps explained. "Wanted to get as much physical evidence on record before it washed away. What happened was, just as soon as I got the MO up on the wires, I get a call from the Mid-Atlantic folks with Minneapolis on the other line—the modus here I guess matches both those deals."

"You got a positive on the vic yet?"

The man on the screen looked at his notebook. "Gilchrist, Madeline Louise, resident of the South Houston area. Age forty-one, single, no criminal record. Understand she was a student at South Dayton Junior College. ME reports just came back, toxicology has a cocktail of thiopental, prescription antidepressants in her bloodstream."

Grove clenched his teeth as he watched the poorly framed high-def image zoom into a close-up of the dead woman's porcelain-white face, matted with blood and hair and seaweed. A cold, sharp knife-edge touched his heart. His eyes watered. "Agent Phipps, Ulysses Grove here—got a question."

"Go ahead, sir."

"What part of Galveston is the scene located in?"

"I guess you could say this part of the island's more of a transitional area. Commercial docks, bait shops, marinas, things of that nature."

The averages clicked in Grove's mind. He stared at the screen. The shaky image panned across the blood-soaked sand, the stains like photocopies of both the blood-spattered wall in Minneapolis and the carnage-strewn beach in North Carolina. "Let me guess," Grove said. "There's a grand total of eleven sharp trauma wounds between the six vertebra and the sacrum."

On the screen the field agent looked at the coroner's report, then looked up. "That's right, did somebody—?"

"Time of death," Grove went on, staring at the table now, "is somewhere between eleven and noon Central Standard Time."

"Yeah, that's correct, but how did—?"

"Cause of death is heart failure stemming from hypovolemic shock."

"That's correct."

Grove closed his eyes. "Victim was last seen at a public place within fifty miles of the dump site."

Onscreen, Agent Keith Phipps was frowning. "Right again. But how—?"

Corboy let out an irritated sigh. "Grove, that's enough—"

Grove kept his eyes closed. "Victim was kept alive for approximately twelve hours before the fatal wounds were inflicted."

"Grove—"

"There were three distinct shoeprints found at the scene, one of them male, size eleven and a half E."

"Grove, we get it," Corboy grunted.

"Tire marks a hundred yards from the scene indicate a large multipurpose vehicle."

"Grove, I said that's enough!"

The suddenness and volume of Corboy's outburst made Agent Phipps jerk with surprise at the pop in his earpiece. He stared into the camera. "What's going on?" He let out a dry little nervous chuckle. "Y'all didn't tell me I'd be visitin' with a psychic."

"Agent Phipps," Corboy said, his voice laced with thinly veiled anger, "we have reason to believe we got a copycat situation—"

Grove saw something. "Hold on a second, hold on . . . hold on." He stood up, his startled tone of voice making everybody in the room pause. He stared at the shaky video. "Stop the playback—freeze it!"

"What?" Agent Phipps looked confused.

"Freeze the video, please."

Agent Phipps glanced off-camera, whispering something to an assistant.

Grove watched the shaky image panning across foamy waves washing up across the beach. He cocked his head slightly, favoring his good eye, as he stared—an unconscious habit he had developed since his left eye had been injured.

All at once the video froze.

"Okay, now I need you to rewind it, just go back about five seconds."

Agent Phipps glanced off camera. "Johnny, you get that? Back it up five seconds."

Corboy rose. "What is it, Grove? What are we looking at here?"

The image blurred slightly as it quickly rewound. The camera was panning across the beach in reverse, scanning the dirty sand, the shells and trash and shards of driftwood littering the beach. Grove took a step closer to the screen. "Right there! Freeze it there!"

Phipps said, "Pause it right there, Johnny."

Corboy stared at the screen. "What is it?"

The image froze at an awkward angle—right in the middle of a zoom—showing a portion of a bloodstain on the right, a slice of the beach, and part of the sky. Off to the left, the edge of a boardwalk was visible.

"Upper left-hand corner, by the dock." Grove pointed at the screen. "See it?"

"No, I don't." Corboy shook his head. "What are we looking at?"

"In the sand." Grove took another step toward the

screen until he was close enough to touch the pebbled fabric of the projection surface. "See the writing?"

"Writing?"

Grove leaned closer. In his one good eye, the glowing image broke up into a matrix of ten thousand pixel dots, a scarlet pointillist painting. "Bottom of the piling." He spoke in a low, controlled tone now, brushing his fingertip across the screen. "A few inches to the right. See it? I promise you that's not part of your average scene."

Corboy kept shaking his head. "Okay, I see symbols of some kind, chicken-scratch, I just don't—"

"And then the camera pans away." Grove swallowed hard, looked at his watch, a twinge of panic pinching his gut. "When exactly was this video taken?"

Keith Phipps looked at his notes. "Um, let's see . . ."

"Easy does it, Grove." Corboy looked confused, irritated. "You left me in the dust here. Some local scratches something in the sand with a stick—big deal. How do you know that's even part of the scene?"

Phipps looked into the camera. "Video was taken at one-thirty this afternoon."

Grove clenched his jaw, the sudden pain radiating. "You said that's around low tide, right?"

"Yeah. Just about."

Grove glanced again at his watch. "It's almost two." He looked at the screen. "When's high tide?"

Phipps gave a shrug. "I dunno, seven-ish, something like that."

"That's five hours, at the most. Probably less than that. You got anybody out there right now?"

"Couple of uniforms maybe, I don't know. The scene's taped off."

Grove's heart thumped as he stared at the partial image of something scrawled in the soggy, dirty sand on-screen. It looked like worm tracks curling and spiraling back on themselves, crisscrossing, looping, slashing. "Get the lab guys back there, Phipps. Get a cast of that stretch of sand near the piling."

"I understand what you're saying, but I'm not sure we can get a cast before the tide comes in."

"Then get a goddamn backhoe and lift the whole thing out of the beach."

"Again it's a matter of time—"

"Get them back there, Phipps. Trench it off from the water somehow. Get digitals of it, plenty of close-ups. Get shots of it at least."

"But—"

"Less than five hours from now the sea's gonna take that message." Grove whirled toward the Director. "Let's go ahead and scramble a plane out of Andrews; we can make it out there in three hours if we catch a tailwind."

Corboy looked as if he'd just swallowed a chicken bone. "Goddamnit, Grove, slow down. How the hell do you know that was left by the perp? Even if it's fresh, it's just some kid with a stick."

Grove barely heard the man. He threw his notes in his briefcase, snapped the attaché shut, then headed for the door. Corboy grabbed him. The two men came nose to nose. Everybody in the room waited. "Goddamnit, Grove, it's a kid with a stick."

Grove stared at Corboy. "How many kids in Texas with sticks have a command of Sumerian, you think?"

"A command of what?"

"Sumerian, Lou. It's written in Sumerian. It's a dead language."

Corboy released his grip on the profiler, then turned and glowered at the two-dimensional image of worm tracks on the projection screen.

Grove had already vanished out the door.

FOURTEEN

Grove raced the moon to the Gulf Coast that afternoon, riding in the navigator's seat of an Air Force C-17 as the sun dipped behind the rolling purple spires of the Smoky Mountains. Strapped into a tattered, rickety contour chair behind the flight deck, his notebook open on his lap, he bided his time by nervously doodling sketches of the Archetype—that bulbous black demonic silhouette from his class, now sprouting horns and forked tail in his imagination—while the pilot in front of him, a middle-aged female captain named Villalobos, snapped her chewing gum and casually flipped switches.

The C-17 Globemaster was the workhorse of the Air Force, designed to carry troops or humanitarian aid across long distances. This one had been to Afghanistan, then Iraq, then back to the states for FEMA duty. Grove could sense the cavernous, empty cargo hold stretching behind him like the belly of a whale, creaking and echoing with every bump or gust of headwind. The ghosts of long-forgotten paratroopers and war-wounded kids lurked back there. Grove tried to focus on the clock.

They crossed the southern-tier states in record time, climbing to thirty thousand feet over Alabama in order to avoid a spring storm, then coursing westward over the patchwork cotton fields of Mississippi at 400 knots. At just past five, the jet banked to the south, soaring down over the coastal plains of western Louisiana, the fuselage creaking.

Grove gripped the armrests as the aircraft plunged toward the rugged estuaries of southeast Texas, bumping and rattling on currents of ocean turbulence. Through the window to his left, way out in the distance, the low sun shimmered off the Gulf like fire crawling on glass. Another banking turn, and the C-17 began its descent into Ellington Air Force Base, where the 147th Fighter Wing was waiting for them with a Black Hawk helicopter for the quick jaunt down to Galveston Island. Grove leaned over the bulwark and gazed down through the Plexiglas portal at the vast arid prairies rushing beneath them in a blur. The tide would be coming in very soon. The tiny hairs on the back of Grove's neck bristled.

Over the sibilant roar of the engines, Captain Villalobos hollered something in her heavily accented English. Grove leaned forward, pressing a finger to his headset to hear better. "What was that?"

"Sir, put your ears on!" she said, cupping her hand over her mouthpiece. "CSI vehicle's calling from the ground."

Grove stashed his notebook and quickly switched over to the ground channel. "Grove here."

Static in his earpiece. He shook his head at her and tapped his headset. "Can't hear anything!"

"Switch over to channel two!"

He did as he was told, and immediately heard a voice crackling in his ear. "—you copy—?"

"Copy that, you got Special Agent Grove here. Who am I talking to?"

"Phipps here, got the Houston CSI team with me, en route to the scene."

"Copy that, Phipps—what's your ETA?"

"About ten minutes out," the voice sizzled in his ear. "Already got forensics there. Concentrating on a twenty-five-square-foot area around the piling closest to the body dump—is that correct?"

Grove glanced down through the portal. The aircraft was on its descent, low enough now for him to make out Galveston Bay in the far gray distance, maybe twenty miles away, the tide already flirting with the edges of the causeways. He looked at his watch. It was eleven minutes past six.

"Phipps, listen to me. Chances are, the tide's going to obliterate the message before we get full coverage. Do you have the cryptologist with you?"

No answer.

"Phipps?"

Static.

Special Agent Keith Phipps tapped the plastic enclosure around his earpiece. "Agent Grove, hello? Agent Grove? You copy? Hello?"

Static crackled in his ear, Grove's voice cutting in and out. Phipps could not quite make out what the profiler was saying, but it sounded critical.

Ramrod straight in his double-knit sport coat and flattop hairstyle, Phipps rode on the passenger side of the Bureau's tricked-out panel van, reinforced with bulletproof glass and refurbished in the back to accommodate heavy machinery, extra tactical personnel, or specialized lab equipment. A rail-thin young lab assistant from Corpus Christi sat behind the wheel, nervously whistling as he white-knuckled the wheel.

A few seconds ago, the vehicle had reached the last leg of Highway 45, the Galveston Bay causeway, the van's massive tires drumming over speed bumps. Now the vehicle roared down the narrow connecting road bordered on either side by a wall of tangled cypress and sea grass, the aqua-gray estuary visible in all directions. The vibrations felt good to Phipps. The former Marine and Special Forces group leader craved emergencies such as this, and had always wanted to work with the legendary Ulysses Grove. Better yet, Phipps was now delivering one of the Southwest Region's most prickly, difficult specialists to this rustic crime scene.

"What the hell is going on?!" The shrill voice rang out from the back, and Phipps glanced over his shoulder at Dr. Millhouse, who glared balefully from her wheelchair "What did he say, Phipps?"

Phipps kept tapping his headset. "Lost him there for a second. I'll get him back."

"Amateur hour at the Apollo," the cryptologist grumbled from the rear hold. An emaciated dowager of indeterminate age hunkered down in an elaborate motorized wheelchair strapped to the floor, she was clad in a corduroy stable coat, jodhpurs, and knee-high rubber boots. She looked like Katharine Hepburn's ornery little sister, her salt-and-pepper hair pulled back in a severe ponytail. Her wrinkled visage was sunburned and weathered from decades of poking trowels into the sandy earth

of Old Money ranches. She spoke with the aristo-
cratic twang of Dallas society. "What have you gotten me into here, Phipps?"

"One second." Phipps held up his hand to cut
her off. He listened to Grove's voice crackling in
his ear.

"—cryptologist with you?"

"Copy that, yes, the cryptologist is with me.
We're about five minutes away."

"Good, good—I want him to start the translation right away. You copy that? Have him dive right
in."

"Copy that," Phipps said into the mouthpiece.
"One thing, though—"

Grove's voice cut back in: "There may be nu-
ances in that sand the forensics guys have missed,
and the tide's gonna blow it all away. You follow?"

"Yeah, copy that." Phipps glanced over his
shoulder. "One thing though."

"Go ahead."

"The cryptologist is a *she*—Dr. Emily Millhouse."
In the rearview, Agent Phipps saw the little sun-
wizened crone giving him a sour look.

Through the static: "That's great, that's fine . . .
just get there."

"Copy, out."

Phipps switched off his radio, then pointed to a
fork looming up ahead near a salt-rusted gate between two massive live oaks. "There's your turn,"
he told the assistant.

They careened around a gentle curve and
boomed down Broadway, past rows of storefronts
and tourist traps, past beachcomber inns luminous in the sunset.

The murder scene was located at Stewart Beach

Park, a leprous strip of sand about a mile away. They would be there in a matter of minutes. But that didn't prevent Agent Keith Phipps from shooting worried glances out the side window at the inlet to the left.

The town of Galveston was situated on a long narrow strip of land that ran parallel to the bay, barely a mile across at its widest point. Between the island and the mainland was a good-sized harbor of prime boat docks and summer homes, its mercurial gray currents in constant ebb and flow. Phipps could see the far banks of the Pelican Island nature preserve to the east, the tangled roots of cypress and boulders forming a rugged breakwater.

The tide had already climbed halfway up the crags, and was starting to sluice into the forest.

Phipps looked at his watch. It was 6:31. How long would it take them to get the doctor to the scene? How much time did they have before the tide took this message—whatever it was—away forever?

He glanced up at the sky. The vibrant, cloudless blue had turned a deeper shade of magenta, the shadows to the east elongating, the buildings lining Broadway darkening, coming alive with shrieking gulls. Phipps could literally hear the tide coming in through the window, the distant slosh and whisper like a breath on the back of his neck.

Only minutes remained before the seawater got a chance to wash the scene clean of its sins.

Fifteen minutes later, Grove was on the ground at Ellington, dashing across sun-bleached tarmac, his knapsack over his shoulder. The Black Hawk

waited on the edge of the runway, its canopy
gleaming in the setting sun. Its prop was already
screaming, the wind flapping Grove's pant legs as
he approached. He climbed into the chopper without saying a word, the pilot—a heavyset kid with
acne scars—nodding at the harness.

Grove got himself situated. He yelled over the
din of the prop, "You know someplace down there
on the island called Stewart Park Beach?"

"Hold on!" The pilot secured the hatches, then
kicked the engine up a notch. "Have you there in
no time!"

The chopper lurched, then levitated off the tarmac in a thunderhead of dust.

Grove practically held his breath from that
point on.

FIFTEEN

They found a place to set the Black Hawk down on a sandy outcropping just north of the murder scene, on the edge of an abandoned construction site near the seawall east of town. The skids hit the beach with a sickening crunch that rattled the undercarriage and nearly cracked Grove's teeth, which were clenched with nervous tension as he clawed at his harness buckles.

"What the hell are you doing?" the pilot wanted to know, twisting around in his seat.

"Outta time!" Grove unsnapped himself, tore off his helmet, and tossed it to the floor.

"Wait a minute! Wait a minute!" The pilot looked stunned. "They got a jeep on the way!"

"Not enough time!" Grove glanced at his watch. "Tide's almost up!"

He yanked the hatch lever, the canopy door clanging open. It took major effort to slide it the rest of the way, the salt wind rushing into the cabin on the reverse currents of the rotor.

He slipped outside the fuselage, then leapt off the running board.

He landed hard on the sand, the impact rattling his skull. He instinctively kept his head low, spinning toward the west, then loping up the rocky bank toward the dusty road.

Once he reached flat pavement, he clenched his fists, put his head down, and started sprinting—full bore—toward the scene a quarter mile away. Armani coat flapping in the wind, laminate tag fluttering around his neck, he looked a little ridiculous, but he was still in good shape. His gait was strong and fleet, and he made amazing time.

The deserted beach came into view ahead of him. Huffing and puffing, chugging along like an escapee from some white-collar work camp, he strained his good eye to find signs of the CSI team.

He saw an ramshackle mobile home park off to the right, a few old men futzing around engine blocks. Off to the left, coming into focus, a dilapidated dock jutted out over trash-strewn sea grass. The long shadows of dusk cooled the salt winds.

A state trooper's cruiser was parked at the end of the boat dock, where a tail of yellow tape flagged in the wind.

Grove leapt to the sand, his heart threatening to rend his rib cage open. His designer loafers dug into the filthy sand as he churned his way down the embankment toward the end of the dock, breathing hard, fists clenched. He saw the rear end of the CSI van sticking out of the weeds on the other side of the dock.

The tide had already bubbled up as far as the second row of pilings.

It was already past six o'clock. High tide was due any minute.

A stocky, uniformed officer suddenly stepped

into view as Grove came charging toward the scene. "Hey, hey, hey!" he cautioned, putting his hand on the butt of his Glock. His boots were ankle deep in tidewater. "Slow down, friend, slow the hell down."

Grove raised his laminate tag into the air. "FBI! It's okay! FBI!"

"C'mon up, then." The cop backed out of the way as Grove came splashing around the end of the dock, his Florsheims getting soaked.

On the other side of the dock was a narrow, rustic swimming beach, the crime scene just as depicted in the teleconference video. Evidence flags and dark stains spanned the hundred-square-foot swath of sand, bordered on three sides by yellow tape, now fluttering wildly against the trade winds.

In the heart of the swath lay a crude, white-tape outline of where Madeline Gilchrist had fallen, the outline already half submerged where the tide had licked up the sand.

Grove came sloshing around the lowest piling and he saw many things all at once: the highest piling was still about a foot and a half above the surging water, which was now periodically sliding up the sandy embankment, getting closer and closer to the strange markings scratched into the sand; a couple of men were about ten feet away from the markings, lifting a wheelchair down a makeshift ramp onto the soggy beachhead.

A scrawny woman sat hunched in that chair, nervously gripping her armrests. "I swear, Phipps, if you drop me I will sue your department back to the Mesozoic period!"

Phipps glanced over his shoulder. "Agent Grove, I assume? Looks like you just made it."

"Agent Phipps." Winded, dizzy with nervous tension, Grove approached the threesome. "Can I help?"

"Agent Ulysses Grove, meet Dr. Emily Millhouse."

Grove grabbed one side of the wheelchair and helped heft the thing onto the sand. "See by the bottom of the piling? In the shadow?"

"I may be old, but I'm not blind!" the old woman barked. She had a yellow legal pad tucked under her skinny, arthritic arm. "Please turn me around."

They positioned her next to the piling. At this close proximity, the markings in the sand were clearly visible, about a half-inch deep, too delicate to be scrawled by a human finger and yet too fine to be scratched by a stick.

"Give her some breathing room," Grove urged.

Phipps and the lab assistant backed away, their heels in the encroaching water now. The woman in the wheelchair stared at the sand.

Grove lingered. He knelt down by the symbols. He pulled a pair of rubber gloves out of his pocket and put them on. "Is that cuneiform?" he uttered, almost under his breath, still winded.

The doctor did not reply, just kept staring at the oddly conjoined symbols in the sand: crooked little suns, I-shaped bars, tiny half-moons.

"What do you make of it?" Phipps asked from behind Grove. It wasn't clear who he was addressing, Grove or Millhouse.

"Please be quiet!" the doctor snapped. She laid the tablet on her slender lap, found a ballpoint pen in her breast pocket, and clicked it, never taking her gaze off the symbols in the sand near the front left wheel of her chair. "Oh my . . . oh my my my."

Grove flexed his hands in his rubber gloves. "What is it? What's the matter?"

"This is old." She pulled a protractor from her pocket and leaned down close enough to measure an angle. "This is very, very old."

"How old?"

"Old like Babylonian . . . maybe even Akkadian."

The waves crept closer, the foaming tide only inches away now. The salt winds swirled around them, whistling through the wheelchair, tossing the old woman's gray ponytail.

Grove leaned down closer, gently brushing a rubber-tipped finger across the bottom edge of the symbols.

"Agent Grove?" Phipps sounded restless, anxious, a little angry.

Grove looked at the tiny wet pink smudge on the tip of his index finger. "These were made with the murder weapon." He made his announcement in a low, grave mutter, then stood up and looked at Phipps. "Postmortem."

"Quiet!" The old woman sniffed, then started translating, madly sketching formulas on her legal pad. Her crippled, age-spotted hand, curled around the pen, turned white and translucent as she worked.

A foamy stream of water slid across the symbols, making the edges bleed into the sand.

"Hurry," Grove murmured.

"I could do this a *lot* faster if you would *kindly* stop telling me to do it faster," the doctor snarled, her gaze still riveted to the symbols in the sand.

Another wave came up, sloshing around the chair's wheels, momentarily covering the symbols with a slimy sheet of brine, then rolling away again.

The ancient cuneiform streaked and blurred. It was nearly gone.

"Almost got it," the old woman said.

"Hurry, please." Grove's stomach burned with nervous tension. "Hurry."

"This isn't a damned *spelling bee.*" The cryptologist leaned closer, pressed her lips together, then scribbled something else in her notebook. Then she looked down at the shifting sand with a slight tilt of her head, the wind tossing a stray hair in her eyes. "I don't have the whole string yet but I can definitely tell you what the last word is."

Grove straightened. The others quieted. Grove looked at the old woman. "What is it?"

"That pictogram at the bottom represents the Semitic word *hubur.*"

"Which means . . . what?"

Dr. Millhouse took off her sunglasses and looked up at him with pale blue eyes surrounded by wrinkles. "The word means netherworld . . . or, more precisely, *hell.*"

SIXTEEN

"You gotta be kiddin' me," Drinkwater said from the darkness of the taxi's backseat, gazing out the greasy window at the pathetic excuse for a tavern. A blue neon sign glowed in the darkness above the tops of the trees, adjacent to a broken-down clapboard façade. "That's it? That's the Cherry Pit?"

"Pride of the Low Country," muttered the elderly black gentleman behind the wheel. He flipped down the metal flag. "Watch your pocketbook in there, darlin'."

"Lovely." Drinkwater fished around in her purse for the fare, paid the man, and climbed out.

For a moment she just stood there in the humid swampy air, taking in the timeworn outpost, as the cab belched away in a cloud of exhaust. The bar sat all by its lonesome at the end of a narrow dead-end dirt road, a two-story gallery building buried in overgrown willows and cypress trees. A small gravel parking lot to the west hosted a few rusted pickups. Mosquitoes swarmed around a bug zapper near the door.

Drinkwater took a deep breath. She had traveled all the way to Charleston on a hunch, spent most of her spare cash on the airfare. Now it was the moment of truth. She was either going to shed some light on Geisel's diary tonight, or quit this wild-goose chase and get back to Quantico before she flunked out of the Academy.

She brushed the dust off her denim jacket, smoothed her hand over her braids, and went inside.

The narrow barroom, choked in a fog of blue smoke, reeking of hard-luck cases and sour whiskey spilled on hardwood floors, was mostly silent except for the scratchy drone of a jukebox in the far corner. A few yocals sat bellied up to the bar, one of them head down and sound asleep, while an old black fellow wiped down the counter, giving Drinkwater a lascivious look. "Evenin', sweet pea." His bayou drawl was as thick as blackstrap molasses. "Pull up a stool and name your pleasure."

"Evening, sir." Drinkwater gave a nod as she approached. She casually leaned against the counter. "Why don't you gimme one of them brown bottles of Dixie?"

"You got it." The man fished in a cooler, extracted a beer, popped the cap, and slid it over to her. "You're in luck, sweet thang, 'cuz tonight's ladies' night, so that's just seventy-fi' cent."

Drinkwater tossed the coins on the bar. "Understand Chainsaw Okuba plays here once in a while?"

The bartender showed his rotting gold-plated front teeth and hissed an approximation of laughter. One of the guys at the end of the bar gazed up from his drunken stupor and let out a giggle.

Drinkwater looked around. "Did I say something wrong?"

"Y'all might say old Oky Okuba play here once in a while, 'specially since he owns the joint."

"No kidding?"

"That's a fact. He's just finishin' up his second set downstair as we speak."

"Where?"

The bartender indicated a doorway shrouded in beads on the opposite side of the room. "Right yonder. Go on down. It's okay. He don't bite . . . much."

This last comment roused the sleeping drunk, and all the boys had a good laugh at that one. Drinkwater gave them a convivial nod and laughed along for a moment, then took her beer and her purse and went over to the doorway.

She descended a crooked staircase and found herself in another world. The smoke was so thick it was difficult to make out any shapes other than a general impression of a rotting hurricane cellar. Overturned chairs, battered metal kegs, and peanut shells littered the dirt floor. Broken holiday lights hung from the moldering rafters. Languid, drunken spectators sat on stools along the bomb shelter walls.

Drinkwater strolled through the haze toward a tiny stage at one end of the room, on which an emaciated black musician was putting a guitar back into its case. He looked drugged, spent, malnourished. Sporting a mousy gray goatee, his tight coils of black hair starting to recede, he barely resembled the sinewy bluesman depicted on the wrinkled poster still folded in Drinkwater's purse. "Mr. Okuba? David Okuba?"

The musician glanced up, but didn't say anything, just gave her a nervous smile and snapped the guitar case shut.

"Can I talk to you for a second?" Drinkwater was playing it as casual as possible. "Just for a second?"

"Talk?" His voice was a slow delta wind through a rusty tin can. "Talk, yeah."

He turned and ambled toward a backstage doorway, vanishing in the dark.

Drinkwater shrugged, glanced around the room, then followed the man into the dark.

She found herself in a cluttered hall redolent with the stench of marijuana smoke and spoiled fish; it was too dark for her to identify any of the oblong objects stacked along the floor or against the walls. A single yellow cage light shone dimly at one end of the corridor. "Mr. Okuba?" Drinkwater gazed up and down the passageway. "Hello?"

Something moved behind her.

"Don't you move that big booty one more inch," a new voice oozed in her ear from the darkness, a deep, gravelly, baritone drawl.

Drinkwater froze stiff at the sensation of cold sharp steel against her throat. "Okay, easy, easy there, I'm not moving."

The blade remained against her jugular, the sharp edge digging in.

"I'm trying to tell you there's something strange about the use of cuneiform here." Dr. Millhouse navigated her wheelchair around a makeshift chalkboard that was leaning against an oil drum, her palsied hand curled around her chair's joystick, the whirring motor and squeaking wheels echoing in the abandoned boathouse. She had a pen behind her ear. A single ceiling light hung down above her, illuminating a cracked, oil-spotted cement floor littered with her notes. "It doesn't transliterate like most archaic Hittite I've seen."

Grove nervously paced the length of the cavernous boat garage, which had long ago succumbed to Gulf Coast decline and now was overrun with rats and cobwebs and rotting timbers stinking of mold and rancid motor oil. It was the only private room to be procured in Galveston on such short notice in the middle of the night, but that didn't mean it was conducive to delicate linguistic work. Grove had to get out of there or he was going to lose his mind. It was nearly one in the morning, and he was burning up with adrenaline, not to mention a horrible feeling of slippage, of losing control, and the old woman had yet to provide a translation of the killer's message. "Just give it your best shot, Doc, please, it doesn't have to be perfect, just gimme the gist."

"Wait a minute . . . no." The old woman suddenly lifted her hand from the joystick, the wheelchair coming to an abrupt halt. She raised her trembling hand as she stared at the rows upon rows of script that she had scrawled in blue chalk across the back of the signboard. "That's too easy. That's just too dad-blamed easy."

"What is it?" Special Agent Keith Phipps tossed his cigarette to the floor, ground it out with the toe of his wingtip, and came over to the oil drum.

Grove stopped pacing. He stared at the blackboard. "You got something?"

"I shall surely be drummed out of the International Society of Cryptologists, missing this."

Grove clenched his fists. "Doc, you're killing us."

"This symbol here, the Stag head it's called, see?"

The old woman pointed her long quill pen at a primitive line drawing of a faunlike head. The head was at the beginning of each row of pictograms—arrows, spirals, daggers, curlicues, triangles. "At first I reckoned it must be part of the grammar of the message, embedded in the syntax. That's how you transliterate something, in case you're interested, which I'm sure you're not. See this row of pictograms?" She pointed at a series of crude sketches. "Transliteration will give you the Sumerian words." She pointed at the phrase *ES UG IGI E-ZE HUBUR.* "When you do that, you quite often get more context than you bargained for—especially here."

She brushed a long painted fingernail at a row of crudely drawn animals—deer or antelope.

Grove felt a twinge of icy cold travel down his spine. "What does it mean?"

The old woman glanced at Phipps, then back at Grove. "It means this message is directed to someone in particular—someone referred to repeatedly as 'the hunter.'"

Grove stepped forward. "What's the message, Dr. Millhouse?"

"*ES* is three," she said.

"What's the full message?"

"*UG* is death or sacrifice, and *IGI* means to pierce or to open; and finally we have this last string, which is like a mathematical equation."

"Three victims, is that what you're saying?" Grove drilled his gaze into the old woman. He was not even aware that he was clenching his fists so hard his fingernails were breaking the skin of his palms.

Outside the boathouse came the hushed whisper of waves breaking against the beach.

Millhouse looked up at Grove. "Best I can tell ya, the message says, 'After three sacrifices . . . the netherworld shall open . . . for both hunter and hunted.' "

SEVENTEEN

Shivering, dizzy with panic, Edith Drinkwater swallowed the taste of bitter acid at the back of her throat and tried to control her emotions. Puffs of cold white vapor pluming from her nostrils. She wanted to scream, but somehow she held it in—for the moment, at least. Wrists tied with hemp rope behind her back, her legs hog-tied to the legs of the cold metal folding chair on which she now sat, she squinted to see through the gloom of a walk-in freezer stacked to the ceiling with boxes of frozen alligator filets.

"Who sent you here?"

The figure on the other side of the freezer was barely visible behind a veil of icy white vapor. Sucking on a bong, the pale smoke like a wreath around his face, David "Chainsaw" Okuba trembled while he waited for an answer, but it was impossible to tell whether he was trembling from the cold or the paranoia implicit in his question.

"You got no reason to rough me up," Drinkwater managed in an even voice.

"Who the fuck sent you?"

Drinkwater swallowed and spoke very quickly: "I told you, I'm a private investigator, I swear to God, you can look at my ID, you rifled through my purse already, go ahead and look, I'm telling you the truth, go ahead, I'm on a case involving your uncle Baruk—"

"What do you know about my uncle?"

Drinkwater's heart pumped in that crazy way it pumped in her nightmares. She knew men like these men—coarse country types—very, very well. She knew their odors, the smell of lust, fear. Right now she could detect a strong stench of fear on Okuba. "I work for a party wants information on a group of men who followed—"

"Bitch is talkin' shit!"

The other voice came from off to Drinkwater's left, belonging to the enormous mixed-race man who had grabbed her from behind. Clad in faded denim coveralls and porkpie hat, with biceps like great brown muskmelons, he lurked in the shadows now near a stack of frozen hush-puppy boxes, cleaning his fingernails with the same knife with which he had subdued her. "She ain't no private eye."

"Clarence, hush." David Okuba drew a big nervous gulp off the pipe, holding the sweet rush in his lungs. Then he exhaled painfully. Trembling, he gave Drinkwater a suspicious look through red eyes. "What group of men?"

"I got their names written down," she told him. She could see the fear in the man's eyes coalescing into something else. Maybe awe. Maybe a deeper dread. "Bernard Schoenbaum was one—the only one still alive. That's where I saw your poster, in Mr. Schoenbaum's room."

The blues singer stared. "Keep talkin'. . . ."

"There's five others. Your uncle Baruk was one of them; a fella named Goodis. Let's see, a couple of Middle Eastern gentlemen."

Okuba gave her a grave little nod, lowering his pipe. "Mohammad Achmadra and Mr. Norgaru. Thank Christ you ain't from the other side."

Drinkwater looked at him. "No, I'm—I mean, what other side would that be?"

"Untie her, Clarence."

The bodyguard grunted. "But we ain't even sure she's—"

"I said untie the lady!"

The big man grumbled as he came over, knelt down behind Drinkwater, and loosened the ropes. Drinkwater rubbed her sore wrists while Clarence untied her legs. She stood on weak knees and clapped her hands to get some feeling back into them. She felt as though icicles had formed under her nose. "Well, that was fun."

"I'm sorry," Okuba offered. "I had no way of knowin' who you is."

Drinkwater shivered. "All right . . . so. You mind telling me what's going on?"

"C'mon." Okuba went over to the big walk-in door and muscled it open. When the warm air of the kitchen met the coldness of the freezer, a cloud of vapor momentarily obscured Okuba, who had paused in the doorway. "We'll have some whiskey, and I'll tell ya everything I know."

Drinkwater followed him out into the sultry warmth of the tavern's kitchen, wondering if she was ready for this.

*   *   *

Ulysses Grove convinced the Texas Air National Guard to scramble an F14 out of Ellington to fly him through the night back home to Virginia—his fears metastasizing, spreading the terrible notion through him that his family once again could be in mortal danger. When he landed at Andrews, a police cruiser and two uniformed officers were waiting to rush him south across the Virginia state line to his home. It was 3:11 A.M. Driving mostly in tense silence, the sound of the siren howling the whole way, the cops got him up the coast in record time.

The squad car topped the hill south of Pelican Bay right around four that morning.

Grove, hunched in the darkness of the backseat, craned his neck to see his property in the distance. His jacket was off, his oxford shirt unbuttoned and his briefcase open on his lap. He was sweaty from all the frenzied travel and adrenal activity, and when he leaned forward, all his notes and haphazard doodles of faceless demons and black silhouettes with horns and glowing eyes tumbled to the floor of the cruiser. "I don't see any lights on. She usually leaves the living room lights on."

The uniformed officer behind the wheel—a gray-haired vet named Weems—grabbed the radio mike. "Twenty-seven, you got the home secure?"

The speaker crackled: "Fifty-nine, copy that. Secure's an understatement."

"What did he say?" Grove strained to see his place through the windshield, but the predawn darkness obscured his street in a blanket of black. All he could see of his property, still a block away, was the mailbox at the end of the drive. The late moon shone low and huge off the bay to the north, a long broken ribbon of shimmering luminous yellow off the water.

Panic pinched at Grove's chest. He had tried to reach Maura by cell phone repeatedly with no luck.

"Hold tight, be there in a sec," Officer Weems commented.

Grove gripped the back of the seat, stomach burning with nerves. Perhaps he was overreacting, but he had convinced Operations at Quantico to have a black-and-white waiting for him at Andrews so he could get home as soon as possible. He was worried that the killer was likely *inside* the Bureau system and therefore knew where Grove lived. Worse than that, the killer had reached out—albeit in a cryptic fashion—to Grove personally, in the sand on Galveston Island. Not by name. But Grove knew the code. He knew the dance.

The cruiser screeched up to the curb in front of Grove's Cape Cod, lights blazing.

Grove lurched out the rear door and into the cool predawn air, instantly noticing the other three cruisers parked single file along his narrow driveway. The house was dark, a flashlight flickering behind a second-floor window. Grove raced across the wet grass and up his porch steps, taking the wooden stairs two at a time.

Inside the front door he paused, scanning the dark living room. He could immediately see that something was wrong. The lock had been jimmied. The lights were off, the place neat and orderly. Not the usual haphazard clutter that a family with a toddler naturally amasses over the course of a day. The air smelled of disinfectant and change.

Grove's heart started chugging in his chest. "Maura? *Maura!*"

He rushed into the dark kitchen. He didn't see the note at first. His gaze fell on the scrubbed countertops, the gleaming stainless steel of the appliances. The linoleum had that tacky just-mopped quality. Heavy footsteps were creaking down the stairs behind Grove, and he whirled.

A buzz-cut uniformed officer appeared around the corner of the archway, hand cautiously on the butt of his service revolver. He wore yellow-tinted aviator eyeglasses. "Agent Grove?"

"Yes, that's right, what's going on?"

"Sir, I think—"

"Where are they? Where's my family?"

"Sir—"

"Where's my wife, goddamnit?!"

The cop looked apologetic, pointing at the kitchen table behind Grove. "Sir, I think maybe you ought to go ahead and check out the note she left."

Grove spun toward the round Formica table in the corner beneath the antique rooster. He didn't move. He just stared at the business-size envelope leaning against the salt and pepper shakers on the pristine, scrubbed surface. The envelope bore a single word carefully, almost lovingly scrawled across its front:

ULY

EIGHTEEN

Honey—

First of all, I know you're dealing with a lot right now—losing Tom and all—and I know you're hurting, so I'll try and make this as quick and painless as possible. Please don't think this is some kind of "Dear John" letter—I still adore you with all my heart and I know we'll work out our problems. But what I'm about to tell you is just as important as a Dear John letter, so listen up. I've taken Aaron back out West. Someplace where nobody can find us. I guess you could say it's my own version of a safe house because, as you and I both know from past experience, the FBI's version ain't exactly what I would call safe.

I will not go through another fiasco like Indiana. I just won't. I will call you when you get this latest thing safely put to bed and not a minute sooner. And don't waste the Feds' time and money trying to find me, you'll just put your child in harm's way. Again. Just know that I love you with all my heart. I always will

*love you, no matter what. And I always will
believe in you and what you do. I know you
may not believe that right now, but I will.
Please get this one done and come back in one
piece.*

XOXOXOXOXOXOXOXO

M

"Fellas, can you gimme a second here?" Grove kept his eyes on the note still in his hands.

He had read the entire thing twice now, as though it might transform into something less significant, like a grocery list or a note to pick up Aaron at Toddler Town Day Care.

"Gimme a second here," he repeated.

He could not look into the eyes of the two uniformed policemen standing behind him in the archway, waiting. Gaze downturned, jaw tensing like a ratchet wrench, he felt the heavy, leaden despair filling his veins. The dark matter of his life was destroying him now from *inside* his family, like a slow cancer.

"Agent Grove—"

"I'm fine, I'm okay, I just need a second. You guys can take off."

"But they told us to hang around until the morning shift gets down from—"

"Do I have to spell it out?!"

Grove glared hotly at them, the note still gripped in his clenched hand, the shock of his booming cry still bouncing off the tiles.

After a beat of tense silence: "Sir, you left your briefcase out in the prowler."

Grove gritted his teeth. "Go get it, please . . . and then you guys can go ahead and take off."

They both slipped out, and a moment later one of them returned with the attaché.

Grove had not moved from the kitchen doorway in the ninety seconds it took for the cop to retrieve it; he still clenched the note in his sweaty grasp, still reeled with contrary emotions. The cop brought the briefcase over and gingerly set it down on the kitchen table next to Grove. Then the officer turned and got the hell out of there without uttering a word.

For quite a long while Grove remained in that tiled archway, engulfed in silent rumination, the stagnant air smelling of Pine-Sol and desertion—a moment that seemed to stretch interminably, like the passage of time within a fever dream. As he stood there, trying to gain purchase on the tilting angle of events, his thoughts churned.

On one level, it was good that Maura had vacated the place. Grove could now focus on the investigation without worrying about the dangers of bringing the darkness too close to home. But on another level, Maura's exodus woke Grove up to troubling possibility. Maybe he was incapable of having a normal, stable home life. Maybe he was doomed to be a bridesmaid at the Bureau the rest of his life.

For a single instant, the entire arc of his marriage to Maura County sparked across his memory screen. He remembered meeting her in Alaska on the Ackerman case, nearly getting her killed in a storm-lashed New Orleans on the Doerr investigation, and the horrible sequence of events last year when a madman named Henry Splet invaded their safe house. Those were terrifying milestones that would have ripped a weaker marriage apart at the seams, but somehow, in the case of Grove and Maura, these traumatic events only served to more tightly knit the couple together.

On a deeper level, though, it was the small, intimate, seemingly trivial moments—both positive and negative—that Grove remembered the most vividly. He remembered watching goose bumps rise on the small of Maura's back once after making love. He remembered sharing a bottle of champagne in the maternity ward at four in the morning the night Aaron was born. He remembered hearing Maura speak Latin once in her sleep. And maybe most vividly, he remembered the night Maura told him about the young kid from the IT department who had propositioned her.

Looking back on it, Grove still wondered why it had bothered him so much. He should have been flattered. He should have laughed it off. But he could not get that revelation out of his mind. He would never forget the night Maura told him about it. Every little detail was burned into his midbrain: the Middle Eastern food they were eating, the way she pointed out the scene of the crime.

"He hit on me, Uly, right here, in this very kitchen, he comes over one night—you were away—he comes over to drop off a file and he comes on to me."

Grove remembered feeling a weird sort of unresolved dread that night, even after hearing Maura's assurances that she had kicked the kid out immediately after his blunder. Grove remembered working with Benjamin Bard and being annoyed by the young man's beach-punk swagger. Recruited out of graduate school at UC Berkeley for the Bureau's newly retooled Information Technology department, the kid had been a typical young computer geek, socially inept and self-absorbed. Bard had installed all the new firewalls and security systems on Grove's office and home computers and—

Suddenly, in that empty, silent house, Grove looked up on a quick inhalation of air, almost a gasp.

Something sparked in the back of his mind, a synapse firing suddenly, a faulty circuit crackling with a realization: Bard had visited the Grove house once before his awkward little moment with Maura. He had been in the basement. Grove remembered it vividly, a rainy Saturday afternoon, the kid ringing the doorbell, standing on the porch like a wet rat, holding a box of computer cables and disks. Bard had come to Grove's home to install secure software.

Bard had seen Grove's hard drive.

The memories streamed through Grove's brain with the force of a tidal wave. He remembered the young man fawning over him that day, wanting his autograph, talking nonsense about Grove being a legend. More important, Grove remembered leaving the kid alone in the basement with all the computer gear for hours. Bard had access to Grove's class notes, his syllabus, and all the various drafts that ultimately became the finished textbook. Bard had been alone with Grove's entire body of work.

Benjamin Bard was the only other human being on earth who had seen that unpublished computer model of the thornlike bloodstain found at the archetypal scene.

"God *damn* Jesus Christ—*Christ*," Grove babbled to himself in the empty, desolate kitchen.

He dug in his pocket for his cell phone, his hands shaking with adrenaline. He dropped the phone. The phone bounced. He got down on his hands and knees and crawled after it, the memory of Bard's sudden departure from the Bureau bolting through him like a shot of amphetamines: *One day the kid calls in sick. Three days later his weird resignation letter arrives on the desk of the Operations Chief, very short, very terse, almost cryptic, something like "I'm not cut out for this, pressure's too much, I'm off to India to discover myself, so sorry." Follow-ups are made, per Bureau policy, but nobody ever lays eyes on the kid again. They never find him. Ordinarily all this might raise a few red flags, but the kid was such a flake the Operations guys probably just figured it's good riddance to bad rubbish.*

Grove barked into his cell phone after scooping it up and punching in the emergency dispatch: "Tactical, I need Tactical, this is Special Agent Ulysses Grove!"

"Go ahead, Twenty-four," a nasal female voice crackled in his ear.

"Got probable cause on a person of interest, case numbers three-oh-two-A, three-oh-two-B, and three-oh-two-C."

"Copy that, Twenty-four. You want to go ahead with the SIT code?"

Grove quickly gave the dispatcher the eight-digit ID code required to initiate a cold pursuit.

"Copy that, Twenty-four, you want to start with the suspect name and twenty?"

"Negative, negative—current twenty is unknown!" Anger flared in the pit of Grove's stomach, but he stuffed it back down. He would not let his emotions rule. He wanted to find Bard and chew his head off at the neck, but he would not allow his rage and pain to get the better of him. "The suspect's name is Bard." He spelled it for her. "Benjamin David, I believe, a former Bureau employee. You copy?"

"Copy that."

"Start with the staff files, and when you get a twenty, scramble the TAC unit and call me back on this cell. Suspect could very easily be psychotic and packing, highly dangerous, et cetera. I'm going in with them. Do you copy?"

"Got it."

Grove snapped the cell phone off, pocketed it, then hurried upstairs to get his gun.

NINETEEN

"You got no idea what y'all are dealin' with here, girlfriend, but believe me it's real and it's dangerous. All of it foretold in the Gnostic prophesies. Can I pour you one?"

In the predawn gloom of the tavern's kitchen, by the flickering light of a kerosene lantern, David "Chainsaw" Okuba raised the trembling spout of an ancient iron kettle over a coffee mug in front of Drinkwater. She sat shivering at a butcher's table, wrapped in a wool blanket, trying to assess whether this wild yarn Okuba was spinning should be taken seriously. She gestured at the teakettle. "Can I ask what it is?"

"Purely medicinal," the bluesman said with a nervous nod, throwing a glance at his bodyguard, who sat hunched on a stool in the shadows next to the icebox. The man was spooked down to his bones. "Herbs mostly. St. John the Conqueror root, sassafras. Keeps the bad juju out."

She shrugged. "Why not?"

He poured her a steaming, foul-smelling cup of opaque liquid the color of river-bottom while he continued his tale in that intense, smoky wheeze that he employed on dark delta blues songs. "This here prophecy's exactly what my uncle Baruk and his crew was studyin' all their lives—these secret gospel stories—which they believed was as real as that cup o' tea there."

Drinkwater sipped the tea and practically coughed it up. It tasted like paint thinner. "So what exactly did this prophecy say?"

Okuba put the teakettle back on the stove and sat back down. He spoke carefully to her. "It was written in scrolls my uncle found, there was this spirit—long, long time ago—got lost."

The room had begun to blur slightly. Drinkwater felt warm all over. "Lost?"

Okuba put a cigarette between his crooked teeth and fired it up, his slender brown hands trembling fitfully. "That's right. Don't tell me you ain't never heard of no lost spirits."

"I don't know . . . yeah, sure."

"I ain't talkin' 'bout no ghost or goblin here. I'm talkin' 'bout somethin' my Uncle Baruk used to call a displaced spirit. Kinda spirit gets stuck in our world."

Drinkwater chewed the inside of her cheek. "Stuck how? What do you mean?"

"I mean this here spirit's kinda whatchacall *doomed.* Know what I'm sayin'?"

"No. No, I don't. Doomed how?"

Okuba shrugged. "Doomed to wander, I guess. Doomed to be reborn every few generations . . . takin' on human form and all that shit."

Drinkwater sighed. "So you think this has somethin' to do with this guy I'm working for? The FBI agent?"

Okuba wiped his mouth. "I'll tell ya this: my uncle believed he came across a very, very special person. Maybe it's all a buncha damn bullshit, I dunno, but my uncle believed he found the—the hell he call it?—the *good incarnate.* Some kid in Chicago. Must be all growed up by now. S'pose that could be the fella hired you."

"I'm sorry." Drinkwater put her cup down. She felt so light-headed her vision was beginning to tunnel. "I mean no disrespect, but I gotta tell ya I haven't been to Sunday school since I was—"

"I don't give two whits whether y'all believe me or not." Okuba nervously sucked his cigarette, glowering at her. "I didn't ask y'all down here. But I'm warnin' y'all right now—y'all better not fool around with this shit because it's dangerous shit."

Drinkwater raised a hand, a contrite gesture. "I'm sorry, I'm sorry . . . it just takes a little getting used to. Go on, please. Tell me why it's dangerous."

Okuba glanced at the doorway, a creaking noise from the dark empty tavern making him jump. "I never got the whole story, but I understand my uncle believe this one displaced spirit might be in danger."

Drinkwater looked at him. "What kinda danger?"

"Huh?" Again Okuba glanced uneasily out at the doorway. "Say what?"

"What kind of danger?"

Okuba rubbed his mouth again. "I dunno, danger of being destroyed I guess, which is bad news for the rest of us, 'cuz my uncle, he believe that the End Days is what comes after that."

Drinkwater thought about it for a moment. "So

we're supposed to protect this spirit, this incarnate?"

Okuba was glancing over his shoulder again. "I said too much already, I ain't gonna say no more."

"But what about—?"

"Get on outta here."

Drinkwater started to say something else but caught movement out of the corner of her eye, the big man near the icebox rising off his stool with a grunt. "All right, all right." She scooped up her purse and shrugged off the blanket. "I'm going. Thanks for the tea, and for not killing me in the freezer."

She went over to the doorway, through which the darkened, deserted tavern was barely visible. She paused, turned, and looked at Okuba, who still had the jitters, worse than ever now, trying to light another cigarette with shaking hands. Drinkwater measured her words. "One more question and I'm outta your hair forever."

Okuba looked at her, eyes shimmering with fear. "Go ahead, get it over with."

"This incarnate you've been talking about—if it's such a good spirit, why the hell are you so afraid?"

He looked at her for a long time before answering.

The battering ram—about the size of a small tree trunk—broke the cabin door on the third blow. The noise was surprisingly immense, reverberating out across the dark marina, a cannon blast of cracking wood and wrenching metal in the night.

Two tactical officers on either side of the ram lurched past the flapping door and into the dark, disheveled houseboat. The center of gravity shifted, the floor tilting severely, as three more Tac guys followed them in with assault rifles raised and readied.

Grove was behind them, watching all this from the edge of the pier. His Kevlar flak vest weighed a ton under his woolen suit coat, the sea breeze slapping him in the face, the smell of brine and metal bracing him, waking him up. He had his .44 caliber Bulldog gripped firmly in both of his hands, which were already clad in rubber surgical gloves, his feet planted shoulder-width—the Weaver position—an instinctive posture during forced entry.

A gull cried directly above the houseboat, way up in the black sky, echoing over the voices and lapping water.

"Bard, FBI! Identify yourself!" The lead Tac officer, a young Latino with pork-chop sideburns, hollered protocol at the empty darkness of the houseboat. "If you're present identify yourself now please!"

No answer.

The battering ram dropped to the flimsy floor with a loud clang and rolled. The boathouse pitched again. This time, three out of the five Tac officers lost their balance, staggering toward the starboard side. One of them hollered an obscenity and grasped a window ledge. Another banged against a wall, knocking a picture frame to the deck. "Billings, take the lower deck! Now! Now!"

Pork Chop's booming voice got things moving. Headlamps snapped on. Beams of light pierced the musty darkness of the apartment as Pork Chop gave hand signals to the two point men. One went left toward a narrow set of varnished steps leading down into the deeper darkness of the sleeping berths, the other went right toward the tiny galley.

"Nobody touch anything!" Grove entered the boathouse with his gun at the ready, gazing down the front-sight at shadowy corners. Even though dawn had broken over the Chesapeake outside, the houseboat's cabin was bathed in darkness.

Grove didn't expect a maniac to jump out at him; he didn't even expect the Surf Punk to be home. He had gotten the boathouse's location from Dispatch, who had gotten it from Operations: a low-rent marina at the end of Highway 235 near St. George Island, Maryland. The neighborhood was a rusted-out wasteland of crab boats and old retrofitted cabin cruisers inhabited by bohemians, recluses, and retirees who kept to themselves and studiously ignored their neighbors. Eyes adjusting to the dark, Grove saw signs of a struggle: an overturned armchair, a jagged hole in the portside wall, a broken boogie board.

The first rays of morning sliced through mangled, crumpled window blinds.

A strong chemical smell hung in the air, a very familiar smell that Grove could not immediately identify. He spun in a three-sixty, his gun still raised, his good eye taking in fallen bookshelves, dark stains on the walls. The floor leaned and yawed again, and Grove braced himself against the bulwark, as the sounds of the Tac guys doing their frantic room-to-room filled his ears.

"Galley's clear! Clear!"

Formaldehyde. That's what he was smelling—goddamn formaldehyde. He shuffled toward the beams of light flickering in the galley, his arms aching with adrenaline, his hands sweaty inside the rubber gloves. Broken china on the floor. Bootsteps crunching. Light coming through a narrow shaded window. Dirt from an overturned plant. The powerful odor of rancid meat.

"Head is clear! Downstairs john is clear!" Another frenzied voice from belowdecks.

Grove paused near a broken portal, his gun pointing at the ceiling. He listened. He heard an electric motor running somewhere in the bowels of the boathouse, and he felt the floor vibrating faintly. He had been hearing that infernal humming noise, barely audible beneath all the yelling, from the moment he had arrived. He had made note of it, figuring it was a generator or bilge pump or filter or whatever. But now it set off an alarm in his brain.

"Agent Grove, the Sleeper Cabin! In the foredeck! Got a stiff! We got a stiff!!"

Grove lowered the Bulldog's barrel and hustled toward the staircase, sidestepping a stack of cardboard boxes and spilled computer disks like so many shiny plates on the deck. Through the low archway. Down the creaking steps. Toward the furthest hatch in the lower level in which all the flashlights and figures were now convening. Somebody was coughing fitfully inside the cabin.

"Give him some room! Back off, back off!" The Tac officers backed away, their guns going up, allowing Grove passage inside the berth.

Grove entered the cramped, moldering sleeping area—the whole chamber was probably less than a hundred square feet. A beefier stink hung in the clammy air just beneath the chemical stench.

He pulled a penlight from his vest. Flipped it on. Swept the bloodstained mattress on the floor . . . the coils of ropes . . . the blankets bunched at one end of the berth . . . the chains dangling from the light fixture . . . and the huge rusting Frigidaire freezer in one corner, its horizontal door propped open by one of the Tac guys.

In the darkness to Grove's left, the voice of Pork Chop muttered into his two-way: "HQ, we're gonna need the lab guys, the site people, the whole team, pronto."

The body had been stowed in the horizontal deep freeze—petrified in a slab of fishy ice—for many months now, maybe even a year. It was hard to tell from the coloring of the flesh, the milky frozen eyeballs, the gaping rictus of blackened teeth, the swollen purple tongue protruding from the mouth like a fat slug.

Grove gazed down at Benjamin Bard's nude remains and gritted his teeth. Contrary emotions flowed through Grove like a riptide tearing at his sanity: *This was the cocky kid who had come on to his wife, and now look at him, now look at him, with his spiky bleach blond Mohawk and peach-fuzz goatee frozen in a rotting pink sarcophagus, but wait, wait, wait, look more closely, look at the room, Ulysses, look at that gaping mouth, the look of terror in his pupil-less eyes, and the ligature wounds up and down his frozen limbs . . . the man was tortured, he was tortured—systematically, savagely, purposefully.*

All at once, over the space of a nanosecond, Ulysses Grove started fitting together all the tiny puzzle tiles tumbling around in his brain.

The humming sound had been the Frigidaire, running perpetually off the marina's power, and the strange stench *beneath* that chemical smell had been the fishy smell of old frozen meat—better known as freezer burn—but far more important, far more critical, the scene was talking to Grove now, whispering to him in the ancient dead language: *ES UG IGI E-ZE HUBUR—go deeper, deeper, yes, that's right, forget your pain, my brother, forget your ego, go down, down, down into the frozen dead heart like a clock stopped at the precise apocalyptic hour of revelation— this is how the perpetrator knew! This is how the perpetrator knew how to stage the killings! This is how! The surf-punk gave up the information! Benjamin Bard possessed the classified modus operandi, the computer models, the lecture notes. . . .*

"What was that?"

The sound of Pork Chop's voice penetrated Grove's stupor, and Grove turned to the Tac leader like a man stirring from a dream. "What?"

"You said 'This is how he knew.'" The leader spoke in a flat, disaffected voice. "I'm not following."

Grove shone his penlight at the frozen corpse. "See the ligature marks, the superficial trauma— here, here, along the nerve bundles under the feet, along the sides of the tongue—all indicating torture."

Pork Chop frowned, rubbing his nose. The smell was getting to him. "That's a lot of torture."

"He needed a lot of information." Grove looked around the room, then at the Tac leader. "I want you to keep everybody out of here until Cedric Gliane gets here from Quantico—you got that?"

"Yeah, but—"

"I want this place pickled, and I want Latent on every surface, and I want every shrimp rat from here to Virginia Beach canvassed, and I want the lab people to transport the vic frozen."

"Um, yeah, I'm just not sure whether—"

"Listen to me. Don't talk, just listen." Grove fixed his gaze onto the deep-set eyes of the Tac leader. "He's still here, he's *here*. Do you understand?"

"Who's still here?"

"The perp. The killer."

"What?" The Tac leader's hand instinctively went down to the butt of his Glock in its holster. Confusion boiled in his eyes. "What are you talking about?"

Grove closed his eyes. *Let it come to you, Uly*—his mother's voice, deep in his midbrain, her heavily accented Kenyan lilt—*your fate is fixed.* "He spent a lot of time here, left a lot of himself behind. Trust me. He's still here in the woodwork."

Pork Chop looked around. A big sigh. "I'll take your word for it. I'm sure you know this guy pretty well by now, huh?"

"Not as well as he knows me." Grove looked at one of Bard's bluish frozen hands, two blackened fingertips protruding from the ice. "What's that?"

The Tac leader looked down at the remains. "What?"

"By the vic's left hand—see?"

"I don't—"

Grove leaned over, then ran a rubber-gloved fingertip down a series of faint hash marks beneath Benjamin Bard's putrefied frostbitten fingers. The marks were on the *inside* of the ice, lined with flecks of dried blood like pepper flakes. Grove passed his light over the ice and the underside glistened with inch-long parallel lines.

"Holy fucking shit," uttered the man with the pork chop sideburns.

In his death throes Bard had managed to scrawl three crude letters on the inside surface of a large, concave air pocket in the ice:

J Q P

TWENTY

"There's another one, another spirit."

"What?"

"A dark one, an opposite one."

"I don't—"

"Yin and yang. My uncle told me all about it, believed it down to his bones. You understand now?"

"No, I don't understand, as a matter of fact, I have no idea what the hell you're talking about." Edith Drinkwater stood in the doorway of the Cherry Pit's grimy kitchen, a slender beam of sunlight filtering down from a ceiling grate, the column of light specked with dust motes. She felt queasy with nerves and dizziness. Without even realizing it, she had crossed a line, and now she had a horrible feeling she could never go back.

"Your employer, whoever he is, he got a double. A twin. On the other side." Okuba now sat on the edge of a rusty steel counter, nervously wringing an old bandana in his long brown fingers, chewing a wad of tobacco, and spitting juice into a copper pot full of shrimp shells on the floor. His eyes watered with terror as he spoke. "My uncle and his crew searched in secret all their lives for this other spirit, and I ain't sure if they ever found him. I hope they didn't."

Okuba paused, shuddering at the very thought of finding this individual. He dipped his yellow fingertips into a tin of Copenhagen, adding to the huge gob between his cheek and gum. Then he spat again into the pot on the floor. Every time he spat, the dull *ping* off the pot would ring out like the clack of a marimba. "This is pure distilled hundred-proof evil we're talking about here. You have any idea what that is, missy?"

Drinkwater looked at the floor. "I've seen my share of evil, I'm sorry to say."

"This ain't like that, missy. This ain't like *anything* y'all have ever seen before." He swallowed hard, as though staving off maniacal laughter. "This is worse than your worst nightmares. This is the dark rotten thing that lives inside the worst of us, that lives off misery. It's worse than Satan, 'cause even Satan got his weaknesses. Satan's got pride, lust. This thing, this dark spirit—it's just a cold, cold, cold, cold-metal misery machine." David "Chainsaw" Okuba spat into the copper pot on the floor, as if punctuating the gravity of his statement, then wiped his mouth with the back of a trembling hand. "This thing is like a virus you can't even talk about, or think about, for fear it'll infect your brain."

Drinkwater didn't say anything. She thought about that black target silhouette from Grove's class, and she thought of the Archetype, the homicidal sociopath who tortures and kills out of ego and self-gratification. And she also thought about those whispered words of old Bernard Schoenbaum, long-time comrade of Baruk Okuba and current guest of St. John the Baptist Extended Care Center in beautiful downtown Newark, New Jersey: *long way to fall.* Goddamn right it was a long way to fall—especially for a spirit floating around the ether. But it was also a long way to fall for Drinkwater—street-smart girl from the projects, woman of reason.

Okuba was looking at her, chewing a fingernail now. "I ain't even doin' this thing justice. Words ain't enough. You don't want to know."

"All due respect, David, how do *you* know all this?"

He spat again with a *ping!* "What difference does it make? Y'all don't believe a lick of what I'm sayin'. My uncle got drunk once, told me things about the dark one would straighten them corn-rows of yours."

Drinkwater started pacing across the kitchen, the soles of her shoes crackling on the sticky floor. "So what's the endgame?"

Okuba gave her a cockeyed glance. "Say what?"

"The finale, you know."

"What do you mean?"

She stopped pacing, looked at him, and shrugged. "How's it all play out? In the prophesies, I mean. Do these two—whatever you call them—do they ever face each other? Is that the endgame?"

For a moment it looked as though David Okuba was about to yell at her, his eyes sparking with emotion. He balled his hands into fists. But then his face broke into a sideways smirk and he began to laugh.

He laughed and laughed, as though the sick irony of it all was too much to bear.

TWENTY-ONE

Two things instantly assaulted Grove—who was now livid with anger, exhausted, and running on very little sleep—as he exited Benjamin Bard's houseboat and hustled over weathered planks toward the nearest police cruiser: one, daylight had broken with a vengeance, the cloudless sky over the Chesapeake now blazing brightly, driving an ice pick of pain down between Grove's eyes. And two, somebody was calling out for him behind the yellow tape that had been strung up since he arrived at the scene.

"Special Agent Grove! Over here!"

Grove paused at the end of the pier and glanced over his shoulder in the general direction of the voice. Something about the grating, shrill sound was familiar, but at first Grove didn't see the owner of the voice in the small crowd of gawkers who had gathered at the edges of the cordons—a few old geezers in Bermuda shorts, a baker in stained whites wiping his hands in a bread towel, a grease monkey from a local marina up early to fix motors.

At last Grove saw the prematurely balding white

man in low-riding baggy jeans, a big medallion, and a T-shirt about ten sizes too big for him waving his hand. "Agent Grove, it's Byron Haskell from *The Weekly World!*"

Grove felt his stomach clench at the sight of the tabloid reporter. "Not now, not now," he grumbled, turning in the opposite direction, heading toward a SWAT van that had parked on the edge of an adjacent lot.

"Yo, Agent Grove—wait!"

The reporter scurried around the crowd, then hopped over a low barrier between the boardwalk and the parking lot. He moved with the jackrabbit energy of a skateboarder, despite the fact that he was nearing forty and his fringe of hair was starting to salt with gray. He darted across the edge of the parking lot toward Grove.

Grove paused near the rear doors of the SWAT van, then turned to face the approaching pest. "What do you want, Haskell?"

"Whassup?" the reporter panted as he reached the rear of the SWAT van and pulled his mini-recorder from the back of his baggy denims. "Long time no talk, dawg. Quick couple of questions."

"I'm in a hurry."

"Promise I won't keep you more than a sec." He raised the tape recorder as though asking permission. "Y'all mind if I roll on this?"

"Why bother?" Grove stared into bloodshot eyes. "You're gonna make it all up anyway."

Haskell feigned a hurt look, his little soul-patch goatee twitching. "Now why you gonna go and do me like that, my brother? I'm here to get the four-one-one from the source, get the inside scoop."

"We're not brothers."

Haskell thumbed the record button with a *click*. "This one here, is it connected to the ones in Minneapolis, North Carolina, and Texas?"

Grove stuffed his rage back down his throat, and tried to breathe through it. Years ago, Byron Haskell had stolen some candid photos of Grove and Maura courting in Alaska, publishing them in *The Weekly World News* right under the banner headline *J-LO'S BUTT IMPLANTS EXPLODE!* The unauthorized photos had made Maura a target of the psychopath Richard Ackerman, nearly getting her killed. To add insult to injury, the tabloid subsequently started an absurd continuing series on "Ulysses Grove, the manhunter from the FBI with mystical methods and mysterious past." Grove had considered initiating a lawsuit; though he ultimately opted for simply ignoring it, his contempt for Haskell becoming harder and harder to stanch. "Get out of my face," Grove warned.

"Just tell me whether they're connected."

Grove's jaw throbbed. "This is an ongoing investigation, Haskell, and if you were a real journalist you would know I can't discuss open cases."

Grove turned and started walking away when the reporter grabbed his arm. "Hold up, man— hold up!—please, one more, just one more question."

Grove turned and bored his gaze into the reporter's face like an augur. "Let go of my arm."

Haskell released him with a mischievous smirk. "Just tell me one thing, dawg."

Grove didn't say anything. Just stared. The rage squeezing his guts.

"Just tell me"—and then the reporter lowered his voice, smirk still plastered on his face—"Is the reason your wife left 'cause she was on her way into witness protection again, or is it marital problems this time?"

What happened next occurred with the surreal unraveling of a car accident or a nightmare, as though time had suddenly slipped a belt. Grove was outside his own body, watching the action transpire in flash frames of unreality, like a motion-picture projection flickering on and off. FLASH! Grove shoving Haskell with brutal force. FLASH! Haskell stumbling backward over his own feet, tripping and falling ass-down on the cracked pavement of the lot.

And then FLASH! Grove was on top of Haskell, knees pressing down on the flailing reporter's arms, holding him down on the ground. Haskell writhed and spat and grunted inarticulate grunts. Grove wrapped both hands, still in their rubber gloves, around the reporter's skinny neck. Haskell convulsed. Grove squeezed. Haskell twitched and kicked and gasped.

By this point, the rear door of the SWAT van had burst open and two younger Tac officers lurched out with eyes bugging.

Other doors opened across the marina—Bard's houseboat, one of the cruisers, an ambulance— voices almost instantly calling out. In fact, it seemed as though half of St. George Island, on edge due to the grisly discovery at the marina, had come to their doors and were now peering out at the unexpected tussle.

"Hey! Hey! What the hell—?" Pork Chop came hustling around the cordon with his Glock drawn, raised, and pointing at the sky, unsure of the rules of engagement here.

Grove noticed very little of this peripheral action, his attention now locked with welding-iron intensity both on Haskell's reddening face and something within *himself,* something just now flickering in his mind. It was there just for a second like a strobe flash on the back of his blind eye, and it seemed to feed off his rage like a surge of accelerant on a fire, blooming in his brain: the sensation of falling, falling down a long, dark chasm in the ground.

Now there were hands on Grove's shoulders and arms, yanking him off the reporter, but Grove's rubber-coated fingers had tightened a viselike grip around Haskell's stringy neck. The sound of Pork Chop's high, shrill voice: "Jesus Christ, Grove! Let go of him! You're gonna waste the guy!"

At last, the collective heave of all three Tac officers managed to tear Grove from the reporter. Grove and the officers tumbled backward, sprawling to the pavement, while Haskell rolled in the opposite direction across the boardwalk like a bundle of cordwood.

Haskell landed hard against the breakwater and gasped for breath, holding his neck.

Thirty feet away, the Tac officers huddled around Grove, who raised himself up on one knee. He struggled to catch his own breath.

A clicking sound drew Grove's attention over his right shoulder.

A photographer stood against the yellow ribbon, madly snapping pictures.

News of the outburst at Bard's houseboat began wending its way through the system that afternoon, beginning with a clacking-whirring sound in a second-floor office at Quantico, alerting Molly Ryan, the administrative assistant in Dispatch, that a redline fax was coming in. A heavyset woman in stretch pants, she spun on her swivel chair, the wheel bearings squeaking noisily. She pushed herself across the office to the doorway of the communications alcove and peered in at the metal filing cabinets and computer terminals. The fax machine near the window was spitting out transmittal sheets lined with scarlet edges, and Molly immediately went over to the phone.

"This is Ryan in Dispatch," she said after the party on the other end of the line answered. "Is the section chief in today?"

The lady on the other end told her to hold on.

"Kopsinky here," said a voice after a few clicks. "Whattya got, Molly?"

"Just came in, redline out of Maryland, something about Agent Grove having some kind of a breakdown."

A brief, tense pause. "Molly, I'm going to need you to walk that over."

"Be there in five."

She hung up, dropped the ten pages of facsimile paper into a manila folder, hugged it to her breast, and walked out of the office.

The fluorescent corridor bustled. Voices on phones, keyboards clicking busily. Molly Ryan walked briskly, nodding at coworkers and chewing gum as she made her way out of Dispatch, across a light-drenched breezeway, and into the adjacent building.

Here in the executive tower the bustle was more subdued, the noise more muffled, the carpet thicker, the accoutrements more lush—like the halls of a mid-line hotel. Molly strode to the end of the main corridor, then paused at the armed guard manning the reception desk.

Molly flashed her laminate and folder. "Dispatch for Chief Kopsinsky."

The guard waved her in.

Molly navigated the maze of office suites until she reached the corner office and stood in front of the closed walnut door with the brand-new name plaque where Tom Geisel's used to be. The plaque was marked in gold inlay with KOPSINSKY, RAYMOND R., S.C., BEHAVIORAL SCIENCE UNIT. Molly knocked, and a muffled voice told her to come in.

She entered the spacious office.

"Thanks, Molly," the man behind Geisel's desk said with a nod. He was a compact little man with horn-rimmed glasses and thinning hair. He had his coat off, his sleeves rolled up. Most of Geisel's personal items had already been swept away or boxed up—family photos, awards, mementos— but his plaster medical skeleton still hung in all its macabre glory by the corner window.

A second man sitting in an armchair in front of the desk was instantly recognizable to Molly. Dressed in a tailored black suit, the man looked like an aging football coach with his thick neck and hard gaze. "The Unsinkable Miss Molly Ryan," Louis Corboy said with a distracted smile. "How's Howard doing? Heard he had a hip replacement."

"He's as grouchy as ever," she said with a genial grin, handing the folder to Kopsinsky. "Thanks for asking, though. Can I get you gentlemen anything else?"

"We're all set, Molly, thanks." Ray Kopsinsky gave her a terse smile and a nod.

She turned and whisked out of the office, closing the door behind her.

Kopsinky stared at the document. "Speak of the devil," he murmured.

Corboy levered his portly self out of the chair and came over to the desk. "Don't tell me."

Kopsinky looked up at him. "Read it."

Corboy did so. His lips pressed together so tightly they looked purple. At last he looked up at Kopsinsky. "Grove is finished in this unit."

"Can I suggest—"

Corboy shook his head. "There isn't enough Tylenol on the eastern seaboard."

"Boss, we need Grove on this thing; you know it as well as I do."

"Grove's finished." Corboy glared. "He flipped his wig on a goddamn media guy. You have any idea how much shit I'm going to have to eat because of this?"

"But maybe there's a—"

"I told you, I'm washing Grove out!"

Kopsinksy looked down at his desk for a brief and awkward moment of deference. "Got it, sorry. Just thinking of the press here."

Corboy took a deep breath. "Tell them . . . tell them we're reassigning Grove to a top-secret vigilante force, tell them we're submitting him for sainthood, tell them anything you want. But Grove is gone."

TWENTY-TWO

The front door burst open with the force of Grove's kick, and he stumbled into the deserted Pelican Bay house with heavy Pendaflex expandable folders under each arm. He had been alone in the home many times, but not like this, not this woozy with nervous tension and paranoia, and the conspicuous absence of his wife and son only added to his disorientation.

He turned in a fidgety circle trying to decide what to do first. In the stillness, the midday sun glowed behind the front drapes, creating an oven effect. A musty odor filled the house, an odor that always pervaded the place when it was left empty for long stretches. Seaside homes are never completely free of mold. The scent of moisture is always there, in the wallpaper, under the floorboards, along the baseboards. But now the ghostly mildew merely tightened the uneasy knot in Grove's gut, playing a sour counterpoint to the constant refrain in his head.

JQP?

He headed for the stairs to the second floor,

stumbling across the entry hall like some incorrigible derelict, drunk with exhaustion. He tripped on a braided rug, and his feet tangled, and he fell over. He dropped both files as he went down; one flopped open on impact and spilled its contents across the foyer. Forensic photographs of corpses in Minnesota, North Carolina, and Texas, coroners' reports, maps, Xeroxes of Sumerian symbols, notes—all of it fanned across the hardwood.

Grove struggled to get his breath, and tried stop that skipping record in his brain.

JQPJQPJQP?

He rose to his knees, head spinning. He could hardly see through his one good eye. He felt nauseated. He needed sleep badly, he needed to eat, he needed to think. Over the last few hours he had been acting purely on instinct, racing back to his office at Quantico before word got out about the chaotic scene at Bard's houseboat, retrieving all his Archetype files, consolidating his profiles into the two heavy Pendaflexes, then rushing back to his empty house in Pelican Bay to do God-knew-what with the letters JQPJQPJQPJQPJQPJQPJQP JQPJQPJQPJQPJQPJQPJQP—

The sound of the phone ringing in the kitchen shook Grove out of his trance. It was the unlisted phone. Grove had three lines, including his work cell, which was also unlisted. The private line was used only by Maura, a few superiors at the Bureau, and emergency dispatch.

He rose on shaky legs, took a deep breath, and made his way into the kitchen, leaving all the forensic documents on the floor where they had fallen. He snatched the cordless off the wall with a sweaty hand. "Grove."

"Ulysses, it's Ray Kopsinsky."

Grove knew immediately by the edgy tone of the man's normally rock-steady voice that there was major trouble. "Ray, I'm glad you called."

"Yeah, well."

"You got the news from Dispatch? I'm gonna need VICAP on these initials. Right away."

The man on the other end of the line sighed. "Look, I got all the details on Bard and the scene—I also got an earful from Corboy about the reporter you tried to surgically remove from the planet."

"He's not a reporter, he's a hack."

"Be that as it may—"

"Ray, this guy Haskell, his articles were on Splet's walls—he got Maura kidnapped! Remember Ackerman?"

"Grove, listen to me. There's a line you vaulted over here. You tried to wax the guy in front of a live audience *and* a photographer—we're gonna be doing mea culpa for a year. Now, I realize you're in a bad place, with Tom passing and this freak out there who's hooked into your work—"

"We got the guy's initials, Ray. If we don't act, he's gonna kill again. He's going to torture a woman, and then kill her."

"Ulysses—"

"I'm going to find this guy very soon. That's the best PR you can get!"

"Let me finish." The voice on the other end of the line was strained with thinly repressed anger. "Corboy has ordered you on paid leave."

"What?" Grove's sweaty palm was welded to the receiver. *"What?!"*

"It's unavoidable, Ulysses. Pending an investigation—"

"I'm the only one, Ray."

"Grove, I'm trying to—"

"Goddamn it, I'm the only one who can catch this guy!" Pain stabbed the bridge of Grove's nose at the sudden volume of his own voice.

On the other end of the line, Kopsinky's voice changed slightly. "You know, Tom always said you were difficult, but you were worth it because the plain truth is you get these guys off the streets. Fine. I get that. But I don't know the playbook, Grove. I'm not Geisel, I don't know the blocking routes. I don't have the juice."

After a long beat, Grove swallowed. "What are you telling me, Ray?"

"There's nothing I can do."

"Listen to me. You think Haskell is bad press? This perp is the grim reaper, Ray. He's the Antichrist, he's—"

"I tried. I'm sorry. I really am."

The phone clicked in Grove's ear.

United Flight 287—nonstop from Charleston International to Chicago's O'Hare—landed on time that day in a flurry of vapor and noise. The aircraft rattled and roared to a stop on the northernmost runway, then taxied in a light mist to the jetway to the south.

Inside the stale, refrigerated fuselage, passengers stirred and unbuckled and rearranged their belongings in preparation to disembark long before permission to move was given by the flight attendants.

One passenger in particular was exceedingly antsy to exit the plane—a zaftig black woman with cornrows seated in 34A, Business Class. By the time the aircraft shuddered to a stop, she was already standing.

"Ma'am, I'm going to need you to stay seated until the seat-belt sign is off," one of the attendants called out from the galley seats in back.

"Sorry, sorry," Edith Drinkwater said with a wave, plopping back down in her seat. Others were stirring around her, flipping open cell phones, thumbing Palm Pilots like junkies cooking their next fix. Drinkwater gripped her carry-on bag as though it contained a human organ bound for transplant.

Back in Beaufort she had made a last-minute decision to change her plans.

As a rule, Edith Drinkwater was not big on changing her mind. Doubt was not a familiar state of mind for her. But something happened back in South Carolina that had started a mysterious clockwork mechanism of gears turning in the back of her brain. Maybe it was the unmistakable glint of fear in David Okuba's eyes when he spoke of displaced spirits and dark doppelgängers. Or maybe it was just the strange vibe Drinkwater had always sensed radiating off Grove.

Whatever the reason, Drinkwater was beginning to think of Ulysses Grove in a different way.

After leaving the Cherry Pit, she had rifled through her notes and had reviewed all the background she had amassed online and in the FBI archives on Grove. She had found the name she was looking for—as well as the address and phone number—in the Bureau personnel folders. The Kenyan woman had been listed on an insurance information form that Grove had filled out way back in the dark ages when he was a trainee. A couple of phone calls later, Drinkwater was on her way to the Windy City.

A sudden *DING* pierced her thoughts, and again she rose to her feet.

A lighted sign announced the all clear to deboard, and Drinkwater hurried off the plane.

O'Hare Terminal One is notorious for chaos—the worst record for delays on the continent—and always seems under some kind of inconvenient construction. Laid out like the ribs of a vast fossilized behemoth, the underground route to baggage claim is lined with decorative neon capillaries that have seen better days. People don't look at one another much. Echoes of distant jackhammers and jet engines ebb and flow.

Drinkwater hurried through the underground, then up an escalator to the main terminal, her brain swimming with possible scenarios, images of what the old lady might look like, speculations on what she had to say. The woman had not been very forthcoming over the phone—suspicious even—but had suddenly perked up when Drinkwater had mentioned Okuba and his story of demigods and dark destinies.

The appointed rendezvous spot was at the end of the main concourse—a cavernous mall teeming with travelers coming and going amid the Waterstones and Starbucks, the mélange of merchants masking the stale air with burnt sugar and coffee smells. Drinkwater found the meeting place and looked at her watch. It was a quarter to four. The old woman was due in fifteen.

Drinkwater went over to a contour bench against the corner windows and sat down to wait.

At length, a hunched figure loomed at the top of a nearby staircase. Approaching slowly, methodically, hobbling along with a cane, the woman caught Drinkwater's attention before any words were spoken. The afternoon sun haloed the old lady's face in a nimbus of washed-out daylight from the skylights, and the closer she came, the more her frizzy, white-streaked mane of hair glowed like a corona of angelic light. To Drinkwater she looked like a tarot priestess, like a black saint on a catechism card.

"Mrs. Grove?" Drinkwater stood up, brushing a stray hair from her eye.

"Vida, please call me Vida," the old woman croaked in a husky, accented voice as she paused on her shellacked baobab cane, a trace of colonial Brit underneath the Kenyan lilt. She wore an ankle-length sarong-dress dyed in traditional African flora. And everything about her bearing—her long neck, her deeply lined regal face—spoke of hard-won wisdom. She had a leather pouch around her neck stuffed with unfiltered cigarettes like bullets in an ammo clip. "You must be . . . Miss Edith, is it?"

"Edith Drinkwater, that's right." The two women shook hands. Drinkwater thought the old woman's hand felt like sandpaper. "You didn't have to come all the way out here to the airport, I would have met you anywhere."

"I like to get out of the house," the old woman said with a wink. "Doctor says it's good for me. Besides, the bus stop is a half a block from my two-flat."

"Well, I really appreciate it."

Vida smiled and patted Drinkwater's shoulder. "My son's fate is now your fate."

"Excuse me?" Drinkwater wasn't sure she heard the old woman correctly.

Vida gave her arm a squeeze. "You're a strong girl, that's good."

"I don't know about that."

"You'll need all your strength for what is to come."

Drinkwater looked at her. "May I ask what you're referring to?"

The old woman pursed her lips, then looked around the terminal. "Is there a place an old woman can rest her bones and smoke a cigarette?"

TWENTY-THREE

In the nightmare Grove is standing at the foot of Geisel's gurney, gazing upon the pale remains of his mentor and boss, when Geisel sits up like he's on a spring, like he's a puppet, and smiles. His teeth are as black as onyx, and a reverse-sound pours out of him like a yowling cat; Grove tries to run away, tries to escape that horrible room, and realizes he cannot move. He looks down. He is ankle-deep in dirty white sand, beach sand, as damp and heavy as wet cement. The sand is riddled with hash marks, symbols, coded messages, phone numbers, bar codes, puzzles, clock faces, lengths, widths, distances, and more; a seemingly endless array of cryptic data. A slimy gray wave licks across the sand, washing away the symbols, enveloping Grove's ankles in greasy salt water. Grove sinks deeper. He struggles and struggles. He sinks into the mire up to his knees; he cries out, but no sound comes out of him as he continues sinking to his waist. The waves curl around him. He looks at the bed and sees Geisel sitting there like a porcelain doll—on his face a weird mixture of utter desolation and horror and something urgent to communicate—and now he's convulsing as though electricity is bolting through him.

Grove sinks deeper and deeper until he's up to his chin and can't move his arms or legs anymore. He arches his neck so he can breathe, but soon the soupy sand covers his face like a sticky blanket. He gasps. But somehow—this is a dream, after all—he can still breathe under the sand. He notices light above him and cranes his neck to look up at the hole through which he just sank, and then something very strange and unexpected occurs. The hole is freezing, icing over. Grove shivers. He can see a thin rind of frost forming across the opening, which is barely a foot in diameter, as though an invisible arctic wind is rushing over the hole. Soon the membrane of ice is nearly an inch thick, transparent, milky white. It looks like a window. Grove stares at it for some time, until finally a face appears behind the ice, and Grove screams. He screams and screams. The sound that registers in the dream is more like a delicate tinkling-glass noise, like a chandelier in the wind. The face is very familiar—it is Maura's face—but horrible wounds scourge her flesh, gouges and lacerations, blood speckles dried as black as India ink, the precise wounds discussed in Grove's textbook, in his class, in the MO of the Archetype. She's writing something with her bloody index finger, scratching it into the frost. It makes no sense—in the dream, that is—but Grove stares and stares and stares at the nonsensical words:

CILBUP Q NHOJ

Grove came awake with a start. It took a few moments for him to catch his breath and realize where he was: alone, on the living-room sofa in his Pelican Bay home, most of the lights still on. It took him another few moments to realize it was the middle of the afternoon, and he had apparently passed out from exhaustion on the littered couch hours ago. His skin glistened with sweat, his T-shirt and slacks soaked through. His heart still palpitated with alarming irregularity, as prominent in his ears as a shoe banging around the inside of a clothes dryer. His bladder was about to burst, but there was something he had to do before dealing with that.

He managed to sit up and quickly shuffle through a pile of documents on the coffee table next to the sofa. He found a yellow legal pad and a pen, and frantically scrawled the words he had just seen in his dream.

Cilbup Q Nhoj?

"You see, the problem is, I'm dying, honey."

The old Kenyan woman sat on a wrought-iron chair in the far corner of the airport cafeteria, shaded by a giant rubber plant, her baobab cane canted against the table, her proud, wrinkled face like parchment in the bright, diffuse light. Her burnished ebony eyes shimmered with deep sadness.

Drinkwater, seated across the round table, wasn't sure she had heard the woman correctly. "You're what? I'm sorry, say again?"

"I'm dying, sweetheart. Lung cancer."

"Oh God, I'm sorry."

"I've done what I set out to do in this life."

Drinkwater let this amazing statement sink in. "Does Ulysses—?"

"He won't accept it." The woman spoke tenderly. "Bless his foolish heart, he thinks it's all in my mind. Sends me articles on green tea. Relaxation techniques."

"I understand." Drinkwater was having second thoughts about this whole insane detour, about bothering this poor, poor woman, maybe even about the entire surreal scavenger hunt she was on—chasing folk legends and bogeymen, for Christ's sake. "Mrs. Grove, can I ask you something a little personal?"

"Vida, please." The old woman smiled.

"Vida . . . do you mind if I ask you . . . about Ulysses' birth?"

The woman's smile flickered for a moment. "His birth? What about his birth?"

Drinkwater felt her face flush. This was ridiculous. But she had to ask it. "I understand Ulysses was your only son?"

Just the slightest pause here. "That's right."

"And his father . . ."

"Yes?"

"Ulysses never knew his father, is that right?"

"That's true."

"May I ask if you and he were—?"

"If we were divorced? Is that what you're wondering?"

Drinkwater looked down for a moment. "Well, yeah." Then she looked up at the old woman. "I guess what I'm really wondering is whether—God, I know this is real personal—but I'm wondering whether your son was planned?"

Now there was a long pause.

Vida Grove leaned forward then, the light catching the side of her lined brown face. She looked like a ghost. Tears had gathered in her eyes. "I never told a soul about this," she said softly, her liquid gaze holding Drinkwater rapt. "Only a few people ever knew about it, and they are long in the ground. I've waited all these years for this secret to come back and haunt me. I knew that it would. They always do. They always, always come back."

The old woman paused. Drinkwater waited, the hairs on her neck standing up.

That night, Grove furiously paced the cluttered periphery of his living room, his heart chugging, the residue of his nightmare—and that jumbled anagram of a word at the end—still clinging to his racing thoughts. At last he reached down to the coffee table and snatched up the yellow notepaper on which he had jotted the nonsense syllables in large block letters.

He stared at the garbled dream-words. *Wait a minute, wait a minute.* Something clicked in the back of his brain.

The room spun.

He staggered across the living room and into the front foyer. Next to the big oak door stood a coatrack, a little pedestal on which Grove and Maura often tossed their keys, and a Warren Kimball mirror. One of Maura's beloved pieces of folk art, the mirror was framed in tiny American flags and cobs of corn.

Grove held the yellow pad up to the mirror, then cocked his head to give his good eye a clean view of the reverse reflection of CILBUP Q NHOJ:

JOHN Q PUBLIC

TWENTY-FOUR

The telltale ring of the private work line—a low, incessant alarm tone trilling across the darkened room—awoke Ray Kopsinsky from a deep sleep. He stirred, careful not to wake his wife, Cynthia, who sleepily murmured something inaudible before turning over and putting the pillow to her head.

The acting section chief climbed out of bed and padded across the deep shag of his Georgetown bedroom to the phone, which he answered with a whisper that managed to be both alarmed and annoyed. "Kopsinky here."

"Ray, it's Grove—I got an ID on the Archetype killer."

"What?"

"Listen to me—the Archetype killer is a transient, goes by the name John Q Public."

Kopsinsky woke up a little. "How do you know this, Grove? What's going on?"

"The note at the Bard scene—Bard was trying to tell us—it's John Q Public, Ray."

The bureaucrat looked out the window at the predawn streets. "You *know* this individual?"

"Oh yeah."

"John Q Public? I'm drawing a blank."

"Funny you should say that."

Kopsinsky frowned. "What do you mean?"

" 'Blank.' "

"What do you mean?"

A slight pause, then Grove's voice: "That's exactly what our impression of this guy was—tabula rasa, man—a complete blank."

At that moment, a little over six hundred miles to the east, just outside of Habers Mill, Kentucky, at the crest of a narrow mountain pass, in the deepwell darkness of night, a tall black man in a stovepipe hat lit a wooden safety match with a long, curved, nicotine-stained thumbnail. The tiny yellow flame bloomed in the wee-hour stillness. The tall man looked at the flame.

The only other sound—barely audible above the ubiquitous drone of crickets—was the idling engine of a battered panel van, rear doors ajar, its rust-pocked white finish beginning to chip, parked on the dirt road next to the man.

The van was considered by most criminologists to be the preferred mode of transportation for the average American serial killer. So this vehicle had been carefully selected by the tall man, meticulously outfitted, and relentlessly driven, thousands and thousands of miles, from coast to coast, from sacrifice to sacrifice. The interior had been aged and dressed with the loving attention of a museum curator. Every cigarette butt, every gouge, every seam, had been placed with photographic accuracy. Data from *The Psychopathological Archetype: Toward a Statistical Model* by Ulysses Grove, as well as the private collection of Benjamin Bard, had served as a sort of bible for the tall man.

He tossed the match into the van just as those who came before him had done.

There was a *whoomp* as the flame landed in a puddle of lighter fluid and caught. An orange glow rose against the tall man's face, the light momentarily illuminating the elaborate Aboriginal-style tattoos tracing the bone structure of his cheeks, running down the sides of his neck. An African by birth, the tall man had deep mahogany skin and sculpted features. Under his long black duster, his broad shoulders and coiled muscles undulated as he moved—like the pistoning sinew under a panther's coat. His head, crowned with that tattered black Abe Lincoln hat, turned with the hyperalert jerks of an insect. Only his eyes lacked any kind of life force whatsoever. His eyes were inanimate objects. Like gray coins.

The madness had settled there, in those tiny orbs the color of moonlight.

"We brought this guy in as a person of interest in the Karen Slattery case." Grove's voice sounded strange to Kopsinsky's ear—robotic and thin. "Very, very unsavory dude, this guy. We all thought so. Off-the-scale nasty."

Kopsinsky paced back and forth across his gloomy second-floor hallway, absorbing Grove's taut proclamations with a mixture of emotions—suspicion, excitement, even a little dread. The section chief searched his memory. "Slattery, Karen Slattery—you're talking about that kidnapping up in Milwaukee?"

"Yep, that's the case. John Q Public. He's the Archetype, Ray. He's our boy."

Kopsinsky rubbed his face. "I'm not remembering this at all. I thought Slattery's killer turned out to be the boyfriend."

"That's correct, but we had our cards on this John Q Public guy for weeks."

"Because of the MO?"

"That and opportunity."

"Remind me."

"This guy, John Q Public—Milwaukee Homicide gave him that nickname—he was a street person in Chicago. Black guy, big muscles. Prison-yard buff, you know what I mean?" Grove's voice sounded brittle and jittery. "Spent most of his life in mental hospitals, violence wards. All the skels around the Loop knew him and gave him a wide berth."

"Yeah, so?"

"Ray, this guy was a ghost. No family, no background, no records. Never saw anything like it. He was just a complete black hole. Very weird."

"Why Slattery, though? Why'd you like him in that case?"

Grove sounded almost breathless: "Brought him in for a routine lineup—witness saw somebody hanging around Slattery's sorority house, sketchy description. But this guy spooked everybody, so I pulled him out of the lineup. Had a little Q and A with him—if you could call it that."

"What do you mean?"

"It was more like a staring contest. This guy had

the dead lights. Know what I mean? Shark eyes. Nobody home. Covered from head to toe with these crazy tattoos, prison tats, all over him. Didn't make any kinda sense at the time, but Jesus, they do now, the tats make sense now."

Kopsinsky was silent for a moment. "Why the hell would they make sense now?"

Grove told him about the rulers, the measuring devices.

Kopsinsky stopped pacing. "Oh, Christ . . . the fetish component. From your study. Always a fetish with these guys. Jesus Christ, Grove, where do these guys come from?"

There was no answer.

The dark man lingered near the driver's-side door of the burning van as the fire bloomed in the rear, sizzling off the corrugated metal floor, climbing up the sides of torture devices and blood-sodden straps and countless items of physical evidence. The van's accelerator pedal had been locked into mid-position with a brick, the automatic transmission shifted into neutral. The dark man reached in and yanked the shift lever down to drive, then lurched backward with the innate speed of a cobra.

The van jerked and fishtailed for a moment, then roared across the shoulder.

It struck the opposite guardrail with enough force to rip through the metal, sending up a loud rending noise like paper tearing. The rear of the van bucked as it went over the ledge and down a wooded embankment. The tall man had to crane his neck in order to see the vehicle slam through a netting of foliage, then sideswipe a tree, then plunge down the remaining twenty-five yards or so of under-growth toward the flooded quarry.

The vehicle hit the water with an immense splash that filled the night air and scattered a cloud of bats into the black sky.

Ray Kopsinsky rubbed his eyes. "I'm assuming we got the guy's prints on file?"

Grove's voice: "Prints, DNA—you name it. But here's the thing. Something happened in that Q and A in Milwaukee, something I never told anybody about."

"I'm listening."

"I got a little overzealous in the interview, sweating this guy extra hard, trying to get a rise out of him."

"Yeah?"

"Finally the guy pushed himself away from the table and got up, like he had just paid his bill at a restaurant. He was just gonna take off, and I guess I kinda grabbed him. There was contact, and . . ."

Kopsinsky waited. "Go on."

Grove's voice sounded strange. "It was like, something happened . . . when we touched. Like a spark almost, I don't know. It's hard to explain."

"You're going to have to do better than that."

"When those dead eyes focused on me, Ray, I saw something new there."

"New like what?"

Long pause. "Like he saw me for the first time. But that's not all of it. It was like . . ."

"What?"

"Like he had been searching for something,

maybe all his life, I don't know, but it was like he had finally found it and it was . . . me."

The dark man went over to the edge of the forest and gazed down at the water as the van sank into the oily black oblivion. A cloud of sparks and steam rose off the back as it vanished, swamping out the fire, leaving behind only a whirlpool of noxious bubbles.

In moments, the bubbles were gone as well. The tall man waited. The surface of the water roiled for a moment, then pieces of evidence began bobbing to the surface. First a knot of bloodstained rope. Then a bottle of sodium thiopental, a linoleum knife, leather leg restraints, and more.

Galvanized by the sight of it, so close to his visions and dreams, the dark man turned and ambled back across the deserted road to his luggage.

The suitcase was a big old Samsonite with a grip of worn brown leather and brass, shiny at the corners, scarred with countless miles and unspeakable secrets. Inside it lay the sacred tools of the tall man's quest—measuring tape, talismans, boning knives, rulers, dried human skin, compasses, needles, snake heads, bottles of ink, protractors, electronic devices, a box of teeth, and coils of rope of all size and description. It was a sort of a doctor's bag for a practitioner of a very old, very secret craft.

He lifted the suitcase with little effort—despite the fact that it weighed close to a hundred pounds—and started down the road toward the next town.

TWENTY-FIVE

That next morning the rains came with a vengeance. A low-pressure cell roared down the eastern seaboard out of Nova Scotia, dumping half a foot of rain on the D.C./Maryland/Virginia triangle. In the nation's capital, sewers flooded and streets became creeks—even the Great Reflecting Pool across from the Washington Monument overflowed across walkways, shutting down the entire Mall.

In Virginia, Atlantic squalls drove gray sheets of rain across the Chesapeake and Potomac corridors. The skies flickered and popped in silver flares like vast photographer's strobes, as the rain billowed and blew across the lush hills of Quantico and outlying areas to the west and north.

Pelican Bay got the worst of it. The gales strafed the cliffs and sent waves pounding up and down the shore. By late afternoon, flood warnings had gone out.

Inside Grove's house, the noise was incredible. Between the gales buzzing off the roof shingles and the barrage of horizontal rain rattling the dormers, he could barely hear himself think, and right now he desperately needed to do just that— think. His brain, overloaded now with urgent minutiae, revved like an engine as he paced across the rain-slashed front windows.

The bulletin had gone out hours ago on John Q Public—last seen eleven months ago at a Chicago homeless shelter—but Grove hadn't heard anything yet. According to Kopsinky, Grove would be apprised of the situation the moment there was any news to report, but until then, he was under no circumstance to go anywhere or do anything heroic. Now he felt like a caged animal. He ached, his stomach twinged with cramps and nerves; he missed Maura, he missed Aaron; he could barely eat—he had managed to swallow a bowl of lentil soup an hour ago, but that was it, and it *had* been it for days now.

He stopped pacing for a moment and peered through a space in the window blinds.

The gray Ford Taurus still sat out there in the rain, idling, a vaporous smudge of exhaust swirling off its tailpipe. The unmarked cop car had been stationed outside his home since nine that morning, parked against the curb on the opposite side of the road, where the abandoned play lot with its dilapidated wooden slide and broken swings shivered in the winds. Ostensibly the cops were there for Grove's protection, but Grove got the feeling they were also charged with making sure he stayed put.

Grove was about to turn away from the window when he noticed a car approaching from the south. It came around the bend at a brisk clip, its brights on, the rain stitching down through its high beams like luminous needlepoint. Grove stared. The car skidded to a stop on wet leaves, nearly sliding into the unmarked Taurus.

The driver's door flew open, and a stocky black woman in an FBI Windbreaker came stumbling out holding an umbrella and fumbling with a laminate FBI ID tag.

Edith Drinkwater flashed her Bureau tag at the plainclothes guys, who were lurching out of their Taurus now with urgent expressions, fingering the stocks of their holstered guns. She waved the ID at them and motioned at the Cape Cod. "Edith Drinkwater, gentlemen—Bureau special, working with Grove."

"Hold on!" One of the plainclothes officers raised a hand, thumbing the hand-mike of his two-way. He said a few words into it in a low voice, that hand still up, the rain drenching him, his irritated partner standing behind him, wiping water from his face.

The drops noisily peppered Drinkwater's umbrella while she waited.

Finally a voice crackled from a tiny speaker in the car, and the cop waved her on. "Go ahead."

"Appreciate it."

Drinkwater turned and hurried up the walk, past Maura's lovely little stand of daylilies and yellow mums, past a wheelbarrow overflowing with multicolored petunias, up the herringbone brick steps, and over to the brightly painted Colonial front door. The quaintness and homeliness of the place proved a bizarre counterpoint to the dark, troubling thoughts sloshing around Drinkwater's brain. How the hell was she going to lay all this out for the man? How do you talk about evil in a house of yellow mums and white chintz doilies?

She didn't even have to ring the bell. There was a click before her hand could reach the button. The door jerked open, and Grove's hand shot out at her, grasping her by the lapel of her Windbreaker. "Get in here!" he ordered in a weird, juiced-up voice.

He yanked her inside, and she stumbled across the threshold, a number of sensations bombarding her in that foyer as the sound of the door slamming shut rang out behind her. Water dripped off her umbrella, which she still held aloft as though the ceiling might cave in on top of her at any moment.

"Just the person I needed to see." His voice was grave, strained, hyper. He wrung his hands as he spoke. Dressed in jeans and a short-sleeved T-shirt, he looked bad, haunted. His face looked gray in the rainy light coming through the window. "I need your help."

"Yeah . . . I can see that." She walked further into his home and gazed around at the disaster area that was Grove's first floor—a battlefield strewn with notes, maps, glossy forensic photos of the Archetype's victims, digital images of pictograms washing away in bubbling seafoam. The air smelled of stale coffee, ammonia, and sweat—the odors of stress—and Grove had apparently been writing in stream of consciousness in Sharpie on odd surfaces: kitchen cabinets, the microwave, the TV. Strange foreign words and phrases adorned the refrigerator door and the hood over the stove. She looked at him. "I read about the Archetype case on the secure site this morning; I heard about the break. You're all over the news, what with that little dustup you had with that reporter."

"They got me locked up. I need you to help me get outta here."

She could not take her eyes off him, hand still white-knuckling the umbrella. "I have to talk to you; I don't even know where to start."

"I'm trying to tell you, I'm the only one's gonna find this guy, John Q Public." Grove paused. "Why the hell are you looking at me like that?"

"What?"

Grove took her umbrella, shook the water off, tossed it across the vestibule. "You're looking at me like I've got two heads."

Drinkwater swallowed hard. "Do you have any alcohol? Any kind of alcohol whatsoever? Anything with a high alcohol content?"

"What? Yeah—here." He turned and went over to a pine dry sink in the living room. Inside the varnished cabinet Grove found a row of bottles, mostly green—Grove's beloved single-malt scotch. "Knock yourself out."

Drinkwater unbuttoned her jacket with trembling hands as she crossed the cluttered living room, sidestepping piles of forensic effluvia. She fumbled with the bottles for a second until she found a half-full pint of vodka. She uncapped it and took a healthy swig, letting it burn all the way down.

"What the hell is the matter with you?" Grove wanted to know from across the room.

She shrugged off her jacket, laid it across the arm of a recliner. "So you wanted me to find out about those old dudes came to see Geisel." A beat of hesitation here. "Been doing traces for years, and I never found out more than I wanted to tell."

Grove looked at her. "I'm not following."

"There's no way to dance around this. It's freaky as hell, and you're not gonna believe a word of it."

"I don't have time for this."

"You *need* to know this, Ulysses," she said, taking another pull off the bottle, grimacing at the fire in her throat. "I'm not sure why . . . but I just have this feeling you need to know this whether it's all bullshit or not."

Grove put his hands on his hips. "You got my attention, Drinkwater, now spit it out."

She looked at him for a long moment. "How do you feel about myths and legends?"

TWENTY-SIX

At 8:32 Eastern Standard Time that night, Jamie Lou Clinger left her boyfriend's house, defiant about being late for supper, knowing her stepfather would probably take out the belt when she got home, but she didn't care.

A skinny eighteen-year-old with a nose ring and a spider tattoo on her neck, she practically skipped down the sidewalk outside her boyfriend's trailer, her head still buzzing from the kick-ass weed Brian and she had just smoked. He had tried to get into her pants, but Jamie had been strong and just gave him a little titty. She wanted to save her coochie for her and Brian's wedding night, at which time she would finally be free of her tight-assed step-daddy and chickenshit mama once and for all.

She reached the edge of the property line, turned left, and headed north on Main Street, buttoning her ratty denim jacket and turning up her collar as she went. It was a typical high Kentucky evening, cool in the hills, damp in the hollows, and Jaimie felt a little shiver of a chill as she strode under pools of yellow street lamps.

Valesburg had already tucked itself in for the night, the windows of Deforest Feed and Seed as dark as black ice, the big neon milk shake over the door to the Dixie Café turned off and swinging squeakily in the breeze. Mining towns are like that—sleepy, stubborn, set in their ways.

Established way back in the early nineteenth century when coal deposits were first discovered a mile below the limestone crags of the Shenandoahs, Valesburg was one of the more stubborn of these enclaves, clinging to the side of Avery Mountain like a calcified barnacle. Ninety-nine percent of the town's population were Pentecostal Baptists, most of them on intimate terms with tribulation and tragedy. The mayor doubled as the preacher out at the Revelation to John church on Gunstock Road, and practically every single family had lost relatives in mining mishaps.

Jamie walked briskly past a row of merchants lining the north side of town, past Doc Felton's office, past the old mining company store, past the Curio Emporium Five and Dime where she got her first ear piercing back in eighth grade (much to the chagrin of the cashier, Betty-Jean Rosseler, who had promptly called Jamie's mom—as well as the rest of the Valesburg bridge club—crowing the scandalous news). By the time Jamie reached the vacant lot at the end of Briar Street, she had decided against her better judgment to take a short cut. For the first time in her life, Jamie Lou Clinger decided to cross the barrens in order to hasten the trip home. She did not make this decision lightly. She didn't want to cross that godforsaken stretch of land, but she also didn't want to show up any later than absolutely necessary. For the last few blocks she had started dreading the promise of her step-daddy's lash, her resolve wilting like a bloom closing up for the night.

She walked over to the edge of the vacant lot, then paused, girding herself for what she was about to do.

"Oh, fuck it."

She hopped over a low rail fence, then ascended the gentle slope into absolute darkness.

"Stop! Goddamnit, stop!"

Grove stood at the front window, gazing through the slats of drawn blinds at the turbulent night sky and the relentless rain slashing the pane. The storm had not let up since dusk—in fact, had worsened—and now the escalating volleys of thunder accompanied by violent eruptions of lightning seemed to echo Grove's rising mania and rage. He had been listening to Drinkwater's bizarre tale—of how those old men had come to Geisel all those years ago, believing that Grove was part of some cosmic duel, a pair of lost spirits in eternal conflict—for almost an hour now, and he was close to the breaking point. "What good does this do me? Huh?" He turned and seared his gaze into Drinkwater. "I'm hunting some kind of supernatural being now? Is that what you're telling me?"

Drinkwater stood across the room, near the fireplace, the pint bottle of vodka in her hand. She had practically polished it off and was starting to slur her words a bit, starting to wobble on her knees. "Look, you hired me to run down these old men, I ran down these old men."

"What am I supposed to do with this?" Grove

thrust his hands in his pockets, dizzy with warring emotions. A voice, maybe his mom's, maybe something else buried deep in his neurons, told him to heed Drinkwater's words: *You got the mark on you, boy, you cannot run away from it.*

"There's more." Drinkwater's voice, low and foreboding, sounded trip-wire taut.

"I'm not sure I want to hear any more."

Drinkwater took one last swig and wiped her mouth. "I'm just reporting what I found out—just the facts, like Joe Friday."

"That's what you call this—*fact?*"

She shrugged. "You hired me to do a job, I did the job."

Grove went over to her, his face flushed with feverish emotion—a lethal cocktail of rage and terror. "All I want right now is to get this guy, this whack job. That's all I want."

"I hear you, I do, I do." Drinkwater set the bottle down on the end table. "But think about it for a second. Maybe this guy knows the same legends."

Grove looked at her. "John Q Public?"

She nodded.

"You're saying John Q Public thinks he's a—a what? A demigod? An evil spirit?"

"If you want me to stop, I'll stop."

"You said there's more."

"That's right."

"Go ahead."

Drinkwater took a deep breath. "I talked to your mom."

Grove stared at her, his center of gravity going all haywire. "You *what?!*"

* * *

The pine barrens lay on the northeast corner of Valesburg, Kentucky, a scabrous rise of weeds and trash enclosed by ancient barbed wire and choked with thick, dense groves of knotty pines and crooked spruce. From the north side of Briar Street, the area looked like an ocean of blackness that stretched all the way to the North Carolina border (although technically the barrens terminated at the county line, a mile or so away).

Local kids loved to tell tall tales about it—how it would eat you alive if you ventured more than ten feet into it, how hapless children had wandered into it only to be eaten by wolves. But Jamie Lou Clinger was smart enough not to be taken in by all those old spook stories. She was a sophisticated eighteen years old now, and she had her sights set on far wilder jungles, such as the University of Kentucky at Louisville, or maybe even Duke down in Raleigh. Duke was a party school, sure, but it was also one of the top rated pre-vet programs. It was Jamie's ticket out of this hellhole hometown of hers.

She entered the barrens at exactly 8:11 P.M.

The first leg of the journey passed quickly—a simple traipse up a narrow dirt path through a thicket of hickories—and Jamie crossed this portion of the trek briskly, eyes forward, ignoring the droning sounds of crickets and burbling frogs on either side of her. Fireflies floated in the darkness like tiny cinders. Her feet, clad in worn Chuck Taylors, scuttled faster and faster up the trail. Her breath huffed.

Soon she found herself engulfed by myrtle and kudzu-fringed whip-weeds so dense they gave the impression she was traveling through a time tunnel. The breeze in the treetops played with the swaying shadows beside her like a puppeteer, and other, more troubling noises crept up on her. The creak of a branch dancing in the wind, the scrape of a limb against a hollow deadfall log. The flutter of something leathery in the sky above the netting of trees.

It was amazing how quickly Jamie lost all her worldly sophistication.

By the time she reached the midway point—a clearing about the size of a baseball diamond, the uneven ground lined with mossy boulders, the dark air hectic with mosquitoes—her heart was pounding. She realized the worst was yet to come, the scariest part of the trip, and she already wanted to turn back and take the long way home. How was she going to face the mine? In all the excitement she had forgotten how close the shortcut came to it. How could she avoid looking at it? The disaster that happened there decades ago had traumatized the little village so severely that the mere act of *looking* at the ruins—even from the distance of Avery Mountain—would place an inexorable hex on the viewer. It was an inexcusable tempting of fate.

I'll just walk on by, won't even look at it, just pretend it isn't even there, just a bad dream, not even real . . .

She took a deep, bracing breath, then began the next leg of the path.

Grove stood very still in the middle of his living room, the soles of his feet feeling as though they were welded to the carpet, as he listened to Drinkwater's slurred words.

"She's a beautiful lady, Ulysses." Drinkwater stood

unsteadily over by the hearth. "She loves you like I can't even explain."

Grove felt his stomach clench. "Who told you to talk to my mom?"

"You said—"

"On the phone you're talking about?"

"I saw her. I connected through Chicago and met her."

Grove felt the top of head coming off. "I don't understand why you thought you had to—"

"This is important, Ulysses. What she said, it all *connects*."

"What are you talking about?"

Drinkwater starting pacing in front of the hearth, searching for the right words. "Your mom told me a lot, but the one thing she told me just about blew me out of my chair—something that happened back in Kenya, before you were born. She was scared, Ulysses. She said one day out of the clear blue sky these mysterious men show up in her village, holy men from somewhere else, priests or prophets or whatever. They kinda stalk her for a while, and she's so messed up and paranoid she locks herself in her shack. They surround her hut and they chant and pray all night, and she has these horrible nightmares, and then . . . the next day they're gone."

"What are you telling me this for?" Thunder boomed overhead, resonating down through the joists. "My mom has nothing to do with this."

"She *does*, Ulysses, she surely does. Because there were six of them."

"What?"

"Those weird-ass guys who came to her village, there were six of them—you see what I'm saying?"

"Drinkwater—"

"These were the same guys, Ulysses, same group of old coots came to see Geisel."

"That's ridiculous."

"That's not even the freakiest part. The freakiest part is what she dreamed that night, okay? Because she dreamed she had sex."

"I don't want to hear this—"

"I'm just saying, this is how it all fits. Your mom had this crazy dream that she had relations with some kind of—how did she put it?—something that wasn't really human." Drinkwater reached into her back pocket, pulled out a small spiral notebook, opened it, and frantically paged through it until she found the entry. " 'An angel of pure white light, he came to me in the dream, he came to me and made me a woman in that dream.' "

"Stop it." Grove felt dizzy, like he was having another out-of-body experience. "Just stop it."

Drinkwater flipped the notebook closed and looked at him with the most intense gaze. "A couple of weeks later she missed her period, Ulysses—"

"Bullshit!" Grove batted the vodka bottle off the end table, and the bottle shattered against the wall. "This is pure *bullshit* and it doesn't help me!"

Drinkwater blinked at the sudden outburst. "Okay, I know it sounds crazy, I know, but lookit, I did some research online on the way home—"

"I told you to stop."

"*Mitochlorians*, Ulysses. There's a term for it. It's like an airborne—what?—like a spore—"

"That's enough."

"—that can be passed during altered states, like a hallucinogen, like in a religious ceremony, but not exactly. It's really hard to explain."

"My dad was Jamaican, he was . . ." Grove's voice faltered for a moment, his vision going watery. "*Trust* me when I tell you this man was no angel of pure white light. "

"All right, but"—Drinkwater was looking at the floor as she wavered drunkenly on weak knees— "that's not what your mama told me."

Grove roared suddenly: "My dad was a lazy-ass fucking truck driver and a coward who ran out on his family!"

After a tense moment of hard-breathing silence, Drinkwater looked up at him. "Whether it's true or not, your mom believes she was a virgin when she—"

"Shut the fuck up!"

Grove's open palm came out of nowhere, a big roundhouse that landed squarely on Drinkwater's cheek.

It was probably a blessing that she was drunk, because the impact of Grove's slap nearly knocked her out of her shoes. She lurched backward and slammed against the wall with a grunt, then bounced to the floor like a deflated punching dummy. Eyes geeked open with shock, hands instinctively raised into a defensive posture, she convulsed and then curled into a fetal position. All of a sudden her voice sounded eerily younger, like a frightened child: "*Please don't hurt me, please, please, please don't hurt me, don't hit me again, please please please please please. . . .*"

Paralyzed, hyperventilating, fists still clenched, Grove stared down at the cowering woman, unsure of what he had just done, or what was happening to him.

TWENTY-SEVEN

In the darkness, batting at the limbs and the switches—the brambles clawing at her thin pants—Jamie Lou Clinger emerged into another clearing and saw the mine in the murky middle distance.

It didn't look like much in the rising moonlight—just a long, narrow, dilapidated building, bordered by a fossilized railroad track and crowned with jagged, broken smokestacks—but in that horrible instant before she reflexively looked away, Jamie felt the malignant power radiating off the place like magnetic waves penetrating her skull.

In its glory days—an era of bathtub gin and flappers and hydroelectric dams, an era long before Jamie Lou Clinger's grandmother was a gleam in *her* mother's eye—the Wormwood Creek Mine had been one of the only deep-shaft coal mines in the southeast, plunging more than twelve thousand feet into the cold, unforgiving Kentucky shale. But that was a long time ago, long before the EPA had come in and cleaned everything up, converting most of the state to strip mining; in fact, long before the Great Disaster of '53.

But tonight, right at this moment, in the deserted darkness—in the instant before she looked away from the mine—Jamie Lou Clinger noticed something tremendously odd out of the corner of her eye that froze her in place. Her breath caught in her throat and she did an almost comical double take. She blinked. And blinked.

And stared.

A ghostly figure crouched near the sealed, petrified entrance to the Shaft Number 1 pithead building: a huge, black, tattooed, muscular, zombie-like phantom dragging a big circular tape measure along the scarred ground.

Liquid terror flooded Jamie's bloodstream as she stared at this incongruous nightmare of a scene— a faceless dark figure measuring the ground along the threshold of the mine, a series of three concentric measuring tapes fanning out from the entrance—and her mind grappled with the logic of it. Was she seeing things?

She only watched for a brief moment, but her eyes took in so much: the figure wore a funky old top hat; and a huge old suitcase lay on the ground near this creep, open, while scraps of rotted timbers the size of hog legs slowly inched across the ground around him, on their own power, as though sliding on ice.

Timbers moving on their own power?

It is amazing how much visual information the human mind can take in over the space of a single instant: especially a young, hyperalert, hyperimaginative teenage mind. In that awful instant before she turned away, Jamie realized just exactly why the wood scraps were moving—

—because the stranger had just turned to the

boarded entrance door and yanked on it, sending up a sudden grating squeak, which scattered the carpet of insects that were writhing under the wood. All at once, a moving wave of beetles, silverfish, and centipedes dispersed across the ground like a school of frightened minnows, leaving behind the boards in the ocean of shadows—

—and that was when Jamie managed to abruptly tear herself away from this otherworldly tableau.

She turned tail and charged like a jackrabbit across the cinder-strewn apron, into the fir trees, and down the other side of the ridge. She ran and ran headlong through the woods, not feeling a thing but white-hot horror, branches whipping at her face as she raced toward the far clearing at the bottom of Northmoor Road.

She didn't stop running until she reached the gate to the trailer park, and even then she trotted nervously through the maze of mobile homes and blacktop courts until she reached her home. She felt as though her heart was going to explode. She could not get the image of that ghostly bogeyman out of her brain, nor would she ever forget what that apparition had been doing in the darkness of the Wormwood ruins, which was something far stranger than a moving carpet of bugs.

He was trying to get *into* the mine.

"I don't know what's happening." Grove stared down at Drinkwater on the carpet across the room, the realization of what he had done cleaving his brain like an ax. All his fury drained out of him, he went over to her. Keeling down beside her, he trembled as he tried to touch her reassuringly, to stroke her shoulder like a trainer calming a cowering wild animal, but she jerked at his touch, obviously triggered by something buried deep within her that had been awakened by the slap.

"I'm so sorry," Grove murmured, "I'm so, so, so sorry."

She turned her back to him and lay there for a moment, as though embarrassed, taking deep breaths and rubbing her face. Her trembling subsided. "I'm okay."

"I can't believe I did that." Grove felt his guts seizing up, his eyes welling with tears. The lack of sleep, the fear, the shame, the fixation on the hunt—all of it pressed down on him now, constricting his throat, scalding his eyes. "I've never hit a woman in my life."

Drinkwater managed to sit up. She looked at him. "I been hit harder."

"I can't—" Grove tried say something else, crouched next to her, but he couldn't get the words out. He tried to swallow, but the lump in his throat was choking him. All at once he became horribly aware of the empty bedrooms above him, the lost dreams of that drafty Cape Cod home, the absence of his family, the broken promises, the darkness winning.

He looked down. A single tear dripped to the floor.

She gently patted his arm. "It's okay, Ulysses. Forget it. I could've said it a little better than I did."

Grove tried to say something else, but he couldn't; he could only stare at the carpet where his tear had fallen. His crying abated into a dizzying, stabbing migraine.

Drinkwater patted his shoulder. "I'm all right, really. I'm fine."

"You sure?"

"You bet."

"I'll make it up to you." Grove stood up. Dizziness coursed through him, his knees wavering severely. What the hell was happening to him? Was it the lack of nourishment and sleep? Was it grief? He was stretched as thin as a razor blade.

"Something else your mom told me. . . ." Drinkwater remained on the floor, taking a deep breath. "She made me swear not to talk about it with anybody, including you."

Grove looked down at her. "I'm afraid to ask."

"She was scared, Ulysses. I could see it on her face. She'd been holding this in all her life."

"Why didn't she . . ." Grove blinked. The dizziness rose in him like a wreath of smoke around his head. He grabbed the edge of the doorjamb. His vision blurred. The room darkened suddenly.

"Are you okay?"

"I'm just—"

"Ulysses?"

"I'm—" The floor seemed to tilt beneath him. His hand slipped off the edge of the jamb.

"Whoa!" Drinkwater reached out and tried to catch him, but it was too late.

Grove never even realized he was falling.

It was as though the floor had levitated, and he barely managed to twist sideways before hitting the carpet. Though the meaty part of his shoulder took the brunt of the impact, the air was still knocked out of his lungs as he landed in a heap, one arm pinned under the other.

"Oh my God, Ulysses! Ulysses?" Drinkwater

crabbed over to him. She cradled his head. "Hey, you okay? You okay? Hey! You okay?"

Grove was only out for a second or two, but in that moment of floating darkness he saw his first glimpse of where he would find John Q Public.

TWENTY-EIGHT

At the precise moment Ulysses Grove was momentarily losing consciousness in Pelican Bay, something of great import was occurring hundreds of miles to the west, in the dead-still darkness of a rural Kentucky night, along the edge of a hole in the earth known as Porchard's quarry. At that exact moment, old Maynard Ferguson saw the first piece of evidence floating near a boulder field on the north side of the man-made lake.

The retired mailman had been ensconced just south of there, perched on a tattered lawn chair in the shadows of a little clearing, his ice chest next to him full of cold Budweisers and warm night crawlers, three of his lines in the water loaded up for bass or maybe, if he got lucky, a decent-size bullhead. At first Ferguson thought his eyes were playing tricks again—since turning the big seven-oh, his peepers had been doing that quite often—but the more he stared at that shimmering black water gently licking at the edges of the rocks, the more he became convinced he was seeing what he thought he was seeing.

At last he levered his creaking bones out of his lawn chair and gingerly made his way through the cattails and weeds to the moss-carpeted stones to the north; then he managed to trundle out to the edge of the water and reached the pale floating object with a long willow switch. He fished it out and held it up in the moonlight.

"I'll be goddamned," he muttered, staring at a pair of white ladies' panties streaked with deep purple bloodstains. Maynard knew bloodstains when he saw them—any good angler knows the color on cotton cloth, especially when it's old and set in.

Other objects floating nearby caught the old man's attention. A tangle of something shiny and wormy-gray that looked like duct tape; a clear plastic container that the sheriff would later identify as an IV bottle; a linoleum knife, also permanently bloodstained; a charred ruler; a torn bench seat from a large vehicle; a knotted phalanx of measuring tape; and perhaps the most disturbing item of all: *a scorched human skull*. Old Man Ferguson saw all this in one wide-eyed gulp before digging in his pocket with his crooked, palsied hand and fiddling open his cell phone.

It only took a little over a minute for him to get Sheriff DeQueen on the line—that night was, as usual, another slow one in Catacomber County— and another ten minutes or so for the sheriff to get his fat Irish ass over to the quarry. Ferguson waited up by the road near his pickup, shivering in the cool night air. When the lights of the cruiser finally materialized to the south, first sweeping across the dense wall of black oaks, then glaring in Ferguson's eyes, the old man let out a relieved sigh and started waving the sheriff over. The cruiser pulled up and the sheriff stuck his big ruddy cranium out the window and said, "You ain't been tipplin' the blackberry brandy again, Maynard, have ya?"

The old man said this was no joke and why didn't the sheriff just get his sizable rear end out of that car and down to the lake to see for himself.

After a split second of thought, the sheriff decided to do exactly that.

The vision came to Grove without fanfare or warning, the fiery flare popping behind his blind eye like a Roman candle, making him flinch at the vivid bright colors: three yellow beams of light shooting toward a dark hole in the center of his field of vision. Then a nimbus of light sparked around the nucleus, as though a match had been struck, and the hole in the heart of his vision coalesced, rimmed in shadows, framed in rotting boards, a portal in the ground, a doorway, a passage.

Then Grove jerked awake on the floor of his drafty Cape Cod in Pelican Bay.

The duration of the vision had been less than a couple of seconds, but the narrative had been clear: a strange doorway sucking him down into the blackness of hell as violently as a jet engine vacuuming a bird out of the sky. When Grove finally got his bearings back and looked up at Edith Drinkwater, his voice was in shreds. "Oh God, that's it—"

She stared at him. "That's *what?*"

"That's it that's it that's it that's it," he muttered softly under his breath, the room going in and out of soft focus, the woozy feeling clinging as he tried to stand. He saw the answer on the floor all around them, scattered across the disordered house.

"What is? What's it?" Drinkwater looked as though she were awaking from a dream herself, her eyes sober and alert now as she stood.

"The measuring man." Grove stood on his feet, wavering for a moment as he rubbed his eyes. He looked at the room. In one corner, black-and-white glossies of poor Barbie Allison contorted on the cracked pavement of a Minneapolis alley lay in disarray across the sofa cushions.

"What?" Drinkwater kept staring.

"He's showing me where it is, the rendezvous, the meeting place." Grove stared into another corner, where pictures of Karen Finnerty's corpse on a North Carolina beach hung off a lamp shade, news photos of her grieving family above them on the wall, the victimology, the backstory, the pain and suffering caused by this freak.

"Ulysses, you're killing me here. What are you talking about?"

"He's telling me where to go." Grove stared at the fax of Madeline Gilchrist's body dump along a deserted windswept boardwalk near Galveston pier. "Galveston . . . North Carolina . . . Minnesota."

Drinkwater looked around at the chaos of paperwork, not seeing it, not getting it. "Okay so?"

Grove looked at her. " 'And the netherworld shall open.' "

"Okay."

"Galveston, North Carolina, and Minneapolis." She shrugged. "So what."

"Get me a straightedge—a long one—like a yardstick, something like that, now, please—look in the coat closet. Quick!"

Drinkwater whirled, nearly falling over, searching the cluttered vestibule, while Grove rushed over to the corner sofa, nearly tripping over a file box.

He tore a map of the United States off the wall, the pushpins flying. "He's telling me where it is— *hell.*"

In the foyer Drinkwater found the closet, threw it open, and found a yardstick just inside the door leaning against an umbrella and a broom. She snatched it up and hurried back into the living room.

Thunder rattled in the rafters suddenly, lightning flickering, as Drinkwater handed the yardstick to Grove. "Show me."

"Look, look—here." Grove dropped to his knees, spreading the wrinkled map across the floor. "He's showing me where hell is."

Drinkwater knelt next to him.

"Here . . ." Grove pressed the yardstick down on the map, connecting Minneapolis in the upper Midwest to Emerald Isle, North Carolina, on the East Coast. He found a pen in an end-table drawer and drew a thick black line connecting the two murder scenes.

Drinkwater waited for it to make sense.

"And here . . ." Grove drew another thick straight line between Emerald Isle and Galveston, then another one back up to Minneapolis. ". . . which makes a triangle, which provides a perfect average, which is an inversion of the trinity, a corruption of the father/son/holy spirit, which is the median of all serial killings in America. You still with me?"

"I guess, yeah."

Grove looked at her, the yardstick still pressed to the map. "Read your *Inferno, The Divine Comedy.*"

"Now you lost me again."

Grove gazed down at the map, then slowly made three more lines connecting the corners. In the exact middle of the triangle was a point where all three lines came together. "Dante wrote that the epicenter of the earth is the netherworld." His voice softened suddenly, lowered an octave. "And the epicenter of the epicenter is where the devil lives."

Drinkwater stared at the map a long time, stared at that three-way intersection of felt-tip lines. Then she looked at Grove. "The devil lives in eastern Kentucky?"

TWENTY-NINE

Sheriff Howard DeQueen of Catacomber, Kentucky, got things rolling that night with uncharacteristic vigor. He pulled his deputy off watch duty over at the Armour Star plant and got him down to Porchard's quarry within an hour with a patrol boat as well as a tow truck from Roberts Machinery (the one with the heavy-duty winch).

They dragged the swimming hole and eventually recovered the charred remains of a recently torched Chevy Econoline van. It took them about an hour to fish the thing out, and the sheriff supervised it all with his ever-present Meerschaum pipe clenched between his big yellow teeth.

They got the heap back up to the road, and the sheriff told the young driver from Roberts to take the metal carcass as well as all the suspicious items skimmed out of the water over to the impound lot out back of the Piggly Wiggly and make sure the damn thing was locked up good and tight.

By the time Sheriff DeQueen got back to his office he was fully immersed in thought, wondering how he should process this thing, wondering what kind of cowshit he had stepped in this time, so distracted, in fact, that he didn't even hear the crackling voice of Dispatch in the other room. The third shift had not yet arrived, and DeQueen was alone. Finally he realized the voice was calling for him.

He ambled into the radio room and picked up the table mike. "This is DeQueen, go ahead," he said.

"Sir, we got a call from a Bureau gentleman out of Virginia for y'all." It was the voice of Carmella Bozen, the morning gal in the Pinckey PD. "Mind if I route him through?"

"Route him on through, darlin'."

A split second later the desk phone lit up, and DeQueen grabbed it. "Catacomber Center here, who am I speaking to, please?"

"Sheriff, this is Special Agent Ulysses Grove, Quantico." The voice was amped up, jittery. "Sorry to bother you in the middle of the night."

"What can I do for ya, sir?"

"Just wondering if you or anybody in the area have seen anything . . . you know . . . out of the ordinary recently?"

"Out of the ordinary?"

A pause. "Yeah, you know. Anything suspicious, signs of foul play."

The sheriff thumbed his big Stetson hat back on his huge head. "Well now, that's funny y'all should ask that."

THIRTY

Grove had a grand total of forty-eight rounds of ammunition in two different calibers in his house—an unopened box of twenty-four liquid-tip .44 slugs for his Bulldog in the basement office, under lock and key in a strongbox, and sixteen .22-caliber zippers on the top shelf of his bedroom closet—which he gathered in tense silence, moving with the grim methodical focus of a commando. The remaining eight hollow points were still in his Bulldog, injected there with a speed loader before he had embarked for Benjamin Bard's houseboat the previous morning.

Over the last half hour, since speaking with the Kentucky sheriff and learning of John Q Public's trail of bloody bread crumbs—proof positive that the killer was luring Grove into a trap—Grove had gone from room to room, gathering up his firearms and taking inventory of his personal off-the-books arsenal. As he did this, he felt as though he were outside himself, watching his body performing these tasks, watching his hands snapping bullets into magazines, stuffing duffel bags full of supplies—topographical maps rolled up in extra pairs of socks, cans of mace, his handgun stowed in a vinyl case, the night-vision goggles he'd used in New Orleans a couple of years ago, a few pairs of rubber gloves, a webbed belt sheathed with three serrated commando knives, and on and on.

Grove had already called Mike Hauser, a friend and fellow instructor at Quantico, a man with connections at a local airstrip, in order to charter a single-engine job to Kentucky. Apparently Hauser had not gotten word yet that Grove was on suspension: he agreed to meet Grove at the airfield in an hour. Valesburg, Kentucky, was only about forty-five minutes away by small aircraft, and Grove wanted to get there as soon as possible, before the developments at Porchard's quarry reached the Bureau task force and the little town flooded with investigators looking for the owner of the panel van.

According to the FBI's secure website, which Drinkwater could still access, the team had already tracked down the man's last known address—the Saint Aquinas Group Home in Chicago—and had collected a busload of leads from the squalid basement room in which John Q Public occasionally lurked, including a journal written in pictograms, a floor plan of the Mall of America, and lots of DNA.

At-Large bulletins had gone out to state police in a nineteen-state swath between Texas and Maryland. The lab had matched DNA from the Galveston dump site to samples collected at the group home, so now the man was a hard target, with enough physical evidence to win him the needle . . . or at least send him up for a half dozen lifetimes without possibility of parole. Grove knew it was just a matter of time now before *somebody* caught him. Big, buff black guys covered from head to toe in surreal tattoos are hard to hide.

Plus this guy *wanted* to be caught, as would the average killer—a self-destructive trait that the Archetype would surely exhibit. But Grove knew something else, something that was hard for him to articulate, hard to explain with words, hard to even face, but clear nonetheless: *Grove had to be the one to catch the monster.*

The universe and John Q Public both seemed to want it this way.

"Ulysses, I need to say something and I need your full attention." Drinkwater's shrill voice warbled after Grove as he carried his duffel bag across the living room. She had been nipping at his heels from room to room, trying to get his attention.

"I'm sorry, go ahead." Grove went over to his briefcase, which lay open on an end table. He put the duffel down on the table, setting it a little too close to the edge, his depth perception still compromised by his damaged eye. He moved it a few inches, then turned to her. "I'm listening."

She licked her lips nervously. "I don't know how to put this exactly—"

"Go ahead, Edith, just spit it out."

"All this woo-woo shit is just—"

She paused, gazing at the wall behind him, where a big white sheet of poster board was tacked up among the clinical forensic photos of carnage. The endless string of Sumerian symbols, scrawled in blood like decorative wallpaper around Madeline Gilchrist's savaged remains, were now hurriedly jotted in black Sharpie pen across every square inch of the poster, the space underneath bearing Dr. Milhouse's transliterations and embellishments: *through the hole in the firmament the hunter must pass through the portal of the earth and down the bottomless pit the hunter must fall and pay with his blood and with his endless torment and with his hopeless soul the hunter must pay.* Above these translations hung a laser printout that Grove had taped there only minutes ago. It was an aerial photograph—a satellite image from Google Earth—of the dark wasteland directly northeast of Valesburg, Kentucky, known by the locals as "the barrens." In the dense, detailed gray tones of the photograph, down on a thickly forested slope, crisscrossed by railroad tracks like delicate tiny sutures, was a minuscule complex of smokestacks and stone buildings just big enough to identify. A white tag, almost like a thought balloon, flagged off the edge of the complex and said: WORMWOOD COAL MINE—CLOSED C. 1972. An intersection of three thick black lines crossed the mine's entrance.

"It's a little out of my comfort zone," Drinkwater said finally, looking away from the satellite photo.

Grove gave out a sigh. "Look, I don't expect you to go down there with me. I just need some help getting there. Then I'll cut you loose. I promise."

Drinkwater wiped her mouth nervously. "This is like off-the-hook insane. You said yourself you've never even seen a coal mine—at least call somebody, call Dispatch, get some backup."

"Those babysitters out there in that unmarked squad would stop me before I got my garage door open. All I need is a little diversion, then your work is done."

Grove turned and strode over to the front coat closet. He threw open the accordion door and reached up to the top shelf. The Derringer was in a wooden cigar box sealed with packing tape and hidden behind a stack of board games.

"You don't know who this dude is—*what* he is!" Drinkwater swept up behind him. "I gotta tell ya, this is over my head."

Grove peeled the tape off the cigar box. His hands were shaking. "You and me both, Drinkwater." He knelt down and lifted the cuff of his jeans, then taped the tiny, two-shot .22 caliber Derringer pistol to his ankle. "You and me both." His mutter was barely audible. "You and me both."

She watched him. "I'm sorry, Ulysses . . . but I gotta get outta here."

He stood and gave her a nod. "I understand. Believe me. I understand where you're coming from."

"I could lose my spot at the Academy. Seriously I could lose my license."

He nodded again. "Don't blame you one bit." He reached into the closet and pulled out his long white canvas duster. "I really appreciate all you've done. I'll be fine. You can go. It's all right." He shrugged on his coat. "And I'm really sorry I got carried away with you like that."

"I have to go." She turned and strode toward the front door. She paused for the briefest instant before opening it. Then she walked out.

The door clicked shut.

Grove stood there for a moment in that empty house, feeling just about as alone as he had ever felt in his life. Then he turned and headed for the basement.

THIRTY-ONE

Edith Drinkwater paused on Grove's porch, standing in a cone of mist, illuminated by the coach light. The rain had lifted, and now the air was as still and dense as aspic. She could feel the gazes of surveillance officers on her, emanating from that unmarked Ford Taurus parked across the street. She could feel the pulse of her heart in her neck, her cheek still tingling hot and cold where Grove had slapped it, the stinging sensation still sending mixed signals down her spine.

It was as though she were caught in a dream, her feet cemented to the ground, her legs seized up by the taffy-glue of indecision.

She knew she should get the hell out of there. She knew it was the smart way to play it—cut her losses, go back to school, pretend none of this ever happened. Let Grove hang himself, get himself killed. That was his choice. Drinkwater had nothing to do with this. She was an innocent bystander, a subcontractor, an intern, a rube. She didn't owe him anything.

She waved at the surveillance officers. It was an odd gesture, paralyzed with regret.

She knew Grove was about to slip out the rear of the house. In seconds he would be gone, and her role in this drama would come to an end, and maybe that was the way it was *supposed* to be. Maybe Fate had engineered it this way.

Drinkwater made a move toward the porch steps but suddenly balked, pausing again on the edge of the top step.

The wizened brown face of Grove's mother flashed in her brain: that ancient, leathery dowager's face, with eyes the color of wet tobacco leaves, and the bearing of a sad Nubian priestess. *My son's fate is now your fate.* Drinkwater's midsection seized up with emotion, her eyes stinging. Maybe the decision had already been made. Maybe somewhere deep down in her core she had already chosen her path.

She looked across the street and offered a second gesture to that Ford Taurus.

The rest of it happened so quickly, the surveillance officers did not register the import of what followed. They caught a glimpse of Drinkwater quickly whirling around, then heading back inside the Grove house, slamming the door behind her, as though she had forgotten something.

They certainly did not register the exact meaning of the gesture that Drinkwater had aimed their way before vanishing back inside the Cape Cod.

Her middle-finger salute was only partially visible in the nimbus of mist.

THIRTY-TWO

"Hey! Excuse me!" Grove rapped his knuckles on the driver's-side window of an idling cab, which was parked at a cabstand in the shadows of a deserted Pelican Bay BP gas station. Dawn had not yet broken, but the dark sky seemed to hang low, glowing like a shroud of black phosphorous. "Got a piece of luggage to put in the back."

The old Pakistani man behind the wheel jumped. He had been dozing behind a copy of the *Post*, and now he rolled his window down, displaying a brown smile, peering up at the apparition looming outside. "Yes, sir, where is it that you are going?"

I'm going to hell, Grove thought in a single awkward instant of hesitation before replying, "Jefferson Davis Field north of Quantico."

The little man climbed out, trundled around to the trunk, opened it, and helped Grove with the enormous duffel. They got the bag situated, and then Grove went around and climbed into the backseat.

He was damp with flop sweat. He wished he had

taken the time to change out of his Reeboks back at the house and into something more suitable for spelunking in coal mines, like his hobnail boots or hikers, but now he would have to make do with the sneakers. Thank God he had paused long enough to grab his duster, which he now wore buttoned up to the neck over his white T-shirt and jeans.

It would be cold and damp and miserable where Grove was going.

The old man climbed behind the wheel, revved the engine for a moment, then slammed the shift lever down into drive. He was just about to pull away from the stand when a loud muffled rapping noise thudded off the back window. Grove jumped, twisted toward the window, and gaped.

Edith Drinkwater was standing there, out of breath from running, gazing through the window at him; she gripped the huge handbag slung over her shoulder, as though she had been fleeing a purse snatcher. "Don't worry, they didn't see me," she said breathlessly after Grove had rolled down the window.

"What are you doing, Drinkwater?"

"There's a lot more you need to know," she said, trying to get air into her lungs.

"Okay, tell me."

"Move over."

"What?"

"I'm coming with you."

Grove looked up at her. "No way."

"You said yourself you need help; you can't do this alone."

Grove fixed his gaze on her. "Alone is how I *have* to do this."

"Bullshit, move over."

"Drinkwater—"

"Move the fuck on over." She gave him that homegirl look with the subtly swaying head and sidelong gaze that Grove had seen many times on the streets back in Chicago. One did not fuck with that look.

"Goddamn it to hell," he grumbled and pushed open the door, scooting across the bench seat.

Drinkwater climbed in and slammed the door.

The driver stepped on the gas and they launched out of there.

They headed north on Highway 3, toward Fredericksburg, the air cool and fishy through the vent, the sky over the Chesapeake just starting to change from the flat black of night to a kind of luminous indigo. It gave everything a dull glow, like a photo negative in a chemical bath—that time of night Grove's mother used to call "voodoo hour," the doppelgänger of dusk.

Drinkwater was digging a legal pad out of her purse. "First of all, you had that deathbed note on your wall, the one Tom Geisel wrote."

"Yeah, that's right. So?"

She looked at him. "I used to be a crossword freak."

"And?"

"Could do the *New York Times* puzzle in five minutes by the time I was twelve."

"Okay, so . . . ?"

"I don't know why I didn't see it at first." She held up the pad, showed it to Grove in the gloomy light. "Here's the first broken-up line."

Grove looked at the pad:

thee ws an o her b y a b d one

Below it Drinkwater had written:

There was another boy—a bad one

Grove swallowed hard. "So the old geezers had their eyes on a bad seed as well. We know this already—"

"Just wait," Drinkwater said, flipping to the next page. "He goes on to say this."

who_ yo have to Ul

And Drinkwater's translation:

who you have to face Ulysses

"I'm just guessing the word was *face*," Drinkwater said softly then, her voice low and discreet enough not to reach the driver's ear. "But it could easily be *kill* or *destroy*, right?"

Grove didn't say anything. His gut burned with nervous tension.

"Now, the last line confirms something your mom told me, which I didn't tell you about, because she made me promise not to; she made me swear to God, under penalty of death, and I did, I swore to her."

Grove looked at the phrase:

h ss yr tn

Then the translation:

he's your twin

"Ulysses?"

Grove sat staring at the line, his entire being going cold and hollow like an empty well.

"Ulysses, look at me. Are you okay?"

Grove could not form a reply.

"Ulysses?"

At last, he said in a very low, grave voice, "Tell me everything my mom told you."

THIRTY-THREE

All through his life, in his secret 3 A.M. ruminations, behind the membrane of his everyday life, Grove had suspected something had not been quite right with his own birth. He knew he was an only child. He knew this for a fact. But he had also gleaned over the years the occasional odd little anomaly, like his being born "in the caul," as Vida had put it, which meant he had been the one-in-a-hundred-thousand baby born with the amniotic sac still clinging to his face. He had also noticed over the years weird little gaps in Vida's recollections of his birth. For reasons that were only now becoming clear to Grove, she had always seemed to be withholding something.

Now, for the first time in his life, as he stood in the chill morning mist, alone with Drinkwater on the gravel parkway of a small airfield north of Quantico, the horrible truth had started to coalesce in his mind. He gazed off at the steel-gray dawn rising over the black horizon and murmured, "I always knew there was something weird somewhere, something wrong. . . ."

Drinkwater had her hands in her pockets, her breath coming out in plumes of vapor backlit by the airfield's silvery sodium lights. "I guess back in the sixties they only had a few clinics in Kenya that were equipped to do sonograms."

Grove looked at her. "Then how did she know for sure? How did she know?"

"She said a shaman told her she had two warring spirits inside her." Drinkwater looked up at him, her eyes glinting with some unreadable emotion in the half-light of dawn. "But she didn't know for sure until the day of the delivery."

Grove nodded, looked at the gravel at his feet. "They found a trace of it?"

"An extra growth, extra tissue in her womb."

He looked at her. "Extra tissue."

"A failed twin."

The phrase seemed to hang in the gloomy air like a toxic fog.

Drinkwater swallowed hard, looking down. "I don't know how much of this you want to know." She looked up at him. "I don't want you to hit me again."

"Very funny." Grove looked out beyond the horizon. "So you're telling me there was a twin."

"That's right. You had a twin brother in the womb. Didn't gestate all the way. Only enough nutrients in the womb for one, so the other twin gets absorbed into the placenta."

Grove shook his head. "Survival of the fittest."

"Yeah, I guess you could say that. Vanishing Twin Syndrome is what they call it."

"Cute."

"This was a rare case, too, according to the doctors in Nairobi. This tissue—the thing, this lost embryo—was something they call a mirror twin."

"Go on."

"One twin is right-handed, the other left-handed; all the features, every little freckle, is exactly the reverse of the other's, a perfect inversion."

Grove stared at the horizon for a long moment. "How the hell did Tom know about this?"

Drinkwater shrugged. "Somehow the old geezers got the hospital records, I don't know. Maybe they knew all along."

In the distance, on the northeast horizon, Grove saw a pair of headlights coming down a switchback road. "Here comes the pilot," he said nodding at the oncoming four-wheeler. "Let me do the talking."

Drinkwater smiled in spite of her nerves. "You don't have to worry about that."

Grove wiped his mouth with the back of his hand. "It's just a few cells got flushed down the toilet."

Drinkwater looked at him. "What?"

"The unborn twin."

"Oh. Right."

"It doesn't mean anything."

"Yeah . . . you're right."

Grove watched the vehicle approach. "Just superstition. That's all it is."

"Sure," Drinkwater agreed. "Absolutely."

Grove dug in his pocket for his wallet. "I don't want to hear about it again. You got that?"

"No problem," Drinkwater said with a nod, then followed Grove toward the oncoming headlights.

THIRTY-FOUR

The single-engine Piper Cub, with its govern-ment-issue olive drab fuselage and heavy array of DIA spy cameras lining the underbelly, took off out of the rising sun shortly after 6:00 A.M. that morn-ing, the surly ex–Navy SEAL pilot named Barkham at the controls. Strapped into the rear jump seats, positioned single file, guerrilla-style, Grove and Drinkwater rode in leaden silence as the aircraft climbed a northerly wind toward Leesburg, reached a cruising altitude of fifteen hundred feet, then banked steeply to the west, soaring over the sprawl-ing emerald ocean of pines south of the Green Ridge forest.

The journey took them over the ancient stone pillars of the Allegheny Mountains, the harsh rays of daybreak creeping with the inexorable slowness of a sundial across the plane's scarred canopy, while Grove brooded in the back about the mean-ing of Geisel's death note, his mother's revelations, displaced spirits, lost twins, and suicide missions. Grove didn't want to die. He didn't want to be a hero. But something in those desolate aerial photographs of the Wormwood property called out to him.

He thought about all this almost subconsciously as the Piper Cub buzzed over the verdant ruins of Civil War killing fields, pitching and yawing gently on the tailwinds. Through the side window Grove could see the passing patchwork of mountain roads and dense wilderness like miniature landscapes in a fishbowl, broken only by an occasional grassy slope upon which thousands and thousands of siblings fought to their deaths in the War Between the States: Gettysburg, Cumberland, Manassas, Bull Run—the fossilized battlefields passed beneath the aircraft with time-lapse speed while Grove burned with adrenaline.

Homicide detectives stumped by difficult cases will often go see victims' families, picking at the scab of human misery and grief in order to work up the righteous rage, the sense of vengeance. Grove required no such visit now. He felt the loss of *all* the souls he had avenged over the years smoldering in his gut, all those ragged poor bodies he had measured and catalogued and averaged, seared into his memory, mingling with a sense of guilt so powerful it took his breath away: *he was responsible, somehow, for all this suffering*.

With his calculations, extrapolations, and prognostications, Grove had unleashed this evil, and now his world had narrowed into a dark tunnel into which he traveled alone and through which he could only see a single egress flickering at the end: find the man called John Q Public and remove him, as if he were a tumor, from the world.

* * *

At a few minutes after 7:00 A.M., the Piper Cub touched down at a small airstrip about three and half miles southeast of Valesburg, Kentucky.

By that point, the morning sun had crested the mountains to the east and now shone harsh and brilliant off the treetops, warming up the morning with the cloying smells of wet black earth and pine sap. The plane came to a shuddery stop on a rough-hewn dirt landing strip flanked by rusted unmarked Quonset huts—typical military Spartan—while the prop wound down, raising a thunderhead of dust.

"I'm gonna need y'all to stay put for a second!" Commander Barkham ordered at the top of his voice, unsnapping his belts, removing his headset.

The pilot climbed out of the cockpit and strode low and fast across the hard-pack to the largest steel building. He vanished inside it for a moment. Grove watched from inside the greasy glass fuselage. The prop died and the sudden silence inside the plane's cabin made Grove's jaw ache. He felt Drinkwater's presence behind him, fidgeting nervously in her seat, but not saying anything.

At last the pilot emerged from the Quonset and hurried over to the plane. "Get your things and get outta here," he said after climbing back behind the stick. "And remember: I did not bring you here, and y'all most certainly did not pay me for my services today."

"Got it," Grove said and pulled the fat envelope of twenties out of the inner pocket of his duster. He gave the man the money, then nodded at Drinkwater. "Let's go."

They climbed out of the plane one at a time—Grove first, then Drinkwater—then reached back inside the hatch and grabbed their belongings from under their seats: Drinkwater's big vinyl purse, Grove's immense duffel bag. Drinkwater started toward the access road in the distance, but Grove lingered by the plane as the prop kicked back to noisy life.

"One more thing!" he hollered over the noise of the engine, knocking on the pilot's window.

Barkham stuck his head out the open vent. "If the DIA guys find out I gave y'all this—!"

"We had an agreement." Grove kept his gaze leveled at the pilot.

Barkham let out an angry sigh. He leaned down to a road case on the floor, thumbed a combination lock, and opened it. He found a small plastic case the size of a deck of playing cards, rooted it out, and held it up. Grove reached for it, but Barkham did not let go of it, not yet. "I don't think you fully understand what I'm giving you here—"

Grove snatched it out of the man's hand. "Thank you for your concern."

Grove slung his duffel bag over his shoulder, turned away, then hurried across the tarmac in the noisy slipstream toward the access road, where Drinkwater waited with an odd expression on her sweat-shimmering brown face—a mixture of concern and outright fear. "What was that about?" she asked as they crossed the road.

Grove was digging in his duster pocket for the topographical map he had downloaded. "You don't want to know," he said, unfolding the map, looking at it. "We want to go this way."

He started off to the north, when all at once she grabbed his arm and spun him around.

"Yes I do! I want to know!" Anger flared in her eyes. "What the hell did he give you back there?"

Grove stood there, looking at her for a moment, the roar of the plane kicking up behind them. "It's from an old Agency field kit. A vial of potassium cyanate."

She stared at him, uncomprehending.

Grove did not look away. "It's fast-acting poison for black-op guys—you bite down on it and you check out in like a minute."

He turned then and hurried toward the intersection of access roads to the north.

It took Drinkwater a moment to recover her bearings and hurry after him.

THIRTY-FIVE

The hike took its toll on both of them. By the time they found their way across the Avery Mountain switchbacks and reached the little Farmers' Market shack on the east side of town—essentially a glorified lean-to of canvas and old pine timbers shielding a dozen or so bushel baskets of local produce—Drinkwater had blisters on both heels, Grove's trick knee was heating up on him, and they were both damp with sweat. The sun had risen high and harsh that morning, and Grove had removed his duster along the way, tying it around his waist. By noon, the backs of their necks were burned and creased with grime, and Drinkwater had a bad feeling they were going to stumble upon another murder scene—but Grove sensed he was walking to his *own* doom, not someone else's.

They entered Valesburg from the east and proceeded directly to the Quik-Stop Service Center, where they gobbled a couple of cheese sandwiches and bandaged their sores. Grove knew they had to stay under the radar of Sheriff DeQueen or they would risk tipping the Bureau, so they concocted a

cover story for themselves—nothing too out-
landish, just a subtle nod to allay suspicion for as
long as possible. Grove bought a sheaf of maps at
the front counter and told the gum-snapping girl
behind the cash register that he was from the University of Kentucky College of Agriculture, taking
soil samples.

Word travels in a small town like influenza germs
in a kindergarten.

By mid-afternoon, Grove learned just how
quickly the cashier had circulated news of these
two strangers from "up to the college" when he
and Drinkwater stopped at Bud and Hank's Tavern
on the west edge of town to see if they could dis-
creetly glean any information about the discovery
of John Q's van, or Sheriff DeQueen's investigation, or any suspicious characters loitering around
the mine. The bartender didn't know much—he
was a former biker who had never even laid eyes
on Wormwood—but there was a gangly underage
girl with tattoos and a nose ring drowning her sor-
rows, at the end of the bar who knew plenty.

"You them two eggheads from the U of K?" the
girl asked after the bartender had gone back to his
game of solitaire. The young lady seemed to be in
a sort of boozy fugue state.

"That's right." Grove wheeled toward the girl.
"Ulysses Grove is the name, and this is my fellow
egghead, Edith Drinkwater."

Drinkwater's gaze seemed to gravitate immediately to the fresh bruise under the girl's eye. "You
okay, honey?"

"Fine and dandy, and I'll be even finer and
dandier when I get another one of these—Earl!"

The bartender grunted and went about the

business of making another pink frothy drink for the young lady. He seem unconcerned that she was still three years shy of legal.

"I'm Jamie, by the way," she said with a forlorn smile, shaking Drinkwater's hand. Something raw and unspoken passed between the two women—Grove noticed it, even in the tense zone he was in. The girl looked over her shoulder, then back at Grove. "Did I hear you askin' Earl about Wormwood? The old mine?"

Grove stared at her. "That's right."

The girl licked her lips. "What is it y'all want to know about it exactly?"

Grove spoke softly. "You haven't seen anything suspicious around there in the last few days, have you? Strangers? Anything of that nature?"

The girl's eyes changed slightly, sobered up a bit. "Maybe . . . I don't know."

Grove spoke even softer, his voice intensifying into a sort of taut hiss: "Think hard. It's very important—did you see anyone around the old mine? You could say this is a life-or-death situation."

The girl's expression filled with a terrible sort of awe right then, her chin beginning to tremble. "You two ain't from no college, are ya?"

Grove looked at Drinkwater.

They could smell fear wafting off the girl like musk.

THIRTY-SIX

Night rolled in with the subtle menace of a plague. The chatter of crickets and katydids filled the dusky air, and darkness crept down into the village from the hilltops. A thin wisp of methane glowed faintly in the distant trees like dull purple neon.

"This here's as far as we go." The old man paused on the weed-whiskered shoulder of the dirt road, the legs of his walker crunching in the gravel. "Folks around here are awful superstitious—guess I ain't no different."

Grove set down his duffel bag and surveyed the deepening shadows off to his right.

It was half past six and already the dense hardwood forest to the north—that raw stretch of wilderness the locals called the barrens—was immersed in shadows. As far as the eye could see, a dark ocean of treetops rolled up the front range of the Green Ridge reservation. The air had turned gelid and fragrant with pine.

It braced Grove like a blast of smelling salts. "How about GPS?" he asked the old man.

"Ain't no good." The old retired miner, Jamie Lou Clinger's grandfather, slowly shook his head, his deeply lined face creasing with a frown. His name was Ryland Clinger, and in the twilight his leathery skin looked almost blue, as though six decades underground had permanently stained his skin. "Once ya get below a hundred feet, the mineral layer throws off the satellite. Let me see your piece."

"My what?" Grove looked at the old man.

"Your piece, your iron—whatever you're planning on carrying in there."

"Um, I don't—"

"I assume you're plannin' on bringin this shitheel down with something a little harsher than strong language?"

Grove knelt down and unzipped the duffel. He had not yet loaded the Bulldog. He pulled it out and handed it to the old miner.

The old man flung the pistol across the shoulder and into the shadows. It landed in the weeds with a thud. "Won't be needin' that," he muttered.

"What the hell—?!" Grove stared, aghast. "What are you doing?"

Clinger looked up at Grove with saggy, red-rimmed eyes flashing with anger. "I already told y'all, she's like an unlit fuse down there."

"Okay, but—"

"What's left of the air's got more damp-black gas in it than a dadburned Molotov cocktail. You start a shootin' match, you're gonna end up on the moon."

"All right!" Grove angrily zipped the duffel shut. "I get it."

"You're not still going down." Drinkwater stood

behind the old man, next to Jamie Lou, wringing her hands. "This is fucking crazy."

Grove rose to his feet, slung the duffel's strap over his shoulder. "You're probably right."

Drinkwater pushed her way past the girl, around the old man's walker, and up into Grove's face. "What do you really want here?" She spoke softly, intensely, drilling her gaze into his eyes.

"Drinkwater—"

"Answer the question. You want to take this cocksucker out?"

Grove nodded in the darkness. "That would be good."

"Then call in the goddamn cavalry." She grabbed his arm, squeezing. "It's your best shot. Listen to me. Get the TAC guys in there. They have remotes they can send down, cameras, you can flush the guy out."

"Getting him's only part of it," Grove said after looking into her eyes for a moment.

"Don't do this."

"I *have* to, I'm supposed to."

"That's just mumbo jumbo." She said this last .phrase in a broken voice, her eyes welling. Grove had not realized until this very moment how far Drinkwater had fallen for him. "At least take your .44 and a speed-loader," she pleaded.

Grove gave her a squeeze. "I appreciate the thought, I really do."

"Ulysses—"

"I'll see ya soon, Drinkwater. And don't worry so much, it's bad for your health." Grove turned and started across the weed-clogged ditch toward the trail.

"Young fella!"

The old man's voice made Grove pause and glance back at the threesome standing in the deeper shadows of the roadway. "Yes, sir?"

"I ain't sure you fully understand what it is yer about to do."

"Again, you're probably right . . . but if it's all the same to you I'm gonna go ahead and do it anyway."

The old man leaned forward on his walker, making it creak, as though punctuating the seriousness of his point. "This here is the U. S. of A., and the last time I checked, American citizens were free to go and get theirselves killed any old time they wanted to."

Grove looked at Drinkwater. "I'm not going to get myself killed."

Ryland Clinger let out a grunt, then trundled closer to where Grove was standing, across the ditch, in the shadows, near the trailhead. The old man was shaking with rage now. "Young fella. You listen to me. What yer about to do, you might as well count on gettin' yourself killed."

"Duly noted," Grove replied with a nod. "Now if you'll excuse me I gotta—"

"That mine is special in a lotta ways," the old man said, fire in his eyes. "Ways that ain't necessarily on no map. It's more than just bad luck. It's sour. The part of the earth, it's cursed."

"I understand—"

"No, I don't think ya do, I don't think ya got no idea what I'm talking about. But you will. When you go down there where it's permanent midnight, you will."

Grove looked at the old man. "I don't have any

choice in the matter." Then he looked at Drinkwater. "Maybe I never did."

And with that, Grove turned and plunged into the darkness of the woods.

THIRTY-SEVEN

In the hours after Grove entered the mine, Drinkwater went through a sort of modified five stages of grief back at the old man's battered RV.

The camper was parked less than a mile from the Wormwood trailhead, in a little scenic cul-de-sac along Rural Route 24, featuring a blacktop turn-off and a single picnic table overlooking a wooded gorge to the west of Valesburg. But that night, in the impermeable darkness that seemed to draw down on the valley like a great shroud, the primeval beauty of eastern Kentucky turned inside out with the grotesque grandeur of bat wings, unfurling in the silence, feeding Drinkwater's dread and guilt and remorse.

Would she ever see Grove again? Would they find him dead at the bottom of a coal mine? Would Drinkwater be blamed by the Bureau for Grove's erratic behavior after it all hit the fan? The questions plagued her throughout most of that night, despite the old man's and his granddaughter's best efforts to distract her. They played gin rummy on a little fold-down table in the reeking camper, they finished the old man's bottle of Jack Daniel's, and they studied old blueprints and maps of the Wormwood mine as it had been in its last year of operation—1972—discussing escape routes and possible exit points up north in the Green Ridge preserve through which Grove might emerge.

Grove's two handguns sat on the table next to a bowl of pork rinds like dead soldiers.

Drinkwater spent a lot of time staring at those two handguns, and the ammo magazines lying next to them—bad-luck charms taunting her. The longer she stared at them, the more sick to her stomach she felt. How could he leave his guns? She wanted to scream. She was getting drunk. She didn't want to play cards anymore. She felt as though fire ants were crawling all over her body.

At last, at around 2:05 A.M. that morning—and seismic readings across the eastern United States would later verify the exact time—Drinkwater rose from her seat to go to the bathroom when an enormous boom rang out from the east.

It was so sudden, so deep and immense—almost like an enormous depth charge rattling the sky— that Drinkwater was thrown right back onto the tattered bench seat next to a yelping Jamie Lou Clinger, who slammed against the window at the shock wave, banging the side of her head and cracking the glass. The entire six-ton camper shuddered sideways onto two wheels, nearly toppling over, throwing the old man—along with his walker— out of his chair and onto the corrugated floor. Cabinet doors flapped on their hinges. Glassware toppled, fell to the floor, shattered, and the entire chassis groaned before slamming down onto four wheels again with a massive bone-rattling thud.

For one horrible instant, the threesome lay there, paralyzed in the silence, gaping at one another, not a single word being exchanged, while puffs of insulation floated down from the cracked ceiling. They all knew where the explosion had originated.

Drinkwater's ears were ringing unmercifully and she felt her entire midsection seizing up with icy panic as she did the awful math in her head. Grove had been in the mine for almost seven hours. Nobody could have survived an explosion of that magnitude—not even the mysterious, resourceful, mystical Ulysses Grove. The RV was parked more than a mile from the mine, and it had felt as though someone had just set off a million sticks of dynamite right outside its door.

"Oh Lordy, no," the old man uttered in a toneless voice then, as he rose on trembling legs, using the bent walker to prop himself up. He was looking around the trailer as though it were filling with demons. "No, no, no, no—"

"You gotta be shittin' me." Jamie Lou struggled to her feet next to the table, her voice breathless with awe. "Holy fucking *shit.*"

"Here it comes," the old man mumbled in a warning voice, gripping the handles of his walker with knuckles so white and arthritic they looked petrified.

"Here comes *what?*" Drinkwater held onto a cabinet for balance.

"This ain't possible." Jamie Lou's eyes were huge and aimed up at the ceiling as though she were watching for some dark miracle.

Drinkwater spun toward a strange sound suddenly coming from outside—actually it was the sudden *absence* of sound: all the droning crickets

and insects and burbling tree frogs, so om-
nipresent in the Allegheny Mountains, abruptly
ceased with the violent suddenness of a CD cutting
off. "What? *What is it?!*"

The old man closed his eyes and braced himself. "Hell's been opened up," he murmured.

Drinkwater gawked at the old man, and was
about to scream something else at him when she
felt the first vibrations resonating like the tines of a
tuning fork beneath her feet. The sensation made
her freeze.

When Drinkwater was a kid, she used to visit a
cousin in Chicago who lived by the elevated train
tracks. Every night, Drinkwater would lie in a bunk
near the window and count the seconds before another deep vibration would begin gently shaking
the darkened bedroom. The shaking would rise
and rise as the train approached, until little Edith
had to slap her hands over her ears and brace herself against the bed frame for fear she would be vi-
brated right out of her bunk and onto the floor.
When the train finally passed in a magnificent
clamor of sparks and noise, it felt as though the
walls were going to fall down on top of her. This
feeling—magnified about a billion times—was exactly how Drinkwater felt right at this moment: as
though a gargantuan train was headed for the RV.

"Get under something!"

Jamie Lou's scream reached Drinkwater's ears
like the echo of a pistol shot, slightly out of synch
with what she was seeing: the teenager lurching
under the table, her mouth moving, but sounds
getting jumbled all together. The noise swirled
around Drinkwater now, glass breaking, the distant
crack of timbers like mortar fire, and a roaring

waterfall sound getting closer and closer, louder and louder, until the rushing white noise started sounding like a runaway train, a mad broken runaway train, as the vibrations made the RV convulse and buckle and crack down the middle.

Drinkwater dropped to the floor, curling into a fetal position and shrieking.

The floor shifted beneath her. Something popped like a firecracker in the wall, a gout of sparks spitting from an electrical outlet. The old man was under the table now next to his granddaughter, who was sobbing uncontrollably, but Drinkwater heard very little of their voices, the noise of broken pipes and groaning metal pounding in her ears. The chassis buckled beneath them.

Drinkwater slammed her eyes shut then, as cold greasy water came spraying down on top of them, and she started praying like crazy, she prayed to God that Grove had not unleashed something unnamable down there, something vast and inexorable—a genie that could never be put back. God would answer her frenzied query soon enough.

Over the next few moments, in fact, Drinkwater would begin to learn the true nature of what Grove had done in that mine—

—which began six hours and fifty-seven minutes earlier, with Grove's journey into darkness.

PART III
The Wormwood Event

And in the lowest deep a lower deep
Still threatening to devour me . . .
To which the hell I suffer seems a heaven.

—JOHN MILTON, *Paradise Lost*

The true nature of the murderous
psychopath may be too painful for the sane
to face: that they are us.

—ULYSSES GROVE, *The Psychopathological
Archetype: Toward a Statistical Model*

THIRTY-EIGHT

The first thing Grove noticed upon entering the Pithead building at exactly 6:51 P.M. Eastern Standard Time, after flipping on his heavy-duty flashlight and playing it across Peg-Board panels laden with rows of old dented miner hats, long forgotten and furry with dust, was the absence of a hole in the ground.

Where the hell was the shaft?

He stood there for endless moments, his back against the wall, his heart thumping. He had no idea when and where and how he would ambushed—the killer could be lurking right there in that vestibule building—so he didn't move for a quite a long while, allowing his eyes to adjust to the darkness, allowing his heart to calm down.

At length he got a fix on the immediate area just inside that rusted metal door—the lock bore the scars of a recent jimmy-stick, undoubtedly the entrance through which John Q had passed at some point over the last few days—and then, very slowly, he scanned the light beam across filthy aluminum walls. The beam flitted across dusty objects that confirmed Old Man Clinger's overview of the place.

An old rolltop desk sat nearby, probably once stationed there to induct new miners or process time cards but now congealed shut in the eternal darkness, lined with filth and age. Ramshackle wooden chairs lay along the wall to the left, most of them overturned and cocooned in spiderwebs. Stalactites of dust-lined calcium deposits hung down from the ceiling like fuzzy icicles. Kerosene lanterns spoke of old-fashioned eras.

It was hard to tell in the dark, with his one good eye, but the room seemed to stretch at least fifty feet or so, terminating at a wall drifted with trash. A doorway to the right—now boarded with Sheetrock—most likely led to the washhouse, and to the left, another sealed door was probably the lamp cabin.

According to Clinger, miners would emerge at the end of each day, exhausted, wheezing, their faces black with dust, hauling their lunch buckets and water jugs. They would go to the lamp cabin and return their headlamp and battery for recharging. In return they would receive a brass tag, like a coatroom token, embossed with their ID number. Batteries were engraved with the same numbers.

A Peg-Board wall full of hooks near the door, like the board on which keys are hung in a parking garage, displayed the brass ID tags of miners currently on shift. In the event of a cave-in or some other disaster, the board would tell rescuers how many souls were trapped. At Wormwood, with all its misadventures, some of the miners had come to call the board "Death Row."

The second thing Grove noticed about that outer building was the smell. The moldy rock floor and cobweb-filmed walls exuded a kind of acrid metallic must, like the inside of a book that hadn't been opened for centuries. Grove's nose—finely tuned from years of failed gourmet cooking experiments—recognized lower notes beneath the mélange of filth. Assorted vermin long since decayed to dust, dried animal droppings, desiccated rats.

He froze.

Right up until that very moment—as his body became very still, very rigid and tense—he had secretly harbored doubts that John Q Public was indeed waiting for him there, somewhere in the depths of that deserted mine. Grove's intuition had tricked him more than once in the past. His calculations had frequently been wrong, his inner voice off the mark. And he knew if he allowed himself to think too hard about the wisdom of walking into a trap, he would check himself into a rubber room. But right then, as the beam of his flashlight brushed along the edge of something shiny on the far wall, he knew with unalloyed certainty that he had come to the right place.

His destiny had brought him here, his whole life leading up to this single act.

Death waited for him in the darkness below.

A few minutes passed. Hard to tell how many. The passage of time had already started breaking down in the dark, like a yolk separating from the white. At last Grove managed to make his legs work and went over to the far wall.

He dropped his duffel bag. It made a loud clanking noise that did not echo in the dark airless chamber. He knelt and unzipped the bag, trying to gather his thoughts, ignoring the voices whispering like night breezes in his midbrain. He found his surgical gloves and snapped one on each hand.

The blood on the wall was fresh. It looked like raspberry jam clinging to the ancient aluminum bulwark.

Grove went over to it and brushed a rubber-tipped finger across the outer lines of the design. Was it human or animal blood? It didn't really matter—the drawing was proof positive that John Q lurked somewhere in the labyrinth below, and it made the back of Grove's neck prickle: *the gun-target silhouette from his class.*

It was a perfect rendering, carefully drawn in simple thick outlines, the bulbous head, the rounded-off shoulders, the circle around it. The style was like a finger painting done by a brilliant child: the faceless archetype in all its blank, dead, impassive glory.

Grove stepped back and shone the light around its edges. There was a second blood-painting about eight feet away: another rendering of the silhouette, almost an exact copy, staring blankly back at him. Two generic silhouettes of every-killers.

A perfect pair.

Grove's spine went cold. It was a message meant for him and him alone.

Wait, wait a minute, wait a minute. He stared at the twin silhouettes, stared and pondered. In the space between the symbols, a stack of uneven panels of plywood leaned against the wall—the wood so old and gray and petrified it looked like flint—and he realized there was something behind the plywood.

He reached for the panels and shoved them aside with a grunt.

The doorway behind the wood was molded out of aluminum casting. About the size of a submarine hatch, it lay wide open, displaying the utter darkness on the other side, a darkness that seemed to have a weight and texture to it not unlike tar. Now Grove remembered the old man explaining the mine's layout, and the fact that access to the shaft would not be in the outer building, but would instead lie further in.

Grove went over to the duffel bag, knelt down, and as carefully and silently as possible started removing his "hit kit."

Since traditional sidearms were out of the question, he pulled out an eleven-inch-long Randall-style knife made by a Kenyan blacksmith. The blade was serrated along one edge and sheathed in buttery brown leather—a family heirloom meant to kill ibex that he had thrown into his bag back at Pelican Bay because he was going on instinct now. The sheath was engraved with a Swahili phrase: *Ukwenda babili kwali wama pa chalo.*

He aimed the flashlight at the sheath, and looked at the engraving. He blinked. The darkness must have already been working on him. He blinked again, and shook his head, because he saw something crawling across the end of the sheath like delicate little veins spreading in the grain, like silken spiderwebs branching in the darkness, beginning to form words: *Nnn nn nn nn n n nnnn d d d d d deya ndeya ndeya no mwana ndeya ndeya no mwana wandi munshila ba mpapula—*

Grove dropped the knife.

It made an inordinately loud clatter in the dead

stillness of the Pit shed, and Grove tensed all over, his testicles shrinking up into his pelvic bone, because the knife sheath was telling him to cross over into the land of shadows, to sacrifice himself, to martyr himself, but if there was one thing Grove didn't need right now it was more advice from visions. He was there to kill a killer, and that's all he was going to do. Nothing fancy. Nothing mystical.

He looked at the sheath.

It had returned to normal.

Grove let out a tense sigh. He realized he was breathing very quickly already, almost panting. He had to get his brain under control.

He attached the sheath to his belt, then dug in the duffel for the rest of his supplies. He found the stun gun—about the size of a cigarette pack, with a pistol grip—its hardwired spike carrying fifty thousand watts of persuasive voltage. He stuffed the stun gun into the back pocket of his jeans. His hands shook slightly. But it wasn't unmanageable.

Nearly a dozen other items came out of the duffel and went into the pockets of his duster, into small nylon packs attached to his belt, or onto a strap around his neck: night-vision goggles, oxygen mask, small digital camera, batteries, stainless-steel handcuffs, a smaller halogen penlight with a head strap, protein bars, a small pickax, a bottle of water, and the poison pellet in its sinister little government-issue vial.

That last item—which he stashed in the inside pocket of his duster—screamed madness at him. The futility of what he was doing, the folly, the hubris, the waste—it all came bubbling up through him like a wave of doom. He was supposed to be the master of this strange obscure corner of law enforcement called behavioral profiling. Now look at him. Obliging a madman, walking into certain death. Was it possible the monster shared his DNA?

His bloodline?

The final item transferred from the duffel to Grove's person was a small handcrafted pouch made of doeskin by an anonymous African artisan. Inside the pouch were essential talismans—bones, feathers, beads, animal paws, and lucky charms—acquired over a lifetime of secret ruminations. He put the pouch in his pants pocket and zipped the duffel bag shut.

It was time to surgically remove the cancer. He rose and took a deep breath.

Then he passed through the door into the darkness on the other side.

THIRTY-NINE

Residents of Valesburg, Kentucky, had good reason to steer clear of Wormwood Mine. First drilled in 1897, the new mine was part of the decadent Gilded Age of industrialization—an era during which the vast, rich coal deposits beneath the Allegheny Mountains began feeding America's insatiable hunger for that black narcotic known as fossil fuel. But there was something wrong at Wormwood from the start.

Maybe it was simply bad luck. Maybe it was something about the soil, or the way the earth had been breached. Or perhaps there was something sacred about this "driftless" region of Kentucky. Geologists refer to areas that remained stationary during the glacial shifts of the Paleozoic period as "driftless."

Today, these driftless regions are as rare as black diamond deposits. They lay beneath the bedrock like stubborn prehistoric roots. Their marrow is as old as the solar system, their minerals and sediments reaching back to the formation of the earth.

Cultists believe these driftless regions offer pipelines to the netherworld.

Since the establishment of their town in 1811, citizens of Valesburg, Kentucky, have preferred *not* to think about it.

Grove found a *second* vestibule-style room, this one smaller than the outer chamber, with a cobblestone floor.

The darkness thickened like a soup, congealing around him, absolutely no moonlight penetrating the low ceiling now. He paused.

He looked over his shoulder, then turned around and around, the beam of his flashlight threading through ancient motes of dust and age, the particles floating like luminous plankton in the sea of black.

The beam landed on a rusted enclosure resembling a construction manhole, surrounded by battered stanchions and sawhorses. Part of the lift had been broken away, the bent pole lying on the floor.

Grove went over to the shaft and shone his light down inside the elevator.

His pulse quickened as he saw the gaping hole in the floor, and the deeper blackness within it, showing through the jagged maw. The mine shaft appeared to be about eight to ten feet in diameter, plunging down into utter darkness darker than the inside of a womb.

Someone had taken a crowbar to the elevator's floor, someone with incredible strength, snapping rivets with the ease of ripping buttons off a shirt. With no electrical power, that someone would have had to climb down the step-pads embedded in the wall of the shaft.

Grove took a deep breath, his duster laden with supplies, already feeling as though it weighed a ton. He climbed into the elevator enclosure, the flashlight hanging around his neck. It took him a few minutes of grunting effort to lower himself through the hole in the floor, guiding his movements mostly by feel.

At last he got his right toe wedged into the first rung of the footholds.

He began to descend.

In the early days of the mine, ponies would power the conveyor belts and coal carts, and gas lamps would light the shafts and corridors. In its second year of operation, twenty-three men perished underground when gas lanterns ignited the flammable coal dust that hangs like veils in the airless tunnels. Cave-ins would occur on a weekly basis. Giant drill bits periodically breached into the nearby Mannehequa River, flooding the labyrinth, drowning miners and shutting down operations for months.

But these mishaps were expected—they were the standard risks of the day.

Wormwood, unlike other mines, had a *second* tier of misfortune that many attributed to otherworldly sources.

In just over seven decades, Wormwood Mining Company lost more than two thousand men in the darkness below its pit sheds. Many deaths were unexplained, many bodies never recovered. Scores of fatalities—often listed euphemistically in company reports as "environmental"—were self-inflicted. Miners ate the muzzles of shotguns, spattering their brain tissue across the lampblack. Or they threw themselves down shafts, or emptied their veins into the cinderdust. Madness at Wormwood was as common as the dry, hacking cough of a lifetimer.

In 1927 a drill operator died of blood loss after severing his own penis with a cable cutter and tucking the organ neatly into his lunch bucket. Four years later an entire crew went blind, just spontaneously lost their sight. And then in 1948 a strange radio transmission came up from the bottom of shaft number four, where a dozen miners had been cutting a new branch.

The message, a nearly unintelligible garble of laughter and sobbing, was received only minutes before the branch caved in, killing all twelve men. Court-sealed transcripts included the following: *"We opened it . . . horrible . . . alive . . . the end of us . . . the end of all of us."*

Grove steadily descended. One step at a time. One handhold after another. His heavy breathing echoed in synch with his movements, his eyes dilated and hyperalert. After every step he methodically glanced downward, but all he could see in the swaying beam of his flashlight—which still dangled from his neck—were the endless footholds plunging down into the black void.

The lining of the shaft, a rough, pebbly surface of minerals and earth, hovered only inches from his nose as he descended, and smelled of mire and offal. A narrow iron rail ran along each side of him, and the rungs, at least a century old, were made of stone, carved into the shaft wall like big thumbnails.

At the moment, Grove felt dangerously exposed on the side of the shaft, a duck in a shooting gallery. He could feel John Q Public's presence below him as pervasive as a shark circling the depths, biding its time. Grove picked up his pace a little, ignoring his creaking knees and his cramping fingers—still clad in their rubber surgical gloves.

According to Old Man Clinger, the front shaft plunged more than a quarter of a mile down to the first level. But how long would that take at this rate?

Grove estimated that the footholds were about eighteen inches apart, and each hesitant step was taking him about two to three seconds to complete. At this rate he would make it to the first level—Junction A, as it was known in Wormwood literature—in about an hour.

Old Man Clinger had drawn up meticulous maps of the mine, mostly by memory, revealing the vast network of shafts and tunnels and passageways.

Essentially, the main work area of Wormwood Mine lay twelve hundred feet under the Kentucky countryside and was shaped like a huge italic E. Junction A was the upper right-hand corner, which served as the threshold to the first level (or the top finger of the E). The back slope was the backbone of the E, plummeting nearly ten thousand feet down, past prehistoric layers of sandstone, shale, and limestone.

It was the longest single deep-mine shaft in the history of Western civilization.

Along that impossibly deep shaft were mazes of chambers and tunnels carved into the coal seams—the middle and lower arms of the E—that defied description. Known in mining circles as pillar rooms, these underground labyrinths resembled black stone ghost towns, honeycombed with dead ends and blind alleys, where mining drills had sucked the pulp out of the earth. They went on and on, literally for miles, until they butted up against another mine or an underground body of water. Grove fully expected to find John Q waiting for him somewhere within these silent, forgotten cities of the dead.

Over the years, three separate religious "interventions" were secretly performed on the Wormwood property. In March of 1939, under the cloak of night, a Catholic priest, garbed in full purple vestment, rode in a coal car down to level one, twelve thousand feet down, waving his smoking incense brazier the whole way, his quavering nervous litany echoing off the stone tunnels. The exorcism apparently didn't take—or perhaps it had been the wrong denomination—because the Baptists tried it again in the fall of 1952, just eleven months before the Great Disaster. Deacon Earl Pritzker spent five straight hours blessing the shale strata in shaft number two with a gold cross procured from the Crystal Cathedral in Lexington.

The following summer, on a sultry July night, a sudden and unexplained fire raged through the mine, sending all 311 workers present to their deaths. The maelstrom burned out of control for seven days and seven nights, turning the twin air shafts into volcanic cannons, scorching a five-square-mile radius around the property and touching off forest fires as far away as Charleston. They called it the Great Disaster, and Wormwood achieved national notoriety for a few years.

Time magazine did a piece on the alleged "Wormwood Curse" the following year. "A Pox on the Earth" read the headline, and miners' families wrote angry letters to the editor demanding that the company shut the mine down, raze the buildings, and salt the earth forevermore.

Wormwood managed to stay in business for one reason and one reason only: it made money. *Hand over fist,* as the old-timers used to say. At the end of the 1950s, for instance, despite its history of misfortune, the mine was generating three hundred thousand tons of coal a year, and grossing over $45 million. Wormwood remained operational, in fact, until the spring of 1972, when the last heir to the Carlisle family, who owned the mine, passed away under somewhat mysterious circumstances. Earlier that winter, ironically, Valesburg town elders had staged a ceremonial protest and prayer service at the mouth of shaft number one. Months later, Harman Carlisle's will, which was disputed in various courts for years afterward, ultimately dissolved the corporation.

After that, the mine, like an unmarked grave, simply lay rotting in the Kentucky wilderness, a grim testament to America's voracious appetite for more of everything.

Grove saw solid ground looming beneath him at exactly one hour and thirteen minutes after he had entered the shaft. *Home at last, home at last, ollie ollie oxen free!*

Grove awkwardly hopped off the last rung with the palsied exhaustion of an astronaut leaping to the surface of the moon. He landed with a grunt, and fell backward, the items in his overstuffed pockets throwing off his balance. He landed on his ass.

The flashlight snapped its strap, rolled, and hit the wall, the impact instantly cutting off the beam.

Grove was plunged into darkness unlike any darkness he had ever experienced.

FORTY

It was darkness that weighed a million tons, darkness that choked the life out of him, that crashed down on him and made his skin crawl. It was the darkness of deep space. *Inner space.*

For a moment he couldn't breathe.

He managed to sit up. His legs screamed and ached from the interminable descent. His heart raced. He instinctively raised his hands and felt the air, which was so thin he had to labor to get a breath. His throat burned. His nostrils stung from the methane and ancient dust fog. He tried to stand, but his balance had gone haywire.

Panic took hold of him then, as he frantically felt the cinder-strewn ground around him for the flashlight. He clenched his teeth and spots of light dotted his blind eye. He started breathing so rapidly and heavily he was nearly hyperventilating. *Calm down*, he commanded himself, *calm the hell down, or you'll die a purposeless, lonely death down here without even engaging the enemy!*

He forced himself to rise to a kneeling position,

forced himself to take deep steadying breaths. His heart rate began to settle.

Tiny radiant artifacts swam like luminous stars across his narrow field of vision as he got very still, trying to organize his thoughts. He needed to get his bearings and strategize. He needed to adjust to the bottom-of-the-ocean darkness, the tomblike atmosphere, the disorienting claustrophobia. Most of all, he needed to find the opening that led into that first level.

In his mind he retraced his movements, trying to extrapolate the position of the flashlight.

At last he gave up and reached in his coat pocket and felt around for the smaller halogen headlamp. He wasn't sure about the night-vision goggles— they required *some* level of ambient light in order to function—but he quickly found the halogen light and untangled it from a jumble of supplies in his side pocket. Working blindly in the dark, working solely on feel, he strapped the light around his head, felt for the switch, and flipped it on.

The slender beam leapt across a fifty-square-foot alcove of hard-packed earth. A wheelbarrow lay overturned to the right, slathered in cobwebs.

Grove managed to stand on weak legs. He slowly turned toward a doorway.

The narrow silver beam of light illuminated the top corner of an arched entrance ten feet away. Petrified wooden timbers framed the low-ceilinged passageway.

Grove looked up. His light brushed a message hastily scrawled in blood across the lintel. A garbled mess of words yammered at him, the same dead language found at the previous crime scenes. Grove sniffed in the silence.

He turned, and the beam of his headlamp landed on a human face.

The face smiled.

Its teeth were bloodstained.

"*Jesus!*" Grove jerked back as though slapped, the halogen light slipping off his head.

In a flash of silver light John Q Public pounced out of the shadows, a sharp object in his hand, going for Grove's throat.

FORTY-ONE

It happened so abruptly, so unexpectedly, so jar-ringly fast, that Grove barely registered it in the streaks of light from the halogen headlamp bounc-ing off the walls: a tall, glistening brown giant, as tense as a coil of steel cable, darting out of the darkness, a sharp metal object raised in his power-ful right hand.

Grove let out a yawp, rearing back, as the as-sailant swung the knife or scalpel or ice pick or whatever it was down toward Grove's jugular—

—but Grove got lucky because he had raised his left hand on instinct to block the blow; and sure enough, John Q's wrist struck Grove's arm, pre-venting the point from sinking into Grove's artery, the tip only kissing his flesh and the sudden iner-tia heaving the two men into the opposite wall with a bone-rattling thud.

Grove managed to shove the immense black man off him before John Q could recover. John Q staggered backward, the heel of his right foot bumping the halogen light, which now lay on the ground.

The lamp skidded, the silver ribbons of light streaking and blurring across the dark threshold.

Grove gasped for air, lurching away from his attacker. He had no time to arm the stun gun; it was tucked too deeply into his pocket.

Meanwhile, ten feet away, the assailant banged into the opposite wall, letting out a feral grunt that sounded like that of a large rabid animal. He still had his weapon clutched in his huge hand.

For a single instant, in a swirling streak of silver light, Grove caught a glimpse of John Q Public, who now looked like a giant hairless biped, his naked tattoo-covered body filmed from head to toe with coal dust. His bald head bore the criss-crossing gouges of self-inflicted knife wounds, still oozing with blood.

Only his dead gray eyes—his fish eyes—seemed luminous with insanity.

Grove managed to get his hand around the grip of the Randall knife against his hip. It came out of the sheath with a dry husky whisper as he squared himself in the darkness. The halogen light had settled against the corner, its beam now glowing up through the fog of dust.

A piercing howl erupted out of the darkness across the threshold, a primordial death wail pouring out of the monster who had once gone by the name John Q Public—

—and then the beast pounced again, coming at Grove with almost robotic fury, those dead eyes like dim headlamps in the dark, filled with sickness.

The next instant seemed to freeze in time as the two men came at each other. Knife fights are like that. Chaotic, jerky, inexact affairs.

"*Come on, come on, motherfucker, come on!*" Grove bellowed as he made a wide swipe toward the man's face, wanting to drive the blade through that diseased brain.

John Q's weapon arced down at precisely the same moment, and the two blades sideswiped each other, metal scraping metal, spitting a single spark like a match tip igniting in Grove's face.

This time the wild inertia drove both men backward, Grove losing his footing, stumbling, falling backward; John Q tripping over his own bare feet, toppling and going down to the floor.

They landed hard on train tracks embedded in the stone, spine-wrenching hard, Grove hitting the rails on the small of his back, the halogen light in his eyes now, the sudden pain stabbing his tailbone, John Q sprawling down on top of him with a gasp.

It felt like a piano had fallen on Grove, the full weight of the killer smashing down on his ribs, compressing his lungs, squeezing the breath out of him. The stench of char-smoke and BO assaulted Grove.

With one great heaving gasp he willed the knife toward the monster's midsection, a sharp thrust, the blade only managing to graze oily flesh.

John Q shrieked, a caterwaul of pain like a cat being skinned, suddenly convulsing, then he rolled off Grove with panther stealth, rolling into the darkness, rolling off into the shadows of the threshold until he bounced off the adjacent stone wall.

Grove rolled in the other direction, seeing stars, ears ringing, gripped in pain, holding his neck with his free hand where he had been stung by something very sharp.

The monster was up again, moving inhumanly fast, a shuffling shadow across the space, which made Grove scoot back against the far wall, gasping, the halogen light on the ceiling, his bloody Randall knife raised in a defensive posture, his guts freezing up.

He did all of this despite the sharp stinging sensation in the back of his neck.

Over the years Grove had seen perps on PCP slam their hands though car windows, tear through jumbles of barbed wire, bite chunks of flesh out of adversaries' arms, and right then he saw a similar miracle on the edges of that flashlight beam, because John Q had just vanished with the agility of a jaguar.

Just for an instant, trying to see in the darkness through his one good eye, trying to catch his breath, his back against the rock, his head spinning, Grove thought the monster had simply ceased to exist, had simply dematerialized, had simply faded back into the utter blackness on the edges of that hellish, reeking, greasy shaft.

Then Grove reached for the halogen and got his hand around it and shined it to his left, then to his right.

The narrow opening through which the killer had fled now gaped in front of Grove, which all at once reminded Grove of the Wormwood layout according to Old Man Clinger. The three-foot wide, five-foot-high submarine hatch led miners into the labyrinth of level one.

In the momentary silence that followed the knife fight, Grove swallowed the pain and rose on aching legs. He had to stand there a moment in order to catch his breath, the knife still gripped in one hand, the headlamp gripped in the other.

He listened.

The distant sound of nimble bare footsteps padding back into the black midnight reached his ringing ears. He let out a pained sigh, wiped the knife blade on his pants, then put the weapon back into its sheath.

The stinging pain in the back of his neck felt hot now, hot and wet. He reached back with his free hand and felt a small object hanging off his skin like a thorn, or a plastic tag. He gently plucked it off.

He looked at it. His heart quickened, his scrotum contracting deeper into his body.

It was a hypodermic needle.

FORTY-TWO

Working in the darkness, breathless with panic, Grove lanced the puncture wound with his knife, squeezing it as though it were a snakebite. The pain was tremendous. It seared his shoulders and burned down between his shoulder blades. Then he rinsed the wound with bottled water. He drank the rest of the water, forcing it down in order to dilute the unknown dose as much as possible.

The good news was, most of the pale yellow fluid contained in that tiny vial behind the needle's plunger had remained there. Grove had no idea how many milligrams of the stuff—whatever it was—had actually reached his bloodstream.

But he knew *some* of it had.

He felt woozy and nauseous and light-headed, and also strangely disengaged, as though he were completely removed now from the passage of time. He had no idea how long he lingered there in that dark antechamber, trying every field remedy he could think of to counteract whatever had been injected into his system. It could have been minutes, could have been hours.

It could have been centuries.

By the time he got himself bandaged and ready to travel deeper into the netherworld, he felt cauterized, denatured—as though he had somehow aged a thousand years and had become a wraith, a shadow of a human being. He stood in that narrow opening for a moment, his legs feeling like stilts, his feet a mile away.

He pulled out the stun gun from his pocket.

The device was in a holster. It weighed about a pound, and had a coil of silver cable on a quick-release loop on one side connected to the projectile dart. It had to be armed in order to operate. Grove had never used one in the field, but had gone through a training seminar back in the midnineties when the things were introduced to the FBI.

He put the halogen lamp between his teeth and used both hands to arm the stun gun. He thumbed the safety off, then pressed the on button—a faint tone rising in pitch like a camera strobe replenishing. He stuffed the gun into its holster, and clipped the holster to his belt next to the Randall knife for quick and easy access.

The passageway lay before him, less than ten feet away, but it seemed to waver and undulate in the beam of his halogen lamp like a mirage drifting farther and farther away. Grove braced himself against the wall of the antechamber, a wave of dizziness washing over him.

He clenched his teeth and began to pray his silent Swahili prayers again, summoning courage, summoning his powers of concentration. It was dawning on Grove that the contents of that hypo might have been some kind of hallucinogen or psychedelic—especially considering John Q's background: the tattooed killer had terrorized the mean streets of south Chicago for years as a sort of mute, meth-head Robin Hood. He would rob dealers at knifepoint without saying a word, then sell their wares at reduced rates back to skels and crack whores for a quick buck.

By the time Grove had encountered the man in the Karen Slattery investigation, though, the killer must have succumbed to his own products, because he was so far gone he could barely hold his head up.

Back then John Q had worn a full Isaac Hayes–style beard, as well as a scraggly greasy mop of a natural. Tonight, however, in the fleeting glimpses and violent flashes of halogen light, the man looked like a different person. With his clean-shaven face, gray eyes, and scourged bald head, John Q looked not only more dangerous and high-functioning than he had years ago, he also reminded Grove of somebody.

At first, of course, in the heat of the knife fight, Grove could not grasp who it was that this guy resembled. The chiseled face underneath the ornate Aboriginal-style tattoos, the hollow eyes behind the coal-dusted visage, and the prominent cheekbones behind the scowling look of madness—all of it strummed a painful chord deep within Grove, and he kept going back to it as he stood there in front of that ancient hatchway, preparing to enter the labyrinth.

Now it struck Grove with the full force of a ball-peen hammer to his skull.

John Q looked like Grove.

"It doesn't matter," Grove muttered under his

breath, fighting the dizziness, steadying himself on the frame of the hatch.

He tossed the halogen light through the doorway.

The lamp bounced and skipped across the rails embedded in the main corridor, sending its narrow beam past pillars of black shale. Grove shivered with bloodlust. He would go in there and kill them all—all the sick monsters who had ruined Grove's life—he would kill them all by killing their Archetype, their dark avatar.

He found the second flashlight on the floor of the antechamber where it had landed during the fight, and tossed it through the doorway as well.

It banged down the corridor, the light streaking in Grove's eyes, forming brilliant tendrils of yellow fire in the blackness, and coming to rest pointing upward, shining on the low ceiling about thirty-five feet away. Grove reached into his duster pocket for the night-vision goggles.

He put them on.

Then he entered level one with his left palm resting on the stun gun.

The plan was to illuminate the mine with enough ambient light to allow him to navigate the far reaches of the pillar rooms with the infrared goggles. It worked for about ten minutes and about five hundred feet. The thick conical eyepieces, heavy on the bridge of his nose, penetrated the darkness with the accuracy of an X-ray machine.

In the green glow he saw the endless grid of dead-end tunnels, excavated and forgotten over the years like bombed-out alleys in a war-torn city. All the empty chambers, visible through rows of doorways like rotted teeth, bore the scars of old mining machines and drills.

The air burned his lungs and twinkled and glistened with flakes of lampblack dust.

Walking was not easy. He could hear his own footsteps crunching in the cinders, his heart hammering in his ears, but they seemed to belong to another body, not his own. The ceiling brushed the top of his head, and the goggles, irised down into a periscope effect by his one good eye, created a sensation of floating.

He reached a junction of tunnels and paused, his hand on the stun gun's grip.

A faint breathing sound came from somewhere off in the labyrinth, maybe fifty feet away, maybe closer. He drew the stun gun from its holster and reared back until his tailbone struck the stone wall.

The strangest thing happened then: it all started getting funny to him.

FORTY-THREE

Some hidden part of him, buried way back in the recesses of his mind, screamed that it was the drug, the yellow fluid in the vial, the tincture of poison that had gotten into him, but the urge to laugh was so strong because the luminous dust motes dancing across his infrareds looked a lot like snowflakes, and that seemed so ridiculous he started giggling and thinking of a Bob Hope Christmas special: *Ladies and gentlemen, a special holiday greeting to all our boys in the service stationed down here in hell, we've got a great show planned for you tonight, we've got Joey Heatherton, Rip Taylor, The Amazing Kreskin, and a nifty apocalyptic battle between two displaced spirits for the fate of the world!*

Grove's breathy giggling climbed the musical register into a full-bodied, intoxicated laugh.

He laughed so hard his eyes watered and he nearly doubled over, which was unfortunate, because he didn't see the dark figure emerging from the alcove thirty feet away until it was too late to take cover.

The projectile jumped up across his infrareds the moment he looked up.

Grove jerked against the wall at the last possible moment; the silver blur whizzed past him, only inches away from his face, striking the wall behind him and making a loud clanging noise as it scraped the stone.

The spark flared green in Grove's goggles, the back of his head tagging the wall—*ouch!*—the sharp pain like a crack across the chartreuse view screen, crawling down the back of his spine.

A knife! In the snow! On Christmas morning! Grove giggled hysterically at the absurdity of it all—one of Santa's evil elves, no doubt, wanting to play Tom-and-Jerry games in the basement toy factory. Okay, fine, great, looks like loads of fun!

Grove darted across the main corridor, his stun gun gripped in his sweaty palm, the view screen lit up with movement in the tunnel about twenty-five feet away, a blurry figure spinning toward an adjacent doorway. Yellow rose petals of light trailed after the evil twin.

"I see you!"

Grove's shrill voice sounded in his own ears as though it were sped up to *Alvin and the Chipmunks* speed, juiced with helium, which made him chortle all the more uncontrollably as he raised the stun gun and fired off a shot at the dark figure diving for cover inside a rock cut.

Blue tendrils of lightning stitched through the darkness and struck the stone wall, five feet short of the rock cut, making the chartreuse view screen bloom with brilliant delicate veins of color in the falling snow. Grove was awed by it and let out a mesmerized laugh.

He ducked inside a ten-by-ten-foot chamber of darkness left decades ago by a mining drill.

The darkness awoke around him. Purple flowers blossomed across the walls in time-lapse, invisible icy-blue candle flames coming to life in the corners. Grove pressed his back against the wall near the opening and thumbed the recharge button on the stun gun.

The bullwhip sound of the cable-spike being sucked back into the gun filled Grove's ears.

Out in the main tunnel, the sound of breathing rose and bounced off the moldering stone bulwark like a beautiful symphony of whispers. Grove looked down at his hand and saw that his rubber-gloved fingers had changed. They had swollen to cartoon proportions. Like fat sausages in white gloves. Great big Mickey Mouse fingers.

God, it was hilarious, and it made Grove let out wild guffaws of laughter in the radiant darkness of that rock chamber, so wild that he dropped the stun gun. It clattered cheerfully across the coal cinders. Grove giggled convulsively for several moments.

Outside the doorway, the breathing sounds had faded away into tomblike silence.

Still giggling, Grove awkwardly scooped up his stun gun, turned, and lumbered out the door.

John Q had vanished. Dematerialized. His presence absorbed into the walls like a vapor.

Feverishly searching that black netherworld known as level one—with its charred ruins and ancient passageways, its gaslit pillar rooms and prehistoric train tunnels—Grove was reminded, much to his ironic, drugged amusement, of Victorian Whitechapel, where Jack the Ripper had similarly eluded authorities with supernatural stealth. It also brought to mind New Orleans, where the Holy Ghost had haunted forgotten back allies of the French Quarter. It was Every-Hell, the *locus malefactum*—the place of savagery that had tainted Grove's dreams for most of his life—and now it had swallowed John Q like a giant gullet . . . until Grove had to admit to himself, still giggling maniacally, that he was hopelessly lost. Lost in the first circle of hell with a few protein bars, a knife, and a brain under the influence of unknown chemicals.

By the time Grove reached the alcove on the far side of level one—a site the older, more grizzled miners used to call The Asshole of the Universe— his hilarity had transformed, almost imperceptively, into the stoic awe of a dreamer regarding a dream.

Or perhaps *nightmare* was a better word.

On his green view screen he saw the massive rusted arms of the block-and-tackle crane like a great fossilized praying mantis standing guard over the second, deeper shaft. He saw the giant oxidized pulley wheel that raised and lowered coal buckets and miners thousands of feet down into the mine's innermost viscera. *How low can you go? You ain't seen nothin' yet, ladies and gentlemen!*

Dizziness washed over Grove then, the darkness popping and fizzing all around him, shadows coming to life on his view screen like noxious black dust devils of poisonous glittering sparks. He dropped the stun gun. The sound clattered and echoed.

He staggered backward, nearly losing his balance. He gripped the side of a stone pillar for balance. The narcotic noose tightened, an anvil pressing down on his head. He fell to his knees. He ripped the goggles from his face and flung them into the deeper shadows near the pit. They scudded and echoed across the stone floor before coming to rest near the lip of the shaft.

The darkness strangled him then. It squeezed its cold fingers over his face. He blinked and stared back at the crackling, flickering abyss. It was impermeable, this darkness, as opaque as onyx, but it was also alive in Grove's mind with a menagerie of shapes and colors and strange denizens of the deep with their cloven tails and rippling antennae and fluorescent eyes floating on undulating stalks.

Grove laughed at the desolate beauty of this absurd world, this anus of the universe.

He laughed and laughed as he threaded trembling hands through his frizzy hair, and he laughed some more, and soon he was tearing hanks of his tightly coiled hair from his scalp, and even these sharp pangs of agony were accompanied by beautiful fireworks of light, right up until the point he heard the footsteps behind him—the heavy, methodical, rhythmic footsteps.

Coming toward him.

FORTY-FOUR

Under normal circumstances Grove would have easily darted for cover—or at least crawled the eleven feet or so between him and the fallen stun gun—but now the drug had gotten its hooks into his nervous system, and all he could manage was a hamstrung attempt at rising to his feet. His partially paralyzed legs tangled immediately.

He collapsed into a heap on the cold cinders. His vision blurring, his mind veiled in narcotic haze, he could very faintly make out the shape of a figure about fifty feet away, coming toward him, closing the distance slowly, steadily, taking careful strides.

Transfixed, gazing through the tunnel of his single functional eye, Grove watched the figure approach. On some level it was a clear to Grove now that it was John Q coming to finish him off. The game was over, and now all that was left was the formality of death. But right then, Grove could not stop marveling at the *manner* in which John Q was approaching.

The strangest part was not that fact that the figure held some kind of a blunt weapon in one hand, a leather sap or an old-fashioned blackjack, the kind used to stun a hog bound for slaughter. Nor was it the fact that the man was as naked as the day he was born, oily with sweat and sticky with blood from the knife wound in his side, or the fact that his long thick penis was semi-erect, bouncing with each stride.

The strangest part was the fact that the man was walking on the ceiling.

Grove blinked and giggled and stared. And giggled and gaped some more. And he tried to register through the drugged laughter what he was seeing: an upside-down doppelgänger, creeping toward him in the pitch-dark with the nimble, jerky motions of a housefly. Grove had to literally feel the floor around him to make sure *he* was still adhering to the laws of physics.

With the spastic tics of a spider sniffing its prey, the monster loomed.

Grove looked up at it, wide-eyed and transfixed. He couldn't move. He couldn't feel his arms. Something pinched him around his ankle, but there was nothing he could do. His legs felt as though they were light-years away right now, as though they belonged to some other solar system.

The monster drew close enough for Grove to smell the coppery odor of his blood and the rancid-meat stench of his breath. Then he paused, maybe two feet away, maybe three, his head cocked, his arm coiled and ready to strike.

Grove gazed up at the upside-down face. And the two souls regarded each other.

For that one mesmerizing instant, as two worlds finally collided, Grove was enthralled. It was like looking into a mirror—albeit a funhouse mirror, a perfect corruption of Grove's own face—which paralyzed Grove with the suddenness of a meat hook to his brain.

In the darkness, the monster's face began to change. Over the space of milliseconds, the face melted and reformed, melted and reformed, again and again, the flickering metamorphosis too swift to delineate individual identities: It was white one moment, then brown the next, pasty-pale one moment, then pudgy and slack the next, a pair of thick greasy eyeglasses flickering there for a beat, then a face with gaunt cheeks, then a stovepipe hat, then a stained John Deere cap.

Grove closed his eyes.

He had seen all these faces over the course of his career, some of them behind bars, some inside interrogation chambers, some in the pages of musty history books: Gacy, Ackerman, Mudgett, Doerr, Manson, Splet, Berkowitz, Jesperson, Dahmer, Onoprienko, Jack the Ripper, all of them, all of them flashing across the canvas of John Q Public's elongated face—the ancestors of the Every-Killer.

Grove held his breath, opened his eyes again, and looked up.

What he saw then, only inches away, sent a wave of cold down his spine and made his head spin. The killer's face had changed one last time.

Grove managed to utter something then, his voice a dry, broken, mewling sound in the dark: "Good trick."

FORTY-FIVE

The sap came down hard and quick, a blue streak in the half-light, striking Grove above his left eye. Grove's head snapped back with the force of the blow, the pain shooting off a fireworks display behind his retinas.

He sprawled to the cinder floor, his breath knocked out of him.

"The archetype is forty-two, to be exact," the monster said with Grove's voice.

The killer had turned right side up now, and loomed over Grove with a miraculous new face. In his fugue state, Grove struggled to peer up through the disorienting pain at the avatar glaring down at him.

"He's married and has a family . . . a bland, ordinary, run-of-the-mill person with no outward eccentricities." The monster's voice was an eerie replica of Grove's voice, right down to the faint Chicago-by-way-of-Kenya accent, the hard R's and the long A's.

It was like listening to a digital recording.

Grove tried to mutter something else from the

floor as the comet trails of light veined through his vision, but it came out more like a grunt. The pain was bad—the sap was a leather-lined pad of iron— but the narcotic haze buffered it somehow, muted it, translated it into a foreign neurological language written in harsh fluorescent colors.

Finally Grove got out a few slurred, drunken words: "Y-you've duhhn yer homework."

The sap came down again—another blow to the side of Grove's skull, which made a dull thwacking noise, accompanied by another fragment bomb of brilliant magnesium arteries across Grove's field of vision, this time launching him sideways against the adjacent wall. He banged his head off the stone and then folded, giggling uncontrollably at the slapstick quality of this beating, his mouth drooling pink frothy blood now.

The darkness glowed faintly around him, probably from the profuse amount of methane in the atmosphere, providing just enough light to illuminate John Q's face: *the face of Ulysses Grove.*

The resemblance was more than mere resemblance; it was a perfect rendering, sans tattoos, right down to the subtlest detail—the strong high cheekbones, the deep-set eyes, every mole, every blemish.

It was Grove.

In reverse.

Grove was staring up at his mirror self.

"Very few serial killers are drifters, as the movies would have you believe," the monster mimicked.

"P-please—"

Grove started to protest before the killer interrupted in that robotic voice: "Sixty-two percent of all children between the ages of six and ten wet the bed on a regular basis."

Another flurry of blows landed on Grove's writhing, trembling body.

Grove curled into a fetal position as the sap struck every sharp angle of his body, every pressure point—his elbow, the back of his skull, the corner of his hip, the side of his knee, the top of his scalp—his maniacal giggling deteriorating into inarticulate grunts of agony.

The pain sent a tommy gun of brilliant sparks through his vision as stringers of blood looped out of his mouth. He held himself against the barrage, eyes slamming shut with each blow, one hand desperately probing the inner lining of his coat. He needed to get to the inner lining before he lost consciousness—he knew that much.

He had to find that tiny object tucked away there before the last shade came down.

The assault lifted—

—and out of that stunning dead silence Grove heard a rustling noise that registered in his brain like a parasite worming its way into his memory.

The killer, his back now turned in the darkness, was unfurling a cloth or a handkerchief of some sort. Grove detected a new odor in the air, a medicinal tang like the smell of a dentist's office.

The monster most likely was about to soak the cloth with ether, the means to make Grove manageable. It was the next step in the Archetype's MO, and Grove realized at once that *he* was the Perfect Victim now, he was the lone middle-aged woman. He was the transient, the working girl, the lost fringe dweller wandering home at night. He was Barbie Allison, he was Karen Wanda Finnerty, he was Madeline Gilchrist in Dante's purgatory, doomed to live out the torments of the damned at the hands of every killer who ever plagued the human race.

Grove's cold, numb, rubber-clad fingers suddenly located something small and hard—about the size of a kidney bean—inside the bunched-up lining of his coat. He froze. The next few seconds were critical. He had to get his fingers out of his duster and up to his mouth before the monster took him down into the black.

With shattering pain and effort he slowly, carefully, silently slid the vial of potassium cyanate from beneath the flap of his coat. Every bone in his body shrieked—the narcotic wooze long burned away now, leaving behind sober agonies.

The cloth appeared above him—a white smudge in the blackness.

Grove managed to get the pellet to his lips and slipped it into his mouth as the tiny pale cloud lowered across his failing vision.

The cloth softly pressed down on his face. The monster held it there almost tenderly. Grove did not bite down on the pellet.

Yet.

It took a few minutes for the anesthetic to fully take effect. Grove had studied this phenomenon over the years through blood and toxicology reports. From mapping the free-histamine levels in

victims' wound sites, he knew practically down to
the second how long the sodium thiopentol—its
faint bitter-almond odor a dead giveaway—would
take to knock him out. The average victim taken
this way reaches total unconsciousness in slightly
less than four minutes, although the immediate effects are paralysis, sedation, and disorientation.

At first Grove felt as though he were sinking
very slowly into the primordial earth, his body
gradually morphing into the black stone floor, a
million years of history flying by with that syrupy
time-lapse speed; his organs, bones, and flesh pu-
trefying, hardening, fossilizing, vanishing into the
ground, never to be seen again.

The killer moved around behind him and started
dragging him headfirst across the pulverized rock
toward the iron scaffolding.

Even in his altered state Grove knew where the
killer was taking him. They were inching toward
the mouth of that bottomless well known as the
Back Shaft—more than ten thousand feet deep.
That's where they were going.

Down the rabbit hole.

There was a bump as Grove's shoulder blades
scraped the lip of the pit, and Grove nearly swallowed the poison capsule, now wedged between
his cheek and molars. Everything began to spin,
the darkness puckering around his one good eye,
the light irising down like a silent-movie fade.
Grove summoned all his strength to keep his eyes
open.

The killer lifted Grove up by the arms and set
him into an antique iron basket—a coal scoop that
years ago had doubled as a conveyance for miners—

that dangled from a cable at the top of the shaft. In the darkness the massive enclosure squeaked with Grove's weight like old bones creaking.

In his dwindling awareness Grove could feel the cold root-cellar air suddenly waft up around him. He could smell the damp, putrid decay. The iris continued closing down. It was so dark now Grove couldn't see anything.

That pinching sensation worsened around his left ankle as though tiny teeth were biting into his flesh. What the hell *was* that? A rat? With his tongue he moved the vial of potassium cyanate between his two back molars. Now all he had to do was bite down.

Bite down and avoid the horrors about to come: from his studies Grove knew that the next stage was torture, and not only could he avoid that by killing himself, he could also ensure at least a Pyrrhic victory.

The monster would be denied.

The enclosure creaked again as the monster climbed into the basket beside Grove, who now lay on his back. A stone fell through the bottom grate beneath them, and it fell and fell and fell and fell and fell and it seemed to go on falling forever and ever. Grove couldn't see, couldn't move, couldn't use any of his senses.

He prepared himself to bite down.

In the last little scintilla of light, probably from the distant dying methane glow, Grove managed to glimpse the silhouette of the monster once known as John Q Public, hovering over him in those close quarters, rippling tattooed muscles gleaming with sweat as he grasped the ancient cable—

—and he began to let out twelve inches at a time, slowly lowering the block-and-tackle-style pulley with a *squeak-squeak-squeak*—

—and the enclosure began to slowly descend into the bottomless pit, the asshole of the world, the last circle of hell—

—and Grove passed out before he got a chance to bite down.

FORTY-SIX

The killer remembers his birth—not necessarily on the surface of his consciousness, but on a cellular level, in his marrow, as a bird remembers its route of migration— an ash tossed on the whirlwind, an invisible parasite lost in the atmosphere. He remembers the years and years of darkness, adrift in the vacuum of limbo. But most of all he remembers the moment he was finally reborn, made flesh: that hot day in August when the FBI man locked him in that airless interrogation room with the coffee stains and yellow nicotine walls and cracked panel of mirrors, a million fractured faces staring back at him, drilling holes in his brain. He will never forget the moment their eyes met like an atom bomb erupting in his soul: the spirit of a vanquished twin entering him.

Now it was time to fulfill the ancient prophecy whispered in the secret passageways of his brain, uttered in Old Languages, a ghostly voice from the abyss. To meet his Other, to face his double in hell.

To bring about the End Days.

To make the exchange.

At the threshold.

Now.

* * *

The enclosure hit rock-bottom, a depth of 12,311 feet, at precisely 1:17 A.M. Eastern Standard Time. The killer—known to African relief workers as "the boy without a name" and to the junkies back in Chicago as "The Measuring Man" and to the Feds as "John Q Public"—finally released his grip on the iron cable, the wound in his side oozing blood.

He fell back against the side of the basket, making the iron struts squeak in the stony silence and utter blackness of the shaft. His big hands were greasy with blood and perspiration. His lungs ached. It had taken nearly three hours to get to the bottom rung of the E, moving slowly and steadily, a foot per second.

Eyes adjusting to the dark, the killer crouched down and blindly felt around the corrugated steel floor of the enclosure. He found the small penlight that he had stashed there in a wad of cloth, picked it up, and clenched it between his rotting teeth like a cigarette holder. He clicked it on.

Black snow danced in the beam. Particles of coal-ash, floating on convection currents, made it impossible to see more than inches beyond the narrow beam of the penlight. The air smelled of scorched brimstone and char, as thick as gauze on his naked body, on his face, in his eyes, as he stood there, very still now, gazing down at that limp form lying in a heap in the corner of the scoop.

Taking pained breaths, the killer tried in vain to get more of the poisoned air into his lungs, but the madness and secret voices inside him drove him on. He needed to get to the sacred site as soon as possible.

It took him a while to get Grove's flaccid body out of that rickety enclosure, then down the twenty or thirty-some yards of obsidian black tunnel to the sacrificial shrine. Legs cold and stiff from the knife wound just below his rib cage, the monster dragged the FBI profiler by the shoulders, the man's heels making tiny tracks in the cinder-dust. When the monster finally reached the slab, he found a single bare cage-light hanging overhead. The light had been hastily wired to a small car battery.

He flipped the light on.

Behind a veil of black snow, barely visible now in the haze of lamp-ash, the six-inch sheet of shale, elevated by boulders, lay at the heart of the killer's sacrificial shrine, which resembled a crude Aztec altar. The hollowed-out skull of a German shepherd that John Q had butchered in a Valesburg parking lot sat upside down at the head of the slab, a bowl for Grove's blood. Countless ribbons of bloodstained fabric, all colors and patterns, dangled over the table like birthday decorations.

Crime-scene investigators had puzzled over the missing strips of fabric torn from the victims' clothing at half a dozen scenes. But Grove knew the moment he saw the swatch torn neatly off the edge of Barbie Allison's lavender Dior scarf that these were talismanic souvenirs—maybe even something deeper and more ritualistic.

With surprising ease the killer lifted Grove's body onto the slab.

The old battered Samsonite suitcase lay open on the cinders at the foot of the platform. The killer knelt down by it and fished through its contents for a moment, until he found the clippers.

He plugged the device into the battery, then came around to where Grove's head lolled off to one side of the table.

Then, in the fog bank of black ash, he started giving Grove a haircut.

It took less than five minutes to shave Grove's head, first with the horse-clippers, then with an old Gillette electric razor. Fine wisps of tightly coiled black fuzz flew off into the flurry of ash flakes, or floated down like tufts of black cotton to the cinder floor, the buzzing noise echoing in the distant bowels of the empty dark tunnel. John Q prayed silently, in a dead language, as he worked. When he was done, he stood back and admired his work.

Something caught his attention on his own chest, and he looked down, the penlight shining off his bulging pectoral muscle. A downy fleck of Grove's fuzzy black hair was adhering to the monster's skin, halfway between the twin tattoos, the ones depicting measuring tape curling around his nipples. He rubbed the hair away and part of the tattoo streaked. The monster looked at it. He rubbed the tattoo some more, and more of it came off. Delicate lines smudged and streaked away like old paint.

The temporary ink had done its job well—the illusion had fooled even the most suspicious authorities. Now it was time to bathe in the profiler's blood and wash the rest of John Q Public away.

And make the exchange.

FORTY-SEVEN

Grove awoke in fits and starts, the searing pain penetrating his narcotic hangover. At first, his eyes managed to only flick open a centimeter or two, letting in a quick flash of something moving across his body, barely visible in the fog of black ash, something resembling the silhouette of a killer hunching over Grove's midsection, working on him in the shifting shadows of that swaying bare cage-light. Then his eyelids sank again, still too heavy to manage.

Another sharp stinging sensation jostled him awake, this one to the left of his belly button, the point of a knife, perhaps, or an ice pick, piercing his skin. Grove's eyes fluttered open—

—and he jerked forward now, fully awake, his brain screaming *DANGER DANGER DANGER DANGER DANGER*, but something held him down, tethered him to the hard cold surface of the table or platform or bed—or whatever it was—on which he was splayed. He sucked in a breath, trying to get air into his lungs, realizing many things all at once: he lay on a stone slab engulfed in black snowfall, like Black Christmas, the air so thick with flyaway ash it looked like a faulty TV signal, a picture obscured by pixels of interference, and Grove right in the middle of it, exposed like a lamb in a slaughterhouse, his duster gone, his shirt off, his pants yanked down to his ankles, and the big naked black man hunched over his stomach hurting him, hurting him badly with something that went BZZZZZZZZZZZZZZZZZZ like an electric razor.

Grove began hyperventilating with terror as his eyesight returned, focusing on his bare stomach.

The pain came from a tattoo needle—this freak was inking tattoos into Grove's skin—and that seemed to awaken some deeper part of Grove's psyche, but none of it made sense yet, he was too groggy, too confused and disoriented. He remembered nothing. He had no idea where he was, or who this motherfucker was, or why he was giving Grove a prison cell mural on his flesh. Maybe this was all a bad dream, and he would wake up at any moment.

He closed his eyes and another tremendous jolt of pain stung his midsection.

Grove let out a yelp, high and shrill, and the freak looked up from his work, grinning a mouthful of blackened teeth at Grove, and then Grove knew this was no dream because he could see what the big man was inking into his skin with that old electric needle that looked like a welding iron stinking of overheating transistors and scorched hair: rulers and tape measures curling like vines up Grove's breastbone and around his pectorals.

Now panic started taking hold, turning Grove's innards to ice.

"S-stop—ss-stop," Grove finally uttered, his mouth feeling as though it were made of sand. He had no idea how he had gotten here—wherever "here" was—but it looked bad, it looked very bad. He lay at the threshold of a narrow tunnel that receded into absolute blackness, and the walls were moldering black rock, and the air swam thick with motes of charred ash, and it stank of methane down here.

That much seemed obvious: he was *down* somewhere, underground, perhaps way underground. The tattoo needle stung him again, sending off alarms in his head, making him cringe, as his fractured brain crackled suddenly with a disjointed memory like a half-formed soundbite playing on a warped phonograph: *"What's left of the air's got more damp-black gas in it than a dadburned Molotov cocktail."*

The mine—Wormwood mine!

Grove realized many things right then in that one gulp as the needle curled around his belly button like an arc welder cutting into his skin: he had chased this son of a bitch, this doppelgänger, this one-man freak show, down a rabbit hole, down the world's rectum, and now it was all over. Grove was done. He was the Every-Victim. Worse than that, he was trading identities with the monster now. He was exchanging souls with the devil.

All through this series of revelations, the killer continued painting his masterpiece, meticulously recreating the markings of the Measuring Man, every curl and filigree carefully etched in Grove's skin now, branding him with madness, igniting his flesh with slow-burning embers of pain. Piece by piece, the transformation formed in Grove's mind. His head had been shaved. The killer's own tattoos were gone. The switch, the trade, the inversion. The Law of Exchange. Quid pro quo. Like shards of broken glass imploding and coming together with crystalline clarity, the Endgame presented itself to Grove for the first time.

"Y-you're gonna die down here, too," Grove told the killer then.

John Q looked up from his work, then whispered something that sounded like "suhssafuss" or "sysiphous"—Grove couldn't tell.

"You're gonna die down here, asshole, right alongside me. You're gonna die!"

The hoarse, breathless cry took all the wind out of Grove, and all the strength flowed out of him as his head lolled back onto the slab.

Then something else occurred to him: *the pellet.* The poison vial.

Maybe that was the only way to prevent the master plan, prevent the switch. Probing his mouth with his tongue, he couldn't feel it. Horrible thoughts popped and crackled in his brain as he remembered the way the tiny vial had been wedged between his left cheek and molar. Gone now. Gone. Had he swallowed it? Was it already too late?

Chills poured down his body as the tattoo needle tracked down his pelvic bone toward his genitals. He looked down the length of his body and saw his flaccid penis lying sideways across his pelvic bone, a slug, the most sensitive part of his body.

He turned away, slamming his eyes shut. *"Get it over with! Getitoverwith!"*

When he opened his eyes he saw the small translucent capsule on the slab next to his head, lying in a tiny puddle of bloody saliva. The side of his face was moist from his pink drool. The vial must have fallen out of his mouth at some point during the torture.

The pellet was intact.

Grove craned his neck toward the capsule of potassium cyanate, his swollen lips close enough now to suck it in with the reverence of a congregant consuming the host.

Something stopped him. Maybe it was the odd and unexpected sensation of warmth. Rising in him. Pouring over him. Taking the pain away. Warmth unlike any warmth he had ever encountered, warmth that spread through his tendons like velvety honey. Or perhaps it was the strange, incongruous flow of thoughts that suddenly ran through his mind at that darkest moment, in that darkest possible place on earth, like a poem—the face of baby Aaron in the sunlight, the sound of Sarah Vaughan's gorgeous voice hitting the high C in the chorus of "Lover Man," the touch of Maura's breath on the back of his neck, the first smoky-sweet sip of espresso in the morning, the smell of sassafras stewing in a gumbo—all of it coalescing into one great ebullient affirmation that made him spit that goddamned capsule out.

Chances are, though, it was none of these things. Chances are it was the pinching sensation around his ankle that had been bothering him since he had entered the mine approximately eight and a half hours ago.

He finally glimpsed, out of the bottom edges of his eye, the source of that pinching.

FORTY-EIGHT

At the bottom of his shackled right leg, where his pants and underwear were bunched around his ankle, the edge of a leather strap peeked out from under coal-stained cotton cuffs. The significance of that strap, which had been digging into the thin flesh just beneath his ankle for hours, registered over the space of a nanosecond in Grove's forebrain, and whether it was fate or divine intervention or sheer dumb luck, Grove realized in that briefest of moments that his chronic absentmindedness had finally paid off.

In the gloomy yellow shroud of light, the killer paused, lifting that infernal buzzing needle from Grove's burning midsection.

Grove sucked in a labored breath, his lungs aching unmercifully, the pain from the needle radiating up the back of his tailbone, up his spine, and throughout his frozen limbs. He marshaled his strength then, focusing his thoughts down to a single act, a single chance, a single opportunity that was about to present itself.

The monster turned his back suddenly to change a color cartridge.

At once Grove quickly tensed his right leg against its leather shackle, and then strained his right hand in its strap, to see if he could reach his ankle.

But it was no good.

It was no goddamn good.

Grove closed his eyes, straining furiously in the dark, straining and straining.

The tips of his fingers, blackened from coal dust and cramping with exertion, would only come to within about six inches of the fabric bunched around his ankle, and no matter how hard he strained to bend his knee backward, stretch his fingers downward, and strain and strain to bring those two extremities together, he couldn't reach the errant strap of leather poking out of the wrinkled fabric.

That strange warmth rose inside Grove again with the radiance of a fever.

The monster turned back to his masterpiece with a new color to inject into Grove's flesh. The ashy snow of dust and gaseous fog had grown so thick now, stirred up by all the hectic movement, it was hard to see the killer's face, the cone of light from the cage-bulb like a whirlpool, sucking everything up into its artificial heat. Grove couldn't breathe. He was burning up with alien warmth, struggling to see through that soupy atmosphere that had fermented over the decades into rocket fuel as flammable as liquid nitrogen.

Then Grove got lucky once again, maybe for the last time, because John Q had reached the point where he needed to expose Grove's lower legs, expose them in order to complete the masterpiece, and the buckles came off first, which set off a chain reaction unraveling at the surreal speed of an ancient silent film running through a broken projector, black-and-white scenes cutting at awkward moments, impossible to track and yet inexorable, unstoppable—

—all of which started when Grove summoned every last ounce of strength he had in his body and drove his knee up into the killer's chin—

—and the killer reared back suddenly with a grunt, the force of the impact driving his jaw up hard against the roof of his mouth—

—which gave Grove enough time to quickly lean down as far as he could lean, simultaneously bending his leg upward, to the point where his fingers could dig inside the bunched fabric of his pants, until he got his hand around the grip of that little Derringer—

—Maura's little .22 caliber single-action pistol that she kept hidden away, almost superstitiously, in the Swisher Sweets box on the top shelf of the front coat closet back in Pelican Bay, hidden behind the Monopoly and Yahtzee boxes, which Grove, in all the excitement, had forgotten was taped around his ankle, taped there in his living room the previous evening, taped there in the rush to prepare for whatever he might encounter in hell, and now he had it in his hand—

—but he only had it in his hand for a single split second, just long enough to thumb back the hammer, before the monster got his bearings back and then pounced on the table with the speed and savagery of a large feral animal drooling with kill-lust—

—and Grove felt the raw strength of John Q's big callused fingers grasping his right hand, which was still shackled, and now the killer was forcing the tiny barrel upward toward the ceiling when suddenly—

BANG! The Derringer barked in the darkness, making Grove flinch at the dry balloon pop and the silver photo-strobe flash in the dark—

—and then the sensation of rock chips biting his exposed hip from the ricochet chewing through the corner of the slab registered in his stunned brain, and the killer was recoiling suddenly, flash-blind from the crackling sparks spreading along the walls, the dense fog of gas almost catching, almost, the dust in his monster's face, stinging his eyes, his inarticulate baritone howl giving Grove one more millisecond of time—

—enough time to thumb the hammer a second time and blindly fire off the second and last round—

—missing John Q by a mile but inadvertently hitting the wall at the perfect angle to kick up a bright silver spark of magnesium light hot enough to bring an end to the dark legacy of Wormwood Mine.

FORTY-NINE

The fireball sucked the remaining oxygen from the bottom shaft in one great paroxysm of searing heat, flinging the killer to the ground with the certainty of a battering ram, reverberating up through two miles of sediment, rocking the surface with a thunderclap heard across six counties, and for one brief horrifying moment filling hell with daylight.

Grove slammed his eyes shut, his wrists still shackled around the topmost edge of the stone, the jet-engine noise rupturing his eardrums. He expected the heat-storm to consume him along with the rest of the labyrinth, hopefully as quickly and as painlessly as possible—

—but instead, the force of the sudden convection current kicked up the edge of the stone slab and flipped it onto its side.

The impact cracked Grove's molars. He couldn't see, he couldn't breathe; he let out a breathless shriek that was lost in the gargantuan surge of fire. The flames, fed by the methane and nitrogen and damp-black gases, pitched the slab sideways—Grove still lashed to it—as though it were a sail tacking on a squall of wind.

The shackle on Grove's left wrist snapped, his body flopping one way, the slab spinning the other. The remaining shackle ripped free at the precise moment the slab smashed into a buttress, shattering the monolith into countless shards of hot smoking stone.

Grove slid, curled into a fetal ball, into an adjacent buttress, the impact sending comets across his vision. Rock particles sleeted down on him, his ears deafened now.

He lost consciousness then.

He had fully expected to die in that frenzied instant of blinding heat and pain, as everything was going mercifully black and silent, but that strange feverish sensation, as he would soon learn, had other plans for him, not to mention further pain, because he gasped awake moments later in a cold pocket of muffled noise and light. Lungs heaving, eyelids fluttering open, he realized instantly, with mounting horror, that he was underwater.

With sudden involuntary spasms he coughed and coughed and coughed, expelling water from his lungs, the noise of his gasps a muffled mewling sound in his ears. The fire flickered above him like a lightning storm.

He kicked off his pants and pushed and fought his way out of the broken pieces of shale, his wrists still tangled in their long leather shackles. He wasn't necessarily thinking straight at this point, merely struggling for air, instinctively seeking oxygen.

Clawing in the only direction that made any sense.

Up.

His head burst out of the water only to bang against the low stone ceiling, stars bursting in his field of vision, his face instantly sunburned by the furnace of superheated toxic air. Flames curled along the surface of the water, which was flooding into the mine at the rate of a half a million gallons a minute.

Grove tried to tread water and fill his lungs with the smoldering stew. The water level sloshed and eddied around him, swiftly rising.

Through his blurred vision he madly searched for the only way out: *the back shaft.*

In his peripheral vision he saw a long pale object undulating on the currents about twenty feet away, and he swam toward it, realizing with his last molecule of sanity that the object might be his only chance of survival. The water spumed over his head, making him gag and gasp, but he kept on, completely nude and greasy with tattoo ink, only a few more inches now, reaching out for the thing, clawing at it—

—until he finally got his hand around the collar of the duster.

All at once the water covered him, filling the tunnel, ominously muffling all the noise at the precise moment he got his around a thin membrane of plastic stuffed into one of the duster's pockets.

* * *

Grove knew he had only a matter of seconds—even a healthy person is able to go without oxygen for no more than a minute or two, and Grove was weak and hurting and out of air—so he tore the slender object out of the duster pocket and slammed it over his face. The oxygen mask was designed for first responders and paramedics who get caught in dangerous chemical fires, a small, plastic, cup-shaped mask attached to a half-liter bottle of oxygen, and not recommended for breathing underwater, but now it was Grove's only chance.

His last chance.

He pressed it tightly over his nose and mouth with one hand while he spun the small valve with the other. Darkness was closing in again, the flames boiling and sputtering above him. He breathed in moist, cold, ammonia-smelling air and spun around, madly searching the surface of the water for any sign of the shaft.

Twenty feet away an oval shadow flickered above the ceiling of water.

The shaft! There it was! The phone booth–size enclosure lay beneath it, leaning against the adjacent stone wall, scorched and dented by the maelstrom.

Grove swam toward it through the dense stew, holding the mask in place with one hand, frantically paddling with the other. His raw flesh scraped an outcropping of stone, and he cringed at the seething pain, but he soldiered on. He felt the water around him begin to vibrate.

He reached the bottom of the shaft and got his free hand around the cable. It took every last shred of energy to yank himself up, but somehow he managed it with one hand. The water level had already encroached into the shaft, boiling upward with the intensity of a turbine. As Grove scaled the cable—using the jagged wall of the shaft for footholds—he gazed up.

A curtain of black lay behind the billowing, rising water. How much oxygen did he have? How long would it take to climb over ten thousand feet with only one free hand? His brain struggled with the math like a clockwork jamming. Could he make it?

That strange unnamable warmth rose in him again as he scaled the shaft in slow, painful, lurching gasps. It tingled in his upper vertebrae, crawling hotly across his newly shorn scalp and sparking images across his mind screen—the tiny fingers of an infant curled around his index finger, a spring flower blossoming in the Chalbi Desert. The unexpected surge drove him on so profoundly that he broke through the surface of the water.

Gulping air into his singed lungs, the mask falling from his face, Grove kept climbing, faster and faster, galvanized by the eerie warmth, so galvanized, in fact, that he ignored the violent currents beneath him, coming toward him.

At last he glanced down at the rising, bubbling surface of the water.

A charred hand burst out of the water and grabbed hold of his ankle.

FIFTY

Grove let out a strangled, involuntary cry, and the hand tightened with the pressure of a boa constrictor. The monster connected to the hand, his face bursting out of the muck, was a charred husk of a human being that used to look just like Grove but now resembled a blackened leech, so ravaged by fire the tissue was peeling away from his face in gelatinous wet flakes. Glistening, bloody eyes locked onto Grove with primordial hate.

In that one frozen tableau the two souls again regarded each other. A wave of pure denatured hate crashed up against a tide of sorrow—sorrow for an endless cycle of grief that would never—*ever*—come to an end.

Something shifted inside Grove then—invisible and inchoate—way down in the depths of his being, that eerie warmth erupting in him like a fragment bomb, cauterizing every molecule, every atom, and all that he knew, all that he was, all that he loved and cherished, the entirety of his soul, his very *goodness*, all of it suddenly sparked around him like an armature singing with electricity, forming an envelope of neon-blue voltage—

—until a single notion filled his brain, distilled down to a single phrase, spoken in all languages, past and present, all at once: *I will never stop.*

The monster froze.

The balance of power changed.

It occurred over the space of a single moment, the water level pitching and sluicing and rising. The killer convulsed in the heat of Grove's implacable gaze and the darkness seemed to turn inside out.

It was as though the earth itself had suddenly rejected this cancerous parasite known as John Q Public in a peristalsis of ectoplasm coming off the stone walls, ghostly synapses of pale antimatter the color of festering wounds, sparks the color of sickness, penetrating the killer, piercing him, instantly metastasizing in him, eating away at what remained of his life force.

The killer's mouth gaped, helpless with ghastly agony, hinging open so wide it threatened to dislocate the jaw of his scorched cranium.

Grove let out a wail of primal rage, the sound of it blending with the roar of floodwaters.

Then he slammed his bare heel down on the killer's face. The killer's neck whiplashed, his grip slipping. Grove slammed his heel down again and again, and at last the killer lost his hold and plunged back into the rising waters.

Something ruptured then in the deepest core of the labyrinth.

*   *   *

Veteran miners have a word for what happened next. They call it a "bump"—a laughably insufficient word for a catastrophic mine collapse when ceiling and floor crash together in a chain reaction not unlike a tremendous earthquake. Grove saw this occur directly beneath him in that frozen moment after the monster plunged back into the black mire.

The very walls of the shaft trembled. The water surged explosively upward, and the bottom of the shaft contracted upward toward the ceiling.

Grove gawked down at the horrible spectacle, momentarily rapt, the spectacular noise like an airliner crashing inside the mine. The bottom of the shaft imploded, slamming together, crushing the burned, mangled remains of the killer.

Grove turned away when he saw the man's skull crack underwater, extruding a cloud of pink bubbling brain matter like the meat of a smashed gourd.

It was a sight that would stay with you the rest of your life. Unfortunately he had no time to even register the horror of it now. The greasy waters were boiling upward, fissures forming in the shaft walls.

The bump had set off an earthquake.

FIFTY-ONE

What happened next—transpiring over the course of roughly twenty-three minutes—would for years to come be partially shrouded in mystery for all those involved in the Wormwood event. Especially for Grove. He would remember tremendous cracking noises down there like a glacier shifting all around him, the fissures opening in the shaft, the cracks traveling up the walls of the well on either side of him. He would remember shimmying frantically up that elevator cable for several frenzied minutes as the mine disintegrated beneath him and the earthquake rent the ground. All the while Grove was clawing and scraping his way up through the smoke and steam as swiftly as his ruined arms would carry him. He also would remember not being fast enough, because the water finally caught up with him, shooting him up the shaft with the force of a cannonball.

At that point, his memory started getting sketchy because he became a virtual projectile, naked and flailing in the rising piston of water. He probably lost consciousness more than once, intermittently coming back to awareness only to upchuck a lung-ful of water, gasp for air, and then resume his fran-tic shimmy up that pulley-line before the furious currents could swallow him.

One of the things that saved him was that an-cient cable, which somehow managed to stay in-tact during the event and keep Grove oriented in the right direction: *upward toward the surface.*

He had no idea how long he flailed and slashed his way upward, upward, upward through the black chaos, the very structure of the earth giving way around him, but at one point he felt the strangest sensation engulfing his greasy nude body in the darkness. It felt like a cushion of air rising beneath him, levitating him, pushing him upward toward the surface. In Grove's scattered brain he saw it as an impassive act of God, a juggernaut of magic, propelling him upward into another earthly pur-gatory—wifeless, childless, friendless, loveless—into another hell from which he would never escape.

But as it turned out, the source of that force was far more prosaic.

Geologists studying the aftermath of the event weeks later would discover that the little-known fault line that lay beneath the Wormwood mine, awakened by the firestorm, had caused the century-old excavation to undergo what is known as an "in-version quake." Rather than shifting the earth sideways, as do standard earthquakes, the inversion quake buckles underground strata deep below the earth's crust, setting off a chain reaction that causes landmasses to crack open like giant eggshells. Bib-lical historians believe that this rare phenomenon

occurred in the first, second, and fifth centuries—
signaling epochal changes, even informing the
creation of *The Revelations to St. John*—which might
explain the phenomenon's legendary status. Plagues
of locusts and rivers of blood were nothing compared to this "Rending of Paradise," as the phenomenon had come to be known in occult circles.

For Grove, the effects of that inversion quake
would ultimately take on mystical proportions in
his memory and imagination. Since Wormwood
had been sunk so deep into the driftless shale, the
result of the event was a sort of evacuation of the
mine's contents, a shitting out of its foreign bodies. Grove was pushed out of that main shaft like
toothpaste squeezed from a tube.

Which is the point at which Grove completely
lost consciousness.

FIFTY-TWO

Somehow—and Grove would never know the true sequence of events that followed—he was disgorged like a chicken bone gagged up by the earth, hurled into the explosive dust and crumbling, churning rock pillars of that first level. In his stupor he had the vaguest sense of being buffeted by violent waves, his traumatized mind transforming the flooding chambers into raging seas, the jagged fingers of rock gouging at his exposed flesh into man-eating sharks. In this dream state he saw a lighthouse dead ahead, a dull spot of light on the liquid horizon. Out of air, bereft of blood, drained and delirious, he swam toward it, refusing to die.

Refusing to ever stop.

Although nobody will ever know what happened then, it is highly likely that the surging floodwaters had wedged Grove inside a piece of machinery—a five-foot-long tangle of twisted metal from a bolting machine—and carried him two hundred yards across the first level, the mine collapsing behind him, his luck holding out long enough for the wreckage to reach the vacuum of the front shaft, which sucked the mangled metal up into the whirlpool.

The inversion phenomenon had caused the entrance of the mine to collapse into itself, a catastrophic landslide that registered on seismometers from Louisville to Memphis, opening up a vast trench in the landscape around the Green Ridge Barrens.

The floodwaters roared up into the chasm with enough force to tear the mine buildings from their foundations, break window glass across Valesburg, and rip two-hundred-year-old live oaks from Avery Mountain by their roots. Not since Deacon Pritzker had delivered his famous End Days sermon at the Gunstock Pentecostal Church four decades earlier—evoking apocalyptic images of match flames multiplied a million times and the earth opening up to swallow the sinful—had Valesburg citizens encountered such a cataclysm.

By the time Grove's broken body had reached ground level—still entangled in that wreckage, careening on the floodwater for a few hundred yards before tangling in a mass of deadfall trees—he had sunken into a semicomatose state. He was barely alive, his respiration so slow a first-year resident might mistake him for dead.

He lay there for some time while the aftershocks shivered across the Allegheny Mountains.

He regained consciousness only once that night before anybody found him. But in that brief interval, alone under that vast canvas of stars, completely senseless, numb from the neck down, hovering near death, he managed to gaze up at the sky for a single moment and shiver with a strange sort of undefined satisfaction.

The cool air on his face was bliss, the floating sensation euphoric. And for one fleeting instant he felt as though he had been resurrected, transformed from something he could not remember into something new.

Then he passed out again, only minutes before the cleansing dawn began to burn off the darkness.

His work done, his fate all that was left.

And the silence.

EPILOGUE
The Law of Exchange

Flesh perishes, I live on
Projecting trait and trace
Through time to times anon
And leaping from place to place
Over oblivion.

—THOMAS HARDY, "HEREDITY"

"Wait! Down there! By the road, by the road!" Edith Drinkwater, drenched in flop sweat and nerves, bundled in an FBI Windbreaker, pressed her face against the canopy of the Huey helicopter at exactly 6:21 A.M. Eastern Standard Time the morning after the earthquake.

She and the others had been sweeping the epicenter of the Wormwood cataclysm for hours, ever since the tremors had torn the surrounding county asunder, and this was the first breakthrough—the dark crumpled outline of a figure a hundred feet below the chopper, stuck in the mud. "In those logs, in the trees!" Drinkwater stabbed her finger against the window.

"Hold on!"

Captain Barkham, a stocky Navy SEAL with a hairbrush mustache—the same man who had dumped Drinkwater and Grove here in his Piper Cub less than twenty-four hours ago—yanked the stick to his right and eased back the foot pedal. The chopper, a loaner from the Floyd County Sheriff's Police, banked and descended with a rattle. Barkham had stayed in the area last night, worried, and had found Drinkwater at the sheriff's office in the wee hours following the earthquake, demanding rescue and recovery for Grove.

"What is it?" Sheriff DeQueen wanted to know, craning his wrinkled neck, his pipe clenched in his teeth. Dawn had broken behind the aircraft, a wan glow around the dark silhouettes of mountains to the east, and now the watery oblivion below them, the place that used to be Wormwood mine, rushed toward the Huey's belly. "Can't see a dad-burned thing!"

"Looks like a body," ventured old Ryland Clinger in the rear of the cabin, his basset-hound eyes aglow as he gazed down at the nude remains.

The helicopter slammed down on a swampy patch of high ground fifty yards away.

All their guns came out. Even Drinkwater drew a .44 caliber Bulldog—Grove's gun—from a shoulder harness under her Windbreaker. The sheriff had a .38 Special. Clinger had a snub-nosed .45 Smith & Wesson, and Barkham had a Glock. Before the engine even started winding down, before the wind had dissipated enough for them to talk, they were on their way out the doors.

Hand gestures guided them along the edge of the fast-flowing waters.

In the dull gray light of dawn they cautiously approached the body tangled in the wreckage of trees and twisted metal. All the gun barrels went up commando-style, bodies tense as coiled springs.

"Stay back for a second," Barkham suggested to the group with a sharp gesture of the hand.

He took the lead, and crept through the muck, his big jackboots *smuck*ing noisily as he trained his

Glock at the motionless figure in the wreckage. At this close proximity it was clear that it was a man, completely naked and mortally wounded, and very possibly dead.

"Grove?" Barkham called out. "Can you hear me?"

Drinkwater watched from the periphery, gripping her gun in both hands. Something was wrong. She felt it on the back of her neck. The body was either stained with coal dust or burned beyond recognition. It looked as though someone had painted it from head to toe with black grease-paint.

Something deep inside Drinkwater sent up an alarm. The man on the ground was bald. "I'm not sure that's Grove," she murmured, almost to herself, her voice barely audible over the idling chopper. "I'm not sure that's him."

"I'm gonna check for a pulse." The beefy pilot knelt down by the body. "Hold on for a second."

Drinkwater said something then, almost a whisper. "That's not Grove."

"What? What was that?" The sheriff couldn't hear a thing, holding his .38 on the body. "Say again?"

Barkham called out: "He's alive! I got a pulse! Got a pulse here!"

Drinkwater stared at the body. "I'm telling you that's not Grove."

"What did she say?" Old Ryland Clinger stood shaking in his big hip waders, gripping his gun with one arthritic hand, leaning on a cane with the other, his yellow rain slicker zipped up to his flabby neck. "What?"

The body jerked suddenly, a wet cough coming out, lungs gagging up bloody water.

Everybody jumped back instinctively—even Barkham, who nearly fell on his ass, snapping his Glock up to the ready position—and all the gun barrels drew down on the coughing man on the ground, the big, lanky, coughing bald man who looked as though he had been dipped in a vat of black ink.

A tense moment passed before the man's eyelids began to flutter open as he regained consciousness. "Ww-wherrrzzz thuh—wherzzz—?"

The voice sounded alien, coal-choked, wrought with hoarseness, as though it were a scratchy recording. Nervous thumbs pressing down on gun hammers, rounds clicking into chambers. The sheriff called out: "Careful, y'all! Careful now!"

"Take it easy, brother," Barkham muttered as he leaned back down near the body.

"Wipe off his face!" Drinkwater held her gun tightly in both hands, heart racing. She kept her distance. "I can't see his face!"

Barkham dug in his pocket, found a handkerchief. Wiped the nude man's face.

The moment Drinkwater saw the face—very similar to Grove's but with darker, blood-rimmed eyes, and a series of Aboriginal tattoos curling down his cheek, hastily drawn, prison-style—she clenched her teeth. "Goddamnit, that's the other guy!"

"Shit!"

Barkham sprang to his feet and aimed his gun at the dying man's head. "He's coming around." He thumbed the hammer back. "Hey! Look at me—I said look at me! What the hell did you do with Grove?"

The man on the ground could barely lift his head; he looked lost.

Grove kept trying to form an answer, trying to focus on his accuser, the big guy with the mustache and the gun hovering over him. But it was very difficult. Very, very difficult. Lying prone on the ground, naked and hypothermic, Grove could barely raise his head. His body was spent, his eyesight split into bleary double vision. His skull rang and gonged with intense pain, his mind scrambled from all the blunt trauma injuries to his brain. He had no sense of time or place, no equilibrium, no idea where he was.

"Git some cuffs on that shitbird!" somebody else was yelling in the background, a gray-haired sheriff holding a .38 Special.

"I'm—I'm not—" Grove's mouth wouldn't work, the words wouldn't come.

"Where's Grove?"

Another voice, enraged, garbled with tears, approached from the back.

"I'm not hhhhuh—" Again Grove tried in vain to speak, when all of a sudden a black woman in a gray FBI Windbreaker came stumbling across the weeds with her .44 Magnum in a two-handed grip.

She charged at Grove, her face full of fury. "Where is he, goddamnit? Where's Grove?"

"I'm not—"

The black woman pressed the barrel of that Bulldog down on Grove's newly shorn head. "What did you do with him, huh? Huh? Answer me, you fucking freak!"

"I'm—"

The blow came out of the darkness to his left, a hard, sharp kick from the black woman, striking Grove in the ribs so hard it knocked him sideways and sent him rolling across the ground. Fireworks of pain launched up his midsection.

"Answer me, goddamnit!"

Grove wanted to so badly to tell this lady he didn't do anything and she had the wrong guy and he wasn't who she thought he was, and please, please, please, give him a chance, but it was futile, because he realized right then and there, as he lay paralyzed and mute and nude on that cold, mushy ground, he not only had no idea what they were accusing him of . . .

. . . he could not figure out who this Grove person was that everybody was screaming about.

They airlifted the suspect to Pennington Air Force base outside Lexington, Kentucky, where he received emergency medical treatment. The man had a hairline fracture in his left leg as well as major contusions requiring scores of stitches, not to mention second-degree burns over at least 20 percent of his body. Both his eyes were hemorrhaged from all the blunt trauma; they were shot through with bloody capillaries the color of eggplant. A rapid blood test showed off-the-scale levels of free histamine and serotonin in his bloodstream, as well as a laboratory-grade hallucinogen called dimethyltryptamine. Under armed guard and heavily shackled, the suspect was fingerprinted and photographed. A quick comparison with latent prints on file in Chicago showed a perfect match with John Q Public's fingerprints.

Throughout these early protocols the suspect was docile and cooperative, albeit outwardly confused, maybe even a little frightened. After a brief interrogation, Air Force doctors diagnosed the man as having acute episodic amnesia, likely brought on by head injuries, but also very possibly a symptom of the drug-induced psychosis.

By mid-afternoon, they'd discharged him into Federal custody, and he was transported, via armored vehicle, to the Federal Dentention Center just outside D.C. The four-hour trip was made in secret. The suspect was accompanied by two U.S. Marshals, a special agent from the Louisville field office named Karpinsky, and a civilian trainee from the FBI's academy at Quantico named Edith Drinkwater. After she revealed the disturbing events leading up to Agent Grove's disappearance in the mine, Bureau authorities agreed to allow Miss Drinkwater to accompany the suspect to Washington.

En route to D.C., Agent Karpinsky gave Drinkwater a few minutes in the rear of the transport van alone with the suspect, who was conscious and fairly comfortable on the shackled bench seat. He was maybe a little woozy from pain medication, but lucid enough to talk. What follows is a partial transcript taken from surveillance-camera footage in the back of the van:

DRINKWATER: And you have no recollection of
   what happened in the mine?
SUSPECT: (*in a hoarse, damaged voice*) None. I mean

... they told me about the mine and the FBI
agent that I supposedly ... (*inaudible*)

DRINKWATER: Can you repeat that?

SUSPECT: I said I could never do something like
that.

DRINKWATER: Are you okay?

SUSPECT: Yes. I mean ... yeah, I'm okay. (*wiping
eyes*)

DRINKWATER: How do you know, though?

SUSPECT: Pardon?

DRINKWATER: If you can't remember who you are ...
how do you know you could never kill
anybody?

SUSPECT: I never said that.

DRINKWATER: Said what?

SUSPECT: That I could never kill anybody.

DRINKWATER: I'm confused ... I thought you just
said you could never do something like that."

SUSPECT: I meant I could never kill an innocent
man.

(NOTE LONG PAUSE HERE)

DRINKWATER: Those tattoos on your neck ... they
look infected.

SUSPECT: I'm sorry ... what?

DRINKWATER: Nothing ... never mind.

(TRANSCRIPT ENDS HERE)

Drinkwater had already gone back to her motel
when she made the discovery about the fingerprints. She was alone, wrapped in a blanket and
slumped in front of her laptop, nursing a water
tumbler full of Glenlivet scotch, just idly listening
to the radio. All afternoon, reports of the apocalyptic earthquake in Kentucky had dominated the
airwaves, stories of heroism and cowardice, epochal

property damage, and an inept FEMA once again getting caught with their bureaucratic pants down. But when Drinkwater stumbled upon the "Elimination Print Index" on the FBI's secure website, she saw a link for the Behavioral Science Unit staff.

Elimination fingerprints are for crime labs faced with messy scenes riddled with nonessential prints. Through the process of elimination, the technicians can rule out the fingerprints of investigators. Ulysses Grove had been printed several times early in his career for this very reason, once in the military, and then again several times at the Bureau.

Drinkwater stared and stared at the screen as it filled with the familiar whorls and curlicues of Grove's fingerprints. She clicked over to her e-mail file, and then compared Grove's prints to the attachment sent to the Chicago field office earlier that day, the one with John Q's prints. She opened her Photoshop program, then superimposed one of the graphic images over the other.

"Jesus Christ," she uttered, dumping her drink across the cluttered desktop.

Her heart raced as she sprang to her feet and started gathering up her stuff. She threw on her coat, threw on some sneakers, grabbed her keys, snatched up her cell phone, and then she went back over to her computer, quickly downloaded the data onto a flash drive, and then charged out of the room.

She plunged into the misty night.

Getting into the Central Detention Center on D Street late at night wasn't easy, especially for an Academy recruit like Drinkwater. But a guard at the receiving gate recognized her from a newsletter on honor students—Drinkwater's renown on the shooting range had caught his eye (as had her large bosom)—and he let her enter the wing under the strict promise that she not implicate him in any way if she got in hot water. Of course she hurriedly agreed.

Pulse pounding faster and faster with each passing moment, she literally ran the quarter mile of deserted white cinder-block corridors—the fluorescent overheads blazing down at her—all the way to the interrogation ward. She found the night receptionist and waved her flash drive of Grove's prints like a talisman, blurting out, "I need to see the Section Chief right away! Is he here? It's an emergency!"

The receptionist, an elderly black man with thick-lensed spectacles riding low on his nose, raised his gnarled hands. "Whoa there, sis, you gotta—"

"It's a matter of life and death, sir, national security, whatever you want to call it!"

"I can't let you—"

"Is this the famous Drinkwater?"

The voice came from across the waiting room, a flat Midwestern drawl, and Drinkwater turned just in time to see Ray Kopsinsky striding toward her in shirtsleeves, the armpits damp, his hand extended genially. He looked exhausted. "So you're Grove's girl Friday."

She quickly shook his hand, measuring her words. "Sir, I know this is highly irregular, but I think I can prove that's not John Q Public in there."

"Calm down, Drinkwater."

"But, sir—"

"We already know." He rubbed his eyes. "VICAP matched the prints up this afternoon."

Drinkwater visibly sagged, all her muscles loosening. "Then you know who it is?"

Kopsinsky gave her a tired smile. "This guy's gonna be the death of me yet."

"I knew it. Even in the van. I knew something was wrong. Then I saw the prints."

Kopsinsky shook his head. "Obviously the tattoos, the hair—it was symbolism, done to trade places with him. I just can't figure out the voice, the voice was so damn different, a different tone."

Drinkwater shrugged. "All that coal dust, the underground gases, whatever, must have done a number on his vocal cords. I would have noticed the droopy left eye if wasn't for the hemorrhage."

"Yeah, well . . . that's not the problem."

She frowned. "What do you mean?"

Kopsinsky let out a sigh. "You know it's Grove and I know it's Grove . . . problem is, *he* doesn't know it yet."

The next day the man sat at a plain rectangular wooden table in a conference room at the end of the main corridor. The room, with its minimal furnishings, single ficus plant by the window, and lingering odor of cigarette smoke, gave off a sense of purgatory to all those who spend any length of time in it. In spite of this, however, the man at the table was thankful. Dressed in a T-shirt and khaki slacks, his arms and neck bandaged, he was thankful that he had been allowed to change out of the hideous orange jumpsuit. Thankful that the shackles had been removed and that he'd been given the freedom to get some fresh air, or make phone calls, or even leave the facility if he so desired.

Unfortunately he knew no phone numbers, had nobody to call, had nowhere to go, and was just as mystified by this sudden mood swing among his captors as he was by their earlier insistence that he had murdered people.

Now they wanted him to know how sorry they were, and how they wanted to help him, and most of all, they wanted him to understand that he was a man named Ulysses Grove who worked as a criminal profiler for the FBI, a man with incredible skills, a venerable career, and a family that consisted of a lovely wife and young son. None of it rang true. None of it sounded even remotely familiar.

The man at the table had a lead shield around his memory. Even the strange tattoos that adorned his wounded body rang no bells. He felt like a featureless outline of a man, a cipher. Strangely enough, though, in some deeply buried capsule of his imagination, his brain reminded him of a target silhouette, the kind you might see on a gun range, an opaque bust of a generic unknown subject. And this image haunted him, disturbed him . . . right up until the moment the outer door of that meeting room clicked open.

Kopsinsky came in first. Dressed in a smart navy suit, a laminate ID tag clipped to his pocket, he approached the table with an awkward smile. "Ulysses, I don't want to throw all this at you at once, but we have a few special visitors to see you today."

The man looked up. "Okay. . . ."

"Let's take this nice and easy, all right? One step at a time?"

"Sure."

Kopsinsky turned and signaled to somebody hovering outside the door. "You've already met Edith Drinkwater, I believe . . ."

The black woman entered tentatively. Decked out in a conservative navy pantsuit, also sporting a laminate tag around her neck, she had her hair in tight braids. She looked nervous. "Got somebody here wants to see you, Ulysses."

The man nodded. "Okay."

A moment later, a thin ash-blond woman in a sweater and jeans came in the room with a plump, caramel-skinned three-year-old on her hip. The woman paused, her face a topography of pain, her child instantly recognizing Grove, transfixed by the shorn head and markings. "Daddeee?"

Grove stood up so abruptly he knocked his chair over.

Momentarily stricken, his breath catching in his throat, he saw this small-hipped woman and curly-haired child casting off a ghostly aura of light. It radiated off them in faint luminous filaments that reached across the room and penetrated Grove with a surge of heat, the stabbing pain in his hips, in his spine, in his temples, all of it suddenly burning away on a wave of cleansing truth.

The lead shield around his memory dissolved, revealing his identity in a sudden and unexpected nickelodeon-flash of raw experience—*climbing down a bottomless well, ocean waves obliterating a message in the sand, trembling hands holding a heart-wrenching note from a forlorn wife, a father reading a fairy tale to a child, an upside-down monster*—all of the memories so vivid and bright that he nearly collapsed.

"Oh Jesus, there you are, there you are, there you are, there you are," he mumbled under his breath as he limped around the side of the table and went to them, reaching out first for the child, then for the mother, embracing both, one in each arm, the tears blurring his vision. "There you are, there you are, there you are, there you are—"

The room became a tableau of almost reverent stillness and silence.

The section chief stood near the window, his head down respectfully, his expression one of weary acceptance, acceptance of genius, acceptance of the inexplicable.

And the woman named Drinkwater hovered stone-still near the door, looking down at her hands as though praying, a certain kind of acceptance passing over her face as well—

—the realization that this strange and terrifying assignment, as well as her role in this man's life, which would forever remain a secret, had come to an end.